THE DOCTOR'S DAUGHTER

The Doctor's Daughter

Donna MacQuigg

FIVE STAR

An imprint of Thomson Gale, a part of The Thomson Corporation

Detroit • New York • San Francisco • New Haven, Conn. • Waterville, Maine • London

LIBRARY OF CONGRESS CATALOGING-IN-PUBLICATION DATA

MacQuigg, Donna.
  The doctor's daughter / Donna MacQuigg. — 1st ed.
    p. cm.
  ISBN-13: 978-1-59414-596-4 (alk. paper)
  ISBN-10: 1-59414-596-2 (alk. paper)
  I. Title.
PS3613.A283D63 2007
813'.6—dc22

2006038263

First Edition. First Printing: May 2007.

Published in 2007 in conjunction with Tekno Books.

Printed in the United States of America on permanent paper
10 9 8 7 6 5 4 3 2 1

To my parents who met and married during World War II.
A young English girl who married
a young American soldier.

ACKNOWLEDGMENTS

In many ways, it's difficult for an author to choose a favorite book from those that they've written. It's true we tell our readers that we love all our heroes and heroines equally. However, once in a while we authors discover that one of our stories holds a special spot in our heart. *The Doctor's Daughter* is, without a doubt, my favorite. However, like any story, it couldn't have come into being without the help of some very special people:

Tiffany Schofield, *via con Dios, mi amiga*. Thanks for your support.

Alice Duncan, thanks for your endless patience and persistence to improve my writing.

Kathryne Kennedy, a great writer, a great friend, and a great critique partner.

John Helfers who gave this book a second chance.

Words cannot express my gratitude.

CHAPTER ONE

England, 1880

"She's in the parlor, my lady," the elderly butler announced as Rebeccah Randolph leaned her wet umbrella against the wall.

"No need to have Mildred make tea, Alfred," she replied as he lifted the black cape from her slender shoulders. "I rather think Grandmama will need a glass of sherry, though, once I'm through." Rebeccah raised her chin as her cold fingers closed around the knob to the parlor door. With one quick motion she opened it. Like Rebeccah, the old woman wore mourning clothes. She gazed out the window, apparently lost in thought, as she stared at the cold March rain.

"Grandmama? You wished to see me?" Rebeccah asked, thankful her voice sounded strong and confident when the old woman turned.

"Louise—"

"I prefer to use my middle name, Grandmama."

"Nonsense. Your mother merely agreed to that name to appease your father. I'm sure I need not remind you that Louise was your mother's name. 'Tis a much more fitting name for a lady of your status."

"My status?" Rebeccah squared her shoulders a little more, wishing her knees would stop their quaking. Saints, why did just being in the same room with the old dowager filet her courage? "I'm not sure I understand your meaning," she lied, hoping her grandmother wouldn't see through her false bravado. But the old lady did, and by her expression, wanted Rebeccah to know it.

"You look exactly like your mother looked at your age—the same fair hair and rebellious green eyes." Her grandmother blinked hard, unwilling to exhibit even the smallest sign of how deeply she grieved. For a moment Rebeccah wished she could go to her—to comfort her—but the thought was quickly dashed when the old woman's features hardened and the corners of her mouth twisted into a smug smile. "However much you resemble your mother, Lydia is still my favorite."

"Think you I am ignorant of that fact?" Rebeccah challenged, the wound too old to be easily reopened.

"You'd be a fool if you were, and a fool, my child, is the last thing you are." Her grandmother moved away from the window and at the same time motioned for her to sit.

"I prefer to stand. Now that the funeral is over, I have something important to say."

"I shall be tolerant of your insolence only because of the circumstances." Katherine Strong, Duchess of Wiltshire, sat in a high-backed velvet chair near the fire, and smoothed her black satin skirt. "I do believe, however, after you hear what I have to say, you may very well wish to be seated. But do go on. You've piqued my interest."

Rebeccah took a calming breath. "I'm leaving London the day after tomorrow to be married in Colchester. It will be a very small, very private ceremony."

Of course she was making the right decision. Edward was handsome, witty, and although not the heir to his father's fortune, had a modest estate and a good position in the family business. "I've respectfully declined Viscount Wellington's offer of marriage for a higher cause."

"Really?" queried the dowager. "Pray tell, what could be loftier than a title and financial security?"

"Love, Grandmama. Something you know nothing about."

Rebeccah jumped at the old woman's bark of laughter. She had expected her grandmother to grow angry, but wasn't at all prepared for her bout of merriment. She cast a wary glance at the table, wishing now that her grandmother would, indeed, offer them both a glass of sherry.

"Love," her grandmother managed to repeat sarcastically once she had collected herself. "There is no time for such fanciful thoughts, my dear. Not yet." She motioned to the table with a sly smile, giving Rebeccah the feeling she could read her mind. "Pour a sherry for us."

Rebeccah obliged, clutching her glass before her as if to ward off evil spirits. "I had hoped you would be more understanding," she began, cringing at the way her voice wavered.

"And I had hoped to leave my title and my holdings to your mother," her grandmother countered. "But our best laid plans sometimes fall apart. Louise, my precious daughter, is dead and buried, spoiling my plans as I am about to spoil yours." Katherine turned and stared into the fire at the same time Rebeccah took several sips of liquid fortitude. "I need not remind you that she married your father against my wishes, and as a result, has left me with two granddaughters, who are, in the eyes of society, unworthy to inherit such a distinguished appellation."

"All my life you've made it very clear that you did not approve of Mother's choice of husbands," Rebeccah stated without preamble. "It seems, Grandmama, in your social circle, marriage to an American army officer is worse than running away with one's butler. The only difference is that the butler has a chance to redeem himself, whereas the American has none."

Her grandmother's features softened a fraction as the old woman laughed again. "You were always quick-witted, but this time, I'm afraid, there is no way out of our predicament. Your mother made one last request before she died, and because she was everything to me, I will see it enforced if it is the very last thing I do."

Rebeccah's chest tightened. "Wh-what was it?" she asked, her voice barely above a whisper. *Why, in God's good name,* she asked herself, *didn't Mother make the request to me in person?*

"First things first, my dear. With your mother's passing, I have instructed my solicitor to leave my entire estate to you and to Lydia. In this way, I will not worry about your futures when you realize your teaching skills and Lydia's nursing skills, though both admirable do not provide for one's security in life." The dowager paused, but when Rebeccah decided not to speak, she continued. "I have made fine matches for you as well as Lydia, to two titled young men who can provide you with all the comforts you are used to. However, your mother's wishes take precedence over my own. Her first wish, as you will learn, was carried out months ago when Lydia left for America."

This bit of news very nearly took Rebeccah's breath. She had assumed the journey was Lydia's idea, as her older sister had always been the more courageous of the Randolph girls. Her grandmother continued to stare, and for a moment Rebeccah wondered if her surprise had been visible even though she had tried her best to keep her expression bland. Finally the old woman motioned toward two envelopes lying on the marble-top table. "Those are for you."

Rebeccah put down her glass. In a rustle of black silk, she crossed the room and picked up the envelopes. The edges of the first were yellow and worn from its long journey, the second crisp and white. Despite the way her fingers trembled, she popped the wax seals, and after glancing at the contents, met the dowager's cool gaze. "What is the meaning of this?"

"I think you know."

"But . . . but, this, this is impossible," Rebeccah said, hating the way her voice quavered.

"Believe me, nothing is impossible, my dear. I suppose your dear mother, God rest her soul, had her reasons, although she failed to disclose them to me."

Rebeccah glanced down at the ticket in her hand. America. She was to sail at the end of the week, and after two weeks at sea, she would arrive at New York where Lydia would be waiting. Three days later, they would take a train west to where the tracks ended, then a stagecoach to the town of Santa Fe in the Territory of New Mexico.

"I cannot . . . will not go. 'Twas Lydia's choice to travel to America six months ago." She paused. Had it been Lydia's choice or had she, too, been coerced? "Didn't you hear me? I came here to tell you that I've met a man—someone other than the middle-aged viscount you chose for me. Arrangements are being made. We are to be married in six weeks."

"Though I doubt the validity of your announcement, the impending nuptials will simply have to be postponed."

"I refuse to do that," Rebeccah said with more conviction than she felt. She took a ragged breath and stuffed the tickets back into the envelope. "I'm a grown woman now and will, from this day forward, make my own decisions. Perhaps Lydia felt obliged to honor our mother's request. After all, she has expressed certain fond memories of Father. However, I've no memories and do not wish to establish any, nor do I desire to visit America. You see, Grandmama, in that way, I'm very much like you."

" 'Twas your mother's last wish that you do."

"Mother is gone. She'll never know." Rebeccah blinked back the sting of tears. "How can you, of all people, ask this of me? My father made his choice sixteen years ago to rid himself of his family. Why now? Why do I have to go and pretend that I care when everything wonderful is about to happen in my life?"

"Foolish child. Do you think I orchestrated this travesty? I promised your mother I would see to it regardless of my feelings, and that is precisely what I've done. However, I had the foresight to know you would resist." The old woman met Rebeccah's rebellious gaze. "Disobey me, and I will leave everything to your sister. You'll be penniless. Now, I suggest you stop sniveling and have the servants begin packing your things. Your ship sails in less than a week."

"What if I introduce myself to your grandmother?" Edward began with an understanding smile. "And if, after meeting me, it's not good enough, I could arrange for us to elope. We could slip away in the middle of the night and be married in Paris."

"Edward, please," Rebeccah said miserably. She rested her head on his broad shoulder and savored the feel of his arms around her. If only she could stay this way forever. If only it wasn't her mother's last wish. If only . . . "Don't make this any more difficult than it already is."

"But a year with those impudent cowboys . . . and what about Indians, my love?" he murmured as he placed a kiss in her hair. "My poor darling, I should demand to speak with your grandmother and forbid you to go. It could be dangerous."

Rebeccah raised her head. "No, please. Lydia assures me that America is quite civilized," she said past the heaviness in her heart. "Oh, Edward, being away from you . . . will be unbearable."

He cupped her face with his warm hands and brushed a tear away with his thumb. "What am I to do without you?" Slowly he bent his head and kissed her again.

When he pulled back, she nearly drowned in the blue of his eyes. "Will you write to me?"

"Of course, my darling, every day."

"Indians?" Colonel Sayer MacLaren repeated, looking up from

the stack of papers on the desk. He and his men were on their way to Fort Union and had decided to stop at Fort Marcy for supplies while they awaited the arrival of their payroll. "I was told they kept to the reservation up north." He stood and crossed the pine floor to glance out the window. "Why now, and . . ." He turned with his question to look at his father's old and faithful friend, ". . . why did they take the payroll?"

Sergeant Fergus Carmichael pushed his hat off his brow to rest on the back of his head. "I don't know, Colonel, sir," he began in his Scottish burr, "but the wounded soldier said he saw 'em and that he thought they were Comanche or Apache. He said after the bullets started flyin', he was runnin' too fast tae be sure." The sergeant held out a broken shaft. "Doc Randolph dug this outta his backside."

Sayer took the arrow and stared at it while he thought about the missing payroll. Memories of battles won and lost against Indians in the Plains Wars flashed briefly before his eyes, but he forced them aside and heaved a long sigh. "Assemble the men. They've got to be told that their pay will be a month late."

"Aye, sir. Anythin' else?"

"Yes, Sergeant, there is." Sayer tossed the arrow on the desk. "See if you can arrange a meeting with the sheriff. He may want me to leave some men closer to town until things settle down."

It didn't surprise Sayer to learn that ten days after speaking with the sheriff, their orders to proceed to Fort Union were suddenly retracted until further notice. He'd learned a long time ago, while serving under his father, General MacLaren, that further notice could be as short as a few days, or longer. Much longer. Word filtered down that the proficient governor of Santa Fe, the sheriff's brother, had wasted no time sending word to Washington requesting the colonel and his regiment, all experienced Indian fighters, be allowed to station themselves at Fort Marcy until such a time that the hostiles were dispatched back to the reservation.

Though Fort Marcy was never garrisoned, it was not unappealing. Its thick adobe walls offered reprieve from the heat for both men and horses. The officers' quarters were neat and clean, with lace curtains and polished wood floors. Left with no other choice, his men soon settled down to their daily routine. Two weeks later, after another incident and another wounded soldier, Sayer met Doctor James Randolph.

"How is he?" Sayer asked as he watched the doctor place a bandage on the corporal's arm.

"He'll be fine in a few days, but I suggest he be given light duty for a week or so."

Sayer helped the young man put on his shirt. "Can you walk?"

"Yes, sir. Just like Doc said, I'll be fine."

"Good, then I'll see you back at the fort later and you can give me the details." Sayer waited until he and the doctor were alone. "I noticed your credentials on the wall. How long were you in the army?"

"Practically all my life. I retired almost eight years ago." James washed his hands, then motioned toward the kitchen. "Like a cup of coffee?"

"Yes, thanks." While the doctor pumped water into the pot, Sayer lingered in the living room, picking up a picture of a very beautiful young woman and a much younger man. "Is this you?"

The doctor nodded. "Yup. Back when I had hair."

While they sat and had coffee, Sayer learned James liked to brag about his daughters, explaining that the elder had gone to meet her sister's ship in New York. His description of Lydia was thick with fatherly pride, but his description of his youngest wasn't as thorough. By the time the pot was empty, Sayer came away with the impression that Rebeccah was still very much a child.

A few days later, some more reports of trouble near the newly founded mining community of Cerrillos trickled in—the town where the doctor's daughters were to catch the stage. It was no surprise when a note arrived amid the morning mail containing an invitation from Doc Randolph to join him for supper.

"I'm glad you could come, Colonel," James began, pausing when Bonnie, the owner of the restaurant where they'd met, handed them both a menu. "I've a favor to ask."

Without too much prodding, Sayer agreed with the older man's request that the army should act as his daughters' escort. Had Doc Randolph wondered why a man of the colonel's rank was going in person, Sayer would have had to admit that he wasn't being entirely magnanimous as he enjoyed a thick steak and the Doc's company. In fact, by the time dessert was served, Sayer was feeling downright deceitful. He consoled himself with the notion that he wanted to show the local townsfolk that, as the new temporary commander of Fort Marcy, he was not one to send out troops while staying safely behind the adobe wall. But, while James picked up the tab, the truth of the matter was that Sayer wanted to satisfy his curiosity about the doctor's older daughter.

"Well," Doc Randolph began, drawing Sayer back from his thoughts. "I'll sleep better tonight knowing that you'll be meeting their train in Cerrillos on Thursday."

"It'll be my pleasure, Doc, and thanks for supper." With these things in mind, he left for the fort to make sure everything would be ready, stopping by the sutler's store on Santa Fe's Plaza to buy a new hat.

As the date of their arrival drew closer, rumors of the doctor's daughter's beauty intensified and floated freely about the fort.

Just yesterday, it had been confirmed by several young privates, who had heard it from several of the townsmen, two of whom had been Doc Randolph's patients, that Miss Lydia's hair was the color of burnished copper. The color was soon amended to be more like that of a shiny new penny. Then there was the matter of the young woman's eyes. Some said they were the color of emeralds while the doctor himself, just moments ago, had mentioned that they were more the color of the sea.

Sayer finally had to admit that, as the week wore on, his desire to make his own decision was most definitely behind his willingness to see Miss Lydia and her little sister safely to their father's home on Grant Street—not far from the fort in case he wanted to call upon her.

Thursday morning he got up early and dressed in his very best uniform to ensure that he looked every part the gentleman. His army-issue Colt .45 had been cleaned and new bluing applied, the holster oiled, and the saber at his side polished to match the sparkle of the brass buttons on his coat. Even his prized chestnut stallion had been groomed to perfection, his stockings and full blaze gleaming snowy white in the bright sunlight. Since Cerrillos was only two hours away, and the stage wasn't due till four o'clock, there was still plenty of time before he had to leave.

Brushing a speck of dust from his navy-blue sleeve, he decided to have coffee with his men. He swung down from the saddle, tying the reins to the hitching post before Pedro's Cantina. Pedro's was a favorite place to pass some time. Many a hot and weary traveler sought to quench his thirst in the shade of Pedro's cedar-post veranda that faced the majestic Sangre de Cristo Mountains. Though it was only nine o'clock, it promised to be another hot day for so early in June. Tugging at the snug fit of his high collar, Sayer stepped inside and was greeted by a dozen of his men and several wolf whistles.

"Driver?" Rebeccah leaned a little farther out the window, trying to keep from knocking her bonnet off as she was jostled around in the swaying coach. "Driver?" she repeated a little louder, but her words were swept away with the wind. Had she not been so completely miserable, she would have marveled at the way huge billowing clouds dotted a brilliant blue sky.

But she was just too uncomfortable to notice the scenery or the sky. Had she known that the railroad tracks stopped at Cerrillos and were under construction to her destination of Santa Fe, perhaps she would have dressed more appropriately. But, she had only learned that discouraging fact upon their arrival, when she saw the many workers bustling about, dragging logs and heavy planks of iron about with mules and chains.

She very nearly flung herself back against the seat, and only when she turned to stare out the window did she realize that the rolling, cactus-dotted plains had slowly transformed into braces of cottonwoods and sprinklings of piñon pines. The sweet, pungent scent of cedar and juniper chased away the musty smell of dust, and in the distance towered the purple peaks of the Sangre de Cristo Mountains.

" 'Tis beautiful, is it not?" her sister stated, drawing Rebeccah's attention away from the view.

"I suppose it is," she answered. She cast Lydia a brief glance, still vexed that each time Lydia spoke of their father, she did so with the sparkle of admiration shining brightly in her eyes. For the life of her, Rebeccah could not so easily forgive her sire. In her opinion, James Randolph was a scoundrel who'd abandoned his family. She adjusted the full skirt of her butter-colored traveling suit, wishing that she had been more inquisitive about their means of transportation.

Had she known that American coaches were not equipped

with the same comfortable interiors of English coaches, she would have chosen something more suitable to wear, something with fewer ruffles. In the back of her mind, she denied that Lydia had tried to advise her about her choice of clothing, refusing to admit that she had simply been too stubborn to listen.

Now she very nearly envied her sister's slightly flared cornflower-blue cotton skirt and crisp white blouse. Her sibling had removed the matching jacket, and looked cool and comfortable and quite content. Rebeccah retrieved a fan from her reticule and waved it before her face, thinking about her destination. Governess to a Mexican rancher sounded much more appealing than being their father's nurse. "How much longer before we are at Don Fernando's home?"

Lydia scooted forward, her excitement evident by the bright gleam in her green eyes and the rosy blush on her cheeks. "Don Fernando won't be expecting us for several more days. And father will be quite surprised when we arrive half a day early."

The sun shining in through the window turned her fair hair into a light coppery color, and once again Rebeccah wondered if that had been the color of their grandmother's hair before it turned white. If it was, then she knew very well why the old woman favored Lydia. Lydia's complexion was smooth, free of the freckles that dotted Rebeccah's nose.

Lydia spoke again, drawing Rebeccah from her despondent musings. "I realize that this wasn't your choice. It wasn't mine either, but I know if you'll just give Papa a chance, you'll see that he never intended to—"

"To what? Abandon us?" Rebeccah finished defiantly.

"Becky, plea—"

"I prefer Rebeccah and I'd thank you, dear sister, to remember that."

"Very well, *Rebeccah,* have it your way. You always were too stubborn for your own good." Lydia leaned back against the seat with a frown that caused Rebeccah to feel a twinge of remorse.

"On the voyage, I wondered . . . no that's not correct," Rebeccah amended. "I *prayed* that there would be some reasonable explanation that would absolve you from lying to me."

Lydia raised one reddish brow. "You're not going to bring that up again, are you?" She heaved another long, tired sigh. "I've no need to be vindicated, Rebeccah, nor do I feel the need to explain why I left without confiding my real reasons for doing so. I made our mother a promise. I think you should be content in the knowledge that, like you, I believe promises are to be kept. Therefore, you should understand that I had no choice."

"Really?" Rebeccah replied rebelliously. "And so, off you sailed like the brave little soldier. How admirable." She turned and continued to stare out the window—something she had decided to do the moment they entered the disgusting stagecoach. "However, you had no reason not to leave, where I, on the other hand, had every reason to stay. By now, I would have been married."

"Oh come now, Becky. My guess is that you hardly know the man." Rebeccah's dark look did not bring its intended results. "You can scowl at me for the rest of your life if it brings you pleasure, but it does not change the fact that Mother did what she thought best. If this young man loves you as you say, he will wait for your return. In the meantime, we must do the very best we can so that when we return home, we will do so triumphantly."

Rebeccah scoffed. "So I'm to be a governess to a Mexican rancher. How quaint." She folded her fan and tapped it idly against her gloved palm.

"I know it's not what you wanted, but then, I didn't think I would ever be our father's nurse either, but I am, and so far, it has not been as awful as I thought it would be. Once you get to know the people of Santa Fe, you'll feel differently. They are unlike any I have ever met. Their needs are simple, Becky. They don't have the schools and hospitals we have back in England. Our father is the only doctor in town."

Lydia waited until Rebeccah looked at her. "I know you don't understand. And I realize that I had the advantage of an explanation from our mother, but as you are now, so was I appalled when I first heard of her intentions. Then I realized that if she felt so strongly about it, the very least I could do was to comply. I knew she was ill," Lydia paused, and Rebeccah could see the sparkle of tears in her sister's green eyes. "I just didn't realize how little time she had left. I'm sure she meant to explain everything to you herself."

Rebeccah blinked several times, refusing to cry. She had cried for days before she sailed, and nothing had changed. If crying would get her on the first ship back to England, she'd be the first to burst into tears, but her situation was hopeless. Without her grandmother's money, she was, just as the old woman had stated, *penniless.*

"So we've both been sentenced, like common prisoners, to spend one year in this . . . this desolate country, and for what? So we can prove that we can endure hardships?" She raised her chin a little higher.

"I do not think that Mother wanted us to suffer, Beck—Rebeccah. I think she wanted us to see people who have made lives for themselves in this rugged country, who really appreciate the simple things that we take for granted. I think she wanted us to know a different way of life. A life she lived until—"

"Until Father put us on a ship and sent us back to England?" Rebeccah opened her fan and began again to try and cool herself. "If she loved being here so much, why didn't she refuse to leave, and why didn't she ever return?"

"I don't know the answer to those questions, nor do I care to speculate. But I do know that once you speak with Papa, you'll come to realize, as I have, that he did what he had to do to keep us safe."

"How noble of him," Rebeccah replied dryly, slipping a finger between her chin and the ribbon of her bonnet to loosen it a bit. "Very well. I can understand that our mother wanted us to visit America and perhaps to establish some sort of relationship with Father. However, I do not understand why she felt compelled to force us to practice occupations neither of us ever intended to use."

Lydia gave her another sympathetic smile. "I believe Mother worried that we would become spoiled. Grandmama's status, as well as her bottomless purse, had, in Mother's opinion, corrupted our sense of worth. I feel she sent us out west to allow us the opportunity to experience what she experienced." Lydia sighed wistfully. "For that reason alone, I have accepted my fate, and I hope that you'll accept yours."

Rebeccah smoothed an imaginary wrinkle from her skirt. "Very well, now I know why we were sent to this God-forsaken country, but why didn't you write to me and warn me what was coming?"

"Mother made me promise not to tell you." Lydia looked down at her hands, apparently wounded. "I'm sorry if you think that I betrayed you, Becky, but I gave my word."

The girls rode in strained silence for several miles, Rebeccah staring out the window, her vision blurred by the threat of tears. How would she ever be able to survive a year in this desolate wilderness teaching the daughters of a Mexican nobleman English etiquette?

'Twas only at her mother's insistence that she acquired her teaching skills, having not the stomach to endure the blood and gore poor Lydia's chosen profession required. Rebeccah cast a quick glance in her sister's direction, feeling a twinge of pity. Lydia was obviously fatigued, and for good reason. Not only had she made this dreadful journey once, but twice.

"Lydia," Rebeccah began, drawing her sister's attention away from the opposite window. "I haven't been a very good traveling companion, and for that I apologize."

Lydia's smile chased away a little of her gloom. "Tell me about the young man you're in love with."

Rebeccah glanced down at her hands while the corners of her mouth turned into a very slight smile. "He's quite the rogue. He proposed to me while clinging to the trellis outside my bedroom window."

"Really, and no one saw him?" Lydia asked.

"No. 'Twas in the middle of the night." She pulled off her glove, exposing a small but elegant emerald-and-diamond ring. "He gave me this and sealed his promise with an absolutely divine kiss."

"What did Grandmama say when you told her?" Lydia pressed on, her smile contagious.

Rebeccah lifted her chin and sniffed in much the same manner as the elderly dame, mimicking her voice. *"Though I doubt the validity of your announcement, the impending nuptials will simply have to be postponed."*

She couldn't contain her own laughter when Lydia broke out in uncontrolled giggles. When they could finally stop laughing, Rebeccah grew more serious. "He was terribly upset with me when I told him I was leaving. I wouldn't blame him if he never spoke to me again."

"I'm sure, if he loves you as you say he does, he'll wait."

Rebeccah returned her sister's gentle smile. "You were right to keep Mother's intentions a mystery to me. I firmly believe a promise is a promise."

"Thank you," her sister replied. "And I shall make you a promise. The year will go by quickly. Santa Fe isn't as horrible as you're probably thinking. In fact, it's quite civiliz—"

Several ear-shattering cracks of gunfire sounded close by.

"Dear God," Rebeccah cried in horror as the coach lurched forward, then turned sharply. "What in heaven's name is going on?"

The color drained from her sister's face. "I-I believe someone's shooting at us," Lydia gasped.

"What are we to do?" Rebeccah cried as she clutched at the leather handhold to keep from being tossed about inside the stagecoach. Just then an arrow splintered the wood above her head. "Indians?" Fear clawed at her insides when her sister dragged her down to the floor between the seats. "I thought they had been sent to reservations!"

"Apparently not!"

CHAPTER TWO

Sayer had no sooner taken a sip of his coffee than a Mexican boy burst inside shouting that the stage was coming into town at a dead run, the team out of control. By the time the colonel could push his way through the crowd, the runaway stage had careened into several support posts, knocking down the sign and part of the overhanging roof at Bonnie's Eatery, scattering shingles. Women screamed, dogs barked and, most of all, everyone scattered as the stage and six galloping horses flew past, leaving a cloud of choking dust in their wake.

"Mount up," he ordered, vaulting into his saddle. He pressed his heels to his stallion's side and gave chase, six of his men hot on his heels. As he rounded the corner, his worst fear became a reality. The out-of-control team was heading at a dead run down its usual route, which led across the Santa Fe River. An early melt had the caused the river to rise up over the usual shallow crossing, clouding the water with mud and silt. The team was forced to a stop as the heavy coach bogged down smack in the middle of the crossing, listing a little to the right and sinking precariously in the mud.

"Damn," Sayer muttered under his breath. His men were soon at his side waiting for their orders, as curious townsfolk began to gather on the grassy bank. "Sergeant Carmichael, ride over and steady the team. Corporal Rogers, help him."

While his men hurried to obey their orders, Sayer guided his horse into the river. Sayer's young, inexperienced stallion danced on the edge of the water, but after a firm reprimand from his master, splashed over toward the stage. Sayer maneuvered close enough to grab the rail near the door, where he balanced precariously on the small footstep, intending to climb up into the driver's seat. His apprehensive mount took several steps away. A moment later the door flew open, hitting Sayer in the side with enough force to knock him backwards into the shallow water. His stallion jumped out of the way, snorting at Sayer's new hat as it floated by.

"Oh my," came a woman's voice as cold water rushed over him, taking his breath. He reached up, grabbed the wheel and hauled himself to his feet, giving the woman a murderous glance before he turned to catch a glimpse of his hat disappearing around the bend.

"What in the hell are you doing?" he very nearly shouted as he adjusted his saber and tugged at his coat.

"I beg your pardon," came her mutinous reply. "Don't blame me for your incompetence."

"Incompetence?" Sayer stared up at the pale young woman and knew the moment he laid eyes on her that the rumors of her beauty were true—all except the part describing her sweet nature, and the color of her hair. She was definitely a blonde, not a redhead, and her eyes . . . well they were green all right— not like the ocean, but more like the tender new growth on a spruce.

He put one water-soaked boot on the hub of the wheel and quickly climbed into the driver's seat, only to be faced with yet another dilemma. The reins had been snapped by the runaway horses. Swearing under his breath, he whistled sharply, pleased that his young stallion responded quickly to his training, even though one of the animal's ears was cocked on the woman still standing in the open doorway—the ruffles of her gown blowing gently in the breeze.

The stallion snorted nervously.

"What do you propose to do, soldier?" the young lady demanded, lifting her chin a little higher as she clutched her parasol.

"I propose to get you and your little sister out of the stage before it turns over," he said through clenched teeth. "Now, put that thing away and hand the child out when I get closer."

Had he not been forced to pay attention to his jittery horse, he would have noticed her confusion. Standing on the wheel to keep from having to step back into the water, he gathered up his reins and was nearly in the saddle when, at the same moment, the beauty in the doorway opened the frilly parasol.

The stallion sank back on his haunches, slipping in the mud in his haste to get away. Once more Sayer found himself in the water as a burst of guffaws carried over from the crowd on the bank. "Damn it! Didn't I tell you to put that away?" he spluttered as he stood and shook the water out of his gloves.

"I shan't be ordered about by the likes of you."

He glared at her, then tugged his clothing back into place. Still muttering, he none-too-gently caught the reins of his frightened horse. It took him several attempts to quiet the young stallion enough for him to mount. Once in the saddle, Sayer raked his wet hair back off his forehead, rode up to the woman, wrenched the parasol from her grasp and flung it downstream, unmindful of her angry protest and ignoring another bout of laughter from the onlookers.

Much to his surprise another beauty appeared. She gazed over her sister's shoulder, her wide sea-green eyes filled with apprehension as she tucked a loose strand of red hair behind a delicate ear. "Miss Lydia?" he said before he realized it.

"Yes. Please, take Rebeccah first," the redhead pleaded. The sisters argued for a moment while he moved his dancing mount a bit closer. Without preamble, he grabbed the blonde around the waist and dragged her up into the saddle before him, paying no heed to her outraged scream. Angry as he was, he was suddenly aware that she smelled like a field of flowers, and was all softness and curves in spite of her accounting of his ancestors. "Who," she clarified, "had to be uncivilized savages."

He carried her to the bank and handed her down to one of his men, who immediately released her as she spun to shout at the poor man before turning to shout another insult at Sayer's back. Her actions drew a few more chuckles from the crowd, but the hilarity rose to a fevered pitch when a gust of wind caught her fancy, feathered bonnet and carried it out to the middle of the river, where it caught on a protruding rock. The stallion shied and Sayer swore as he barely managed to stay in the saddle, and the crowd roared with gaiety.

"Watch out for that hat, Colonel," one man hollered, his voice thick with humor.

"Don't let that hoss get the best o' you, Colonel," another advised him over the crowd's laughter. "It might have feathers, but it's just a hat."

Paying no mind to the bantering from the crowd, the colonel guided his flighty stallion around the bobbing bonnet until he was close enough to lift the second woman from the stage. She, too, smelled good and felt good in his arms, and he was quickly reminded how long it had been since he'd been in the company of a lady. The crowd cheered the moment she was on the ground. Instead of tossing insults, she smiled up at him with a softly muttered, "Thank you."

"What of my hat?" the blond one demanded furiously, drawing Sayer's attention. Several men mimicked her question with feigned distress, but the concern in her rebellious green eyes was as genuine as the sultry pout of her mouth. " 'Tis ruined."

"Yup, it's rui'nt, all right," an old man agreed.

Sayer tossed the man a dark look, then addressed the young

soldier closest to him as he dismounted. "Corporal, fetch the lady's hat." Grinning from ear to ear, the young corporal splashed through the shallow water and snatched it up. He handed it to his commanding officer who, in turn, handed him his reins. Unmindful of the bonnet's delicate feathers, Sayer wrung it out, shook it back into some semblance of its normal shape then handed it to the lady with a curt nod. He thought he heard her call him a scoundrel, but the crowd's laughter drowned out her words as he raked his damp hair out of his face.

Paying no attention to the comical looks he got, he escorted both women back to town and down the boardwalk. He didn't care that his boots made little squashy sounds with each step that caused the children who trailed behind to giggle. Nor did he care that water and mud dribbled from his holster, and that mud nearly covered the sheath of his saber. His only thought was to deposit the doctor's daughters at his home as quickly as possible.

"You may unhand me, soldier," his captive demanded as she tried for the tenth time to pull her elbow from his firm grasp. The other young woman with the red hair leaned closer.

"Rebeccah, in America, as you know it is in England, 'tis considered an insult to address an officer in such a manner." When Sayer glanced at the redhead, she smiled, melting some of the ice around his waterlogged heart. "I'm not well acquainted with rank, but I do believe by the medals upon your chest that you are more than just a common soldier. Am I correct?"

"Yes, ma'am," he said tightly, giving her a brief nod. "Colonel MacLaren, at your service." He let go of the blonde and knocked loudly on the door, leaving wet, muddy knuckle-prints on the painted wood.

"No matter his rank, Lydia," the feisty young woman retaliated. " 'Tis obvious this man is no gentleman." He felt her gaze riveted on his stern features as he knocked again. "A gentleman would have asked before he snatched me from the coach, and he most certainly would not have destroyed my hat nor deliberately disposed of my parasol. They were purchased in Paris. I hope, *Colonel,* you are prepared to replace them?"

He glanced down at his captive, deciding that she was the fairer of the two, but most definitely had the sharper tongue. He briefly replayed the scene at the river, still glad that he had destroyed the damned parasol. It was only fair. After all, he'd lost a brand-new hat. His status as her escort forbade him to say what was on his mind; instead, he forced a stiff smile and replied, "As soon as possible, Miss Randolph." He had answered only to soothe her temper, holding back his own. He knocked again, harder. "Doc Randolph?"

Rebeccah stared up at him, not at all amused at the slight, arrogant smile that tugged at the corner of his firm mouth. My, she thought, he was tall and even wet and muddy he was bold and almost frightening. His dark hair was longer than she was accustomed to, but damp, it was difficult to tell its true color. And his wet uniform, why, it very nearly left nothing to the imagination, clinging to his broad shoulders and hugging his narrow hips and . . . for heaven's sake, what was she doing? Ladies never stared, and certainly not at a man's thickly muscled thighs.

She felt her cheeks warm with color as she looked up and found him watching, lodging the breath in her throat. She quickly turned away, praying he hadn't noticed her brazen inspection. But he had; of that she was sure. The spark of angry arrogance she saw in his vivid blue eyes confirmed that he had witnessed every mortifying moment of it.

"All of my sister's things are on the stage, Colonel," Lydia said. Rebeccah could have kissed her for drawing his attention away from her.

"My men will deliver your trunks as soon as possible." He reached up to knock once more, but the door opened.

"Lydia," Doctor James Randolph exclaimed as he accepted a hug from his eldest daughter. There was an uncomfortable pause as he slowly turned. "Becky?" he said, his voice soft, his gaze strong yet cautious.

Rebeccah stared at her father, trying to remember his face, but nothing came to mind. He was a handsome man, with thinning blond hair, spectacles, and a few extra pounds around his middle. He made no move to grab her and hug her, but stood stiff, staring at her, and when she met his gaze, it nearly broke her heart in two. His eyes were brimming with love and understanding and something more—tears. He was the first to look away, coughing a little to clear his throat, his uncomfortable gesture prolonging the moment.

"I know that I have no right," he said, his voice breaking right there and then in front of everyone. She realized he was trying hard to be strong, pausing a moment to collect himself.

"Oh, Father," she cried, overwhelmed with a deep longing to have him hold her. She took a step forward and he folded her in his embrace, whispering her name over and over again as she did his. Then Lydia was there too and all three of them laughed and hugged and cried.

Sayer watched the scene before him, unwilling to interrupt, yet painfully reminded of his parents. Ill at ease, he waited until Doc Randolph glanced his way. He gave the good doctor an understanding nod before turning to leave.

Rebeccah spent the rest of the day with Lydia and their father. The shield she had so carefully erected around her heart crumbled away with each hour that passed.

"I want you both to know," James said after a long, thoughtful pause. "I loved your mother more than life itself, and when you girls were born, I was the happiest man on this earth." He heaved a tired sigh and touched a match to a lamp as the sun settled into the crevice of the mountains. "I was afraid. Back then I was just a young captain, and when my orders came to transfer to Fort Riley in Kansas—the very heart of Indian Territory—I-I did what I thought best. I sent my family back to England where your mother could be with her family."

"But why?" Rebeccah asked. "Why couldn't we stay with you?"

James's frown deepened. "It wasn't safe. Tribe after tribe was on the warpath. I said I was afraid, and gall darn it, as much as I hate to admit it, I was. I was terrified. I couldn't sleep nights thinking about it. Your grandmother had been pressuring Louise to visit, and . . . and I guess I just wanted the peace of mind knowing you'd be safe." He heaved a tired sigh then turned with a forced smile. "Did your mother . . . well, did she ever mention me or our life together?" Rebeccah flashed her sister a brief glance, very much relieved when Lydia cleared her throat then hurried to answer. "Yes, Papa, she spoke about you all the time."

"She showed us your picture . . . quite often," Rebeccah added. She inwardly winced that she couldn't say more, but how were they to tell their father that their grandmother forbade his name to be spoken in her house. And, with no place to go, their mother had complied.

Uncomfortable with her lie, Rebeccah rose and crossed the short distance to the mantel on which sat several small framed portraits of her mother, one by herself, one holding an infant and Lydia's small hand, and the other a larger picture of both her mother and her father on their wedding day. Instantly a painful lump formed in her throat. "Where were you married?"

"In New York," her father replied. "I met your mother at a ball. She was visiting her elderly aunt."

"Oh yes," Rebeccah stated. "Aunt Lily. I remember Mother speaking of her."

During the course of the evening, Rebeccah learned about her parents' life together, where they were married, and about the town in Pennsylvania where Lydia and Rebeccah had lived as small children.

As the hour grew late, she began to wonder why her mother never returned to be with her father. The moment it sprang to mind, she knew it was a futile question, and one that would never be answered because of her mother's passing. When she and Lydia excused themselves to make ready for bed, their father insisted that they return.

"I'll make us a pot of coffee," he had said, and his expression was such that they couldn't refuse.

"So," James began as he carried three cups to the table with one hand and a plate of cookies with the other. He retrieved the pot and filled the cups with the fragrant brew. "How'd you come to be so early, and—" He looked at them over the top of his spectacles. "—how'd you end up in the river?" The topic turned to the events of their long journey, to their rescue, then lastly to the colonel.

"I'm finding that men here in the West have no manners," Rebeccah muttered. She added a spoonful of sugar to her cup as they sat at the kitchen table in their robes. "First our driver and his companion forsake us, then we are forced to endure public embarrassment at the hands of an uncivilized army officer. An officer in the Royal Army would have never treated ladies of our standing in such an uncouth manner."

Lydia smiled. "I hardly think that if one of our officers had been pushed into a muddy river, he would be as gracious."

Rebeccah felt her cheeks warm when her father turned his full attention on her, his expression urging her to defend herself. "I did not push him. How was I to know he was going to jump on the coach at precisely the same time I opened the door? He could have warned us of his intent. I believe he tripped on his sword."

Lydia giggled. "You should have seen his expression, Papa, when he came out of the water. I do believe the poor man wanted to murder someone, and I can't say as I blame him."

"The first or the second time?" Rebeccah asked, her own expression filling with mischief. Lydia glanced at Rebeccah, then they both burst out in boisterous laughter.

"Well, now," their father began with an interested grin, "I had wondered why the colonel was all wet and muddy. What happened out there?" He rose, retrieved the pot and refilled their cups. "The colonel's a nice man," James began. "Good-looking too, don't you girls think so?"

Lydia nodded. "Most definitely."

"I never noticed," Rebeccah lied, her memory of his clinging wet uniform causing her cheeks to warm again.

"Really?" her father countered with a smile. "Why, the way you were staring at him when I peeked out the window to see who in the blazes was beating down my door, I thought you had most certainly noticed."

Rebeccah put down her cup. If her father had noticed, then her suspicion that the colonel knew as well was true. "I-I was simply trying to determine his rank," she defended innocently.

"But he told us his military status a few moments before," Lydia added with a superior nod. "I think you liked what you saw. Do you agree, Papa?"

"That's absurd," Rebeccah interjected, hoping that she looked adequately appalled, even though memories of how effortlessly the colonel had lifted her flitted through her mind. And his chest. Why, it felt as hard as if the man wore armor instead of a military uniform.

James grinned. "Don't drag me into this matchmaking stuff.

I'll warn you both right now, I'm no good at it."

"Thank you, Father," Rebeccah said with a patronizing smile. "And, there is certainly no reason for you to worry about it. I'm engaged, and after this endeavor is over, I shall return to England and be married." Her father's smile faded, but she sensed that he wasn't saddened by her announcement, but rather the fact that she sounded so eager to return to England. "His name is Edward. He's absolutely divine and the son of Lord Dunlap of Colchester."

"How long have you known this young man?" her father asked.

"Several months. I met him in London while he was visiting his brother." She stifled a yawn. "I beg your pardon. It's the hour, not the company. It's been a long, trying day."

James rose quickly while Lydia carried their dishes to the sink. "Of course, after what happened with the Indian attack and all, I'm sure you're exhausted. Lydia, leave that, honey. Come along." He led them both upstairs. "It's not as fancy as your grandmother's estate, but I think Lydia will tell you that you'll be comfortable." He stepped aside and let them enter. "Tomorrow, Lydie and I'll show you around town. Before you know it, you'll be miles away, and we've only just come to really know each other."

Rebeccah hugged and kissed their father. "Good night, Father," she murmured, feeling wretched at the glint of sorrow in his eyes. "I shall see you in the morning."

She quietly closed the door, and then leaned back against it for several moments while Lydia turned up the lamp. Lace sheers peeked out behind velvet curtains and reminded her of their mother's room back in England. Terribly homesick, Rebeccah slipped off her borrowed dressing gown and sat on the edge of the bed clad in one of her sister's nightgowns.

"I told you you'd think differently once you met him," Lydia stated as she turned down the quilt and fluffed the pillows.

Rebeccah let out a long sigh. "Yes. He is different. Not at all as I imagined him to be." She slipped between the cool, crisp sheets. "I wonder why he never wrote to Mother asking her to come back."

Lydia bent down and kissed Rebeccah's cheek. "That, dear sister, is something I've wondered about too. Perhaps, in the morning, we should ask him." She blew out the lamp then went across the hall to her own room.

CHAPTER THREE

Standing back from a long, oval-shaped mirror, Rebeccah fingered a wisp of curly blond hair into place as she inspected her lavender gown. The French-designed square neckline left just enough flesh exposed to be daring, yet not enough to be wanton.

"Do you think this is too much?" she asked, turning to see if the bustle was adjusted correctly. A disturbing thought entered her mind. Just whom was she expecting to impress?

"I'm sure if we happen to see the colonel," Lydia replied, as she looked at her sister a moment before placing some of Rebeccah's things in the closet to air, "he'll think it's lovely."

Rebeccah cast her sister a quick glance then turned once more to her reflection. Was she that obvious? "I'm not trying to attract the colonel, Lydia. I'm simply trying to look nice to please Father. Must I constantly remind you that I'm engaged?"

"Oh, yes. I'd almost forgotten. You're engaged," Lydia teased. "Though I doubt you're in love, I apologize. I shan't mention the handsome colonel again."

Rebeccah ignored her sister's goading. "I thank you for that. Now, what about you? You've been here longer than I. Do you find the colonel attractive?"

Their eyes met in the mirror then Lydia gave a sly smile. "A blind woman would find him attractive, but . . ."

"But what?" Rebeccah asked as Lydia stepped into her gown then lifted her long red hair to make it easier for Rebeccah to help with the buttons.

"I, like you, do not know him. I assume he arrived after I left. However, I can assure you, he is not my type."

"Really? Why not? He's handsome, though a bit on the uncivilized side, wearing his gun on his hip, as well as that long, deadly dagger on the other."

"It's called a Bowie knife."

Rebeccah shook her head. "Nevertheless, you were always the adventurous one when we were growing up, not I. Remember the time when you stole Lord Watson's pony?"

"Rebeccah, I did not steal it, I simply borrowed the cute little thing. And, if my memory serves, you had a ride as well."

"Yes, but I wasn't the one who brazenly walked into our neighbor's barn, ordered their befuddled groom to saddle little John Watson's pony, then trotted the animal down the lane as if it were a normal occurrence." When her sister turned, Rebeccah laughed at her innocent expression. "And, if I may add, without an ounce of fear."

"I believe I was a little bit afraid."

"Well, you didn't show it." Rebeccah gave a firm nod of her head. "That is precisely why it makes perfectly good sense to me that you'd find an Indian-fighting, devilishly good-looking soldier most intriguing." They giggled again.

"I suppose . . . if he were back in England," Lydia began. "It would be fun to show him off in his uniform. However, I've heard it said that American cavalry officers don't usually live long enough to grow old with their wives. And when I marry, I shall marry a man who is not, by his profession, required to put himself in danger unnecessarily."

Sayer hung another new hat on the rack then sat down at the only vacant table at Bonnie's Eatery. He had just ordered some coffee when Sergeant Carmichael came in and handed him the broken shaft of an arrow. "I dug this out of the stage," the Scotsman said, his bushy brows drawn together as he sat across from Sayer.

Sayer examined the shaft for a moment then glanced over at his friend. "I don't recognize it as Apache, but that doesn't mean it isn't. In speaking with some of the men who have been here awhile, I understand Comanche have been known to raid these parts on occasion. We'll ride out tomorrow and see what their tracks tell us."

He put the arrow on the seat of the chair next to him. "Did you manage to find my hat?" Sayer could have sworn his old friend was trying hard not to smile.

"Yes, sir, indeed I did. It caught on a piece of driftwood a ways downstream. I hung it up tae dry. It'll be as good as new with a good brushin'. Private Harris cleaned and oiled your Colt, as well as your father's saber, and when your holster and sheath dry, they'll be right as rain." Fergus paused when Bonnie came over.

"What's your pleasure, gentlemen?"

Fergus smiled up at the older woman. "You're looking lovely tonight, Miss Bonnie."

"Why thank you, Sergeant. Now, what can I bring you fellas to eat?"

"I'll have my usual," the sergeant replied with another smile. Sayer ordered a steak, smiling when the woman turned and Fergus heaved a long sigh as he watched her leave, reminding Sayer of a lovesick hound.

"Now there's a woman tae please any man alive." Fergus nodded, then took a sip of his coffee. "Not only can she cook, but she's as pleasin' tae look at as they come. Not too thin and not too plump." The sergeant added a little more sugar to his cup then grinned at his commander. "Speakin' of lovely lassies, which one of the gude doctor's daughters did you think is the prettiest?"

"Prettiest?" Sayer repeated, trying to ignore the grin on the sergeant's weathered face.

"Aye. Miss Lydia or Miss Rebeccah?"

"I'm afraid I didn't notice," Sayer stated. "The blond one was too busy shouting at me."

"Oh, sure, of course you dinna notice," Fergus added, skeptically. "You carried them both tae the bank in your arms, and you're tryin' tae tell me that you dinna notice?" Fergus scratched his chin as if in thought. "I, for one, saw the little blonde lookin' you over even whilst she was shoutin'. She'd be more tae my likin', if'n I was a young buck like you, of course."

"Let me get this straight," Sayer mused as he leaned back in his seat with a grin. "You were thinking about which one was the prettier the whole time?"

"Well, there was hardly anythin' more tae do once I had hold of the horses, now was there?" His expression told Sayer he was still a bit peeved at having to steady the team. Obviously the Scotsman thought the job beneath his status.

Sayer gave his sergeant a doubtful smile. "No, I suppose there wasn't. However, as I was the one dodging her insults, I just didn't think to make a comparison."

"Understandably so," Fergus said. "However, I'll expect you'll have plenty o' time tae make your decision."

"What decision?" Sayer asked, knowing full well that his old friend would not be dissuaded from his matchmaking.

"Why, which one is the prettiest, of course." Fergus smiled, then winked. "My money is on the blonde, though the redhead is pleasin' tae look at as well." The sergeant fell quiet as he glanced at the door when the little bell above it jingled. "Seems you might have another chance tae decide. Look who's comin' in."

Doctor Randolph and his daughters paused to greet another couple sitting by the door. "Mr. Winters, Mrs. Winters. This is my other daughter, Rebeccah. Rebeccah, Mr. Winters owns the bank. When you start teaching, I'm sure he'll be delighted to help you with your accounting."

When the formalities were over, the doctor glanced around the crowded room then spotted the colonel and the sergeant and the three empty chairs at their table. With a wide grin, he guided his daughters in Sayer's direction.

"Doc Randolph, ladies," Sayer acknowledged, standing with his sergeant. "Will you join us?" Fergus hurried to pull out a chair for Lydia.

"Thank you," James said, ignoring the subtle shake of Rebeccah's head. "I was beginning to think we'd have to come back another night." He smiled at his daughters, then motioned to the chair the colonel had pulled out. "Sit down, Becky."

"Please do," the colonel said, matching her father's grin.

The memory of the colonel's strong arms lifting her from the coach caused a strange little flutter in the pit of her stomach, and once more she had to fight the urge to gaze up at him to confirm that her memory was correct. As hard as she fought the urge, she lost the battle and gave him a quick glance, inwardly pleased. His were the bluest eyes she had ever seen—that is, except for Edward's, she quickly amended.

"How nice of you to invite us, Colonel," Lydia said as she accepted a place next to her father.

"Yes, thank you," Rebeccah added as she sank down, then immediately jumped up. "Oh my," she gasped, staring down at an arrow.

The colonel snatched it up, and then slid it under his chair. When she met his gaze, she was almost sure a spark of amusement twinkled in the depths of his eyes. Much to her surprise, his brown hair, now dry, was quite wavy and streaked with gold.

"I trust you're not the worse for your little mishap in the river?" he asked as she took her place and arranged her skirts.

"Now that you mention it—"

"Rebeccah, what are you going to have for dinner?" her father interrupted, smiling when she glanced his way. He nodded toward the two-page menu.

At first she thought to question the colonel about the army's obligation to travelers, but a stern look from Lydia banished the thought. "What do you recommend, Colonel MacLaren?" Rebeccah asked, inspecting the menu. "I'm sure you're more acquainted with the fare than I."

"The roast beef is usually a good choice," he answered, drawing her gaze back to his. Again her stomach did a little dance. He looked exceptionally handsome, more so than he had at the river. Surely she was just captivated because she had never met a man of his caliber before. After all, it was rather exciting to sit next to an Indian fighter.

"Yes, indeed it is," her father agreed.

"Then that is what I shall have," Lydia hurried to comply. "What are you going to have, Becky?"

Rebeccah looked away from the colonel, feeling the heat of a blush color her cheeks. My God, she'd been staring and now everyone at the table knew it. She quickly pretended to scan the menu, only slightly annoyed that Lydia used her father's pet name for her. "I-I'll have the same . . . unless they have buffalo steaks?"

The colonel almost choked on his coffee. "N-no, ma'am, I don't believe Miss Bonnie has any buffalo."

Bonnie came out of the kitchen and after the doctor introduced Rebeccah, the portly woman took their orders. "Bonnie is a wonderful cook," Lydia stated, placing her napkin in her lap. "Once you taste her pastries you'll think you're visiting Paris instead of Santa Fe." Bonnie reappeared with more cups, filling them with coffee.

"Is this what the cowboys drink?" Rebeccah asked. "Father made some for us last night. It's quite popular at the gambling houses in London, but my grandmother never allowed Alfred— our butler," she clarified, "to serve it. But now that I've tasted it, I can't imagine why. It's quite palatable." She hardly noticed as two unkempt men came in and joined some men at the table next to theirs. When she glanced over at them, they both grinned and nodded. Bonnie came, took their orders and served them their drinks.

"You must be the new commander," the first man said when he caught Sayer's eye. The colonel acknowledged them with a polite nod, and then deliberately turned his attention back to Rebeccah, asking if she would like some cream for her coffee. She accepted, and a few minutes later, their food was served.

"Tell me, Colonel," she began, "how do you explain the attack on our stage? We were told all the hostiles were on reservations." She glanced at her father, but like Lydia, he seemed oddly interested in the design on their napkins.

"To assume that men will stay where they are told simply because the government orders it, is not a safe assumption, ma'am."

"Really?" she countered. "Why is that?"

"I can't say for sure, but I expect it would be the same as if I told you to do something you didn't want to do." The gleam in his eyes reminded her that she had blatantly disobeyed him when he'd told her to put away her parasol.

"So, am I to believe there are no agencies, willing or otherwise, to keep these savages under control?" she asked with a superior smile.

"Only army patrols, ma'am." The colonel cut another bite of his steak.

Her father cleared his throat, but she wouldn't be swayed.

"Pray tell, when you capture these men, what do you do with them?"

"They are taken back to the reservation."

"I see." She took a sip of coffee then lifted her chin slightly higher. "Then perhaps, Colonel, the penalty for escape should be harsher."

"Yeah," came a voice from the other table, drawing her attention. "I'd think shootin' at white folk oughta be a hangin' offense."

"Now that's a little too harsh," James stated, shifting nervously in his chair as the colonel turned his attention to the man speaking.

"I've heard it said, Colonel, that you and your pa kilt more Injuns single-handed than ol' Pete and me will ever see in our lifetimes. If that's so, what's a few more?" His remark drew some chuckles from his tablemate.

This time, the colonel didn't bother to acknowledge the man's question. He simply turned back to the table and reached for his coffee. Rebeccah cast her sister a quizzical glance at the sudden tension that filled the room, but Lydia only gave a subtle shake of her head.

"He don't look very mean," the man said to his companion, obviously irritated by the colonel's rebuff. Rebeccah glanced at the sergeant. The older man's reddish, hawk-like brows where pulled together, and she wondered if he would intervene on his commander's behalf. Like the colonel, he appeared to ignore the men, tending to his food. Yet she had the distinct feeling that, if given the opportunity, the Scotsman would have gladly thrown them out.

While they ate, Lydia seemed content to listen to her father, who had changed the subject from Indians to one of his patients. Nevertheless, when Rebeccah glanced at the colonel, a tiny muscle ticked above the tight set of his jaw, even though it appeared he gave her father his full attention. The next instant, he glanced at her and caught her staring. His friendly smile was immediate, but it didn't quite soften the hardness around his eyes.

Bonnie came out with more coffee, and no sooner had she disappeared into the kitchen than the short man at the next table leaned closer to his scruffy companion, whispering loud enough to be easily overheard. "He's kind of young to have such a fearsome reputation. Are you sure he's the one?"

Rebeccah's father paused in the telling of his story to cast the man a quick, irritated glance over his shoulder, before he began again. He was immediately interrupted.

"It ain't how you look, Pete, but how fast you can draw and shoot your gun, I reckon." This time the colonel's gaze drifted past her father to settle once more on the men.

"Everyone says you were transferred out here to keep the peace, but after your Pa was kilt, I heard you just couldn't stand it no longer." The room grew uncomfortably quite. Rebeccah glanced at the colonel, wondering if he would answer.

Once again her dining partner ignored the man even when his rowdy companion asked, "Stand what, Johnny?"

"Injun killin', ya dad-blamed idiot, what else?"

Uncomfortable, Rebeccah glanced at Lydia, who had grown unusually quiet. Her cheeks appeared to have lost their color.

"I reckon a man can take only so many scalps 'afore it ain't no fun no more," one of the men added.

"Nope, it weren't that. My daddy used to say that when a man loses his nerve, he ain't worth his salt."

This time, the colonel put down his knife and fork, and then put his napkin on the table. Rebeccah's heart thudded against her breast as she realized he was preparing to stand. How exciting. Would they have a fistfight right here in the restaurant? Just then Bonnie came out of the kitchen with a pot of hot coffee, and by the look on her usually smiling face, she had more on her mind than refilling cups.

"Got bad new for you boys, we just ran out of steaks. You want more coffee?" Bonnie asked, holding the steaming pot directly over the man's head. The one called Pete ducked down at the same time he shook his head. She gave them a dark look. "If you're done, I'll be taking your cups."

"You got any—"

"Nope, fresh out."

"But I was hopin' you'd at least have some of that apple pie of yours, Miss Bonnie. Got any of that left?"

"Sorry, boys." She plunked the pot on the table, accepted their money, and then watched as they shuffled out. Smiling to herself, Bonnie stuffed the money into her apron, then turned toward their table as she tucked a wisp of greyish-brown hair back into her bun and smiled sweetly at the sergeant. "More coffee?" she asked everyone. Her voice sang with kindness. She filled their cups, then added, "Anyone care for dessert? I've fresh-baked apple pie just out of the oven."

"Why, yes," Dr. Randolph said with a relieved sigh. "I'd like some for sure. How about it, girls? You've got to try it to believe it. Why, it'll melt in your mouth, isn't that right, Colonel?"

"Yes, sir, Doctor. That's a true statement."

When Rebeccah looked over at him, Sayer's expression had relaxed, but nevertheless, he stood, took out his wallet and placed a few bills on the table. "If you'll excuse me, Doctor." He smiled at Lydia, but his warm gaze stopped on Rebeccah. "I've got some business to see to." The sergeant looked disappointed, but rose and fetched their hats.

"I wonder what they're up to?" James asked, once they were gone.

"I do believe that if Miss Bonnie hadn't come out of the kitchen, we would have been witness to those men getting a good thrashing," Rebeccah replied with a rebellious gleam in her eyes.

"You can't beat a man up for being stupid, Becky," James argued. "The colonel knows that."

"I can't believe they were so openly rude. Is that how men behave here, Father?"

"No, not usually," James began. "But sometimes, when a man's new in the area, rumors about his past tend to show up like unwanted relatives at Sunday's dinner." James paused while Bonnie placed three plates of pie before them. "You see," he continued, "a few years back, the colonel and his father, General MacLaren, had fearsome reputations for Indian fighting."

"From what I overheard, it sounded as if those men accused the colonel of being a coward. Why would they make that implication?" Rebeccah asked.

James swallowed, then dabbed at his mouth with his napkin. "That's a good question, but one to which I have no answer. Though Sayer and I have become pretty good friends, he's not real talkative about his past." James shook his head and stabbed a sliced apple. "My guess is that he's no coward, just tired of the fighting."

Rebeccah took another bite of her pie, thinking about what had transpired. She was just about to speak when Lydia voiced her next question.

"Only Indians take scalps, isn't that correct?" Lydia put down her fork. "Yet those men . . . they implied that the colonel killed and scalp—"

"Lydia," their father interrupted, "we shouldn't be discussing this at the table."

"Father, please," Rebeccah implored. "We're not squeamish little schoolgirls. This is most interesting. True, Lydia and I have lived rather sheltered lives, but stories of the uncivilized West were often recounted in vivid detail at some of the finest tables in England." She nodded at her sister. "We found them to be quite exciting."

James heaved a defeated sigh. "I suppose it would be entertaining . . . unless you've lived through it, Becky. But a lot of people died, both white men and Indian. It was a brutal time. A time that's still too painful for many to speak about. And with the recent attacks, it still isn't over."

His somber expression left no room to argue. "It would be best, I think, if we didn't talk any more about it, especially when we're around the colonel." James gave her a fatherly smile. "Now, finish your pie. We don't want Miss Bonnie thinking you're finicky."

Sayer sat in the muted light of the kerosene lamp, staring at the papers on his desk. There had been sixteen reported Indian attacks since March. Most of them were insignificant—a few missing chickens, some sacks of grain, but four of them stood out among the others. In these incidents, men were hurt and money taken. Where the stage was attacked, the ground was hard-packed and badly trampled. There could have been three or thirteen Indians. There was simply no way to tell. But that wasn't what disturbed him. What bothered him more was that some of the horses were shod.

He reached for his cup and found it empty. Instantly he remembered the doctor's younger daughter and her fondness for his favorite drink. One thought led to another, and even though he had tried not to think about the two men that had come in for supper, the insinuations they made weighed heavily on his mind.

He rose and stepped outside, glancing up at the multitude of stars, but he didn't see them. In his mind he saw the bodies of hundreds of men, whites and Indians alike. He closed his eyes, pressing his thumb and forefinger on the bridge of his nose until the grisly vision passed.

Taking a deep, cleansing breath, he went back inside to his bedroom. The lamp cast ominous shadows on the wall as he slowly undressed. He stood before the mirror hanging above the dresser and once more revisited a scene from his past—innocent women and children—his father's rage—the massacre that followed. Slowly Sayer raised his right hand and touched an old scar on his upper left arm, then turned and blew out the lamp.

"Bastard," he muttered as he stretched out on his bed.

CHAPTER FOUR

The next week passed quickly, and all too soon it was time for Rebeccah to leave her father's home and move into the house that had been provided for her at Rancho de Gutierrez. The long drive from Santa Fe north toward the mountains was pleasant. The sky was clear, clearer than any she could remember, its sapphire splendor unspoiled by clouds. When she had inquired about the bushy cactus that bore bright pink flowers, her father told her it was called *cholla*. When she had asked how it was spelled, her brows snapped together. "Then shouldn't it be pronounced cho-la?" she had asked.

"You'll learn, Becky my dear, that double L's are pronounced 'ya.' It takes a little practice, but you'll get used to it." Her father's smile was quick, and once more she was glad that the week they'd spent together had dissolved most of her resentment toward him.

As her sister had said, there were a few adobe houses along the way, but absolutely no sign of a school. The only structure that was large enough to be a school turned out to be a church, which, as they drove closer, stood out among the cactus and scrub pines, its bell tower and cross a grim reminder of the mother she had recently lost.

It wasn't very long before a sprawling adobe house loomed ahead. There, tall cottonwood trees towered over the shorter junipers and cedars. Her father turned their small carriage down the well-worn, fence-lined road, stopping at a hitching post several yards away from the flagstone walkway to the house. Though nervous butterflies danced in the pit of her stomach, Rebeccah smiled as she was introduced to Don Fernando Gutierrez.

"How do you do," she said politely, extending her hand. The Mexican rancher was younger than she expected. Like a true gentleman, he took her hand in his, bowed and placed a chaste kiss on its back. As tall as her father, Fernando's hair and moustache were as dark as pitch. He wore a burgundy jacket with silver trim and silver *conchos* that matched those on the sides of his trousers. When he let go of her hand, she had the strangest thought. His shoulders were nearly as broad as the colonel's.

"The pleasure is all mine, *Señorita* Randolph," he stated formally, drawing her away from her unexpected comparison. His dark eyes twinkled when he smiled and instantly some of her nervousness dissipated. "Allow me to introduce my daughters."

Two little girls dressed entirely in white, their black hair done up in white and red ribbons, stood beside an older Mexican woman. The dowager's grey hair was covered with a lace shawl, and she wore a very elegant white gown that appeared to be layers and layers of lace.

The moment Don Fernando waved, the girls dashed to his side, wide-eyed and trying to hide their giggles behind the little bouquets of colorful flowers they held. He put his hands upon the taller one's shoulders. "This is Elena. She is seven." The child stepped forward, curtsied, then gave Rebeccah the flowers.

"*Buenos tardes, maestra,*" Elena said. The little girl cast a quick glance over her shoulder and upon her father's nod, cleared her throat, then said in broken English, "Good afternoon, teacher."

Rebeccah smiled. "Thank you, Elena, and good afternoon to you, too." Don Fernando did the same with the littler daughter, introducing her as Maria. Just like her sister, the five-year-old curtsied, handed over her smaller bunch of flowers, then recited what she had been instructed to say, stopping in the middle to look at her father for assistance, and repeating what he told her. Instead of returning to her father's side as Elena had, she dashed back to her great-grandmother, peeking out from behind the old woman's skirts. The elderly lady smiled, then spoke rapidly in Spanish, taking the little girl's hand as she stepped forward to be introduced as Don Fernando's grandmother.

"Welcome, *Señorita* Randolph," the older woman said with a warm smile. "I am *Señora* Gutierrez. Please, come inside out of the heat. Ramon, Diego," the older woman called out, and two boys appeared. Once more she spoke in Spanish, but it was easy to guess what was said as they ran to the carriage and lifted out Rebeccah's trunk. "The boys will take your things to your *casa* while we have something cool to drink."

"Will you join us, Doctor?" Don Fernando asked.

"No, no, but thank you for asking. It'll be getting dark soon and . . . well, Rebeccah needs some time to unpack and settle in." Her father took her hand and gave it a gentle squeeze. "You're sure you'll be all right?" he asked for the tenth time since leaving Santa Fe early that morning.

Rebeccah smiled at his feeble attempt to keep her under his wing. "Yes, quite sure." She looked around at the neatly swept stone patio with flowering plants in colorful pots. "This is a lovely place. I'm sure I'll be happy here." She reached up and kissed him on the cheek, whispering in his ear, "There is nothing to worry about, so stop frowning."

"Very well, then." He held her at arm's length for a long moment, nodding proudly. "I'd best be on my way." She walked with him to the carriage, stepping back as he climbed up and gathered up the reins. "If you need anything—"

"I will see that she wants for nothing," Don Fernando added

with an understanding smile. "Come and visit as often as you like, Doctor Randolph."

The two men shook hands, and then, as Rebeccah watched, her father drove away, turning several times to wave. "I can see that he is having second thoughts," Don Fernando added, offering his arm as he and Rebeccah walked back through the patio toward the elegantly carved double doors.

"Yes, I believe you're correct."

"And you, *Señorita*, are you also having second thoughts?" His smile was kind and inviting as he patted her hand.

"Absolutely not," Rebeccah stated with renewed conviction, liking Don Fernando and the way his perceptive smile put her at ease.

"Good. I am much relieved." He led her inside, where she admired the pristine beauty of his home. Mexican rugs in various colorful designs graced a tiled floor. The smooth plastered walls were adorned with oil paintings in heavily carved, gilded frames. Tall-backed chairs, their cushioned seats covered in a rich, caramel-colored leather, accented a long trestle table, carved to match. On the wall, behind the chair that she guessed to be Don Fernando's, hung an elaborate silver crucifix.

"Your home is very beautiful, Mr. Gu—"

"Please, let us not be so formal. You may call me Fernando." He held up his hand, halting her protest. "Trust me, *Señorita*. My vanity is at risk. You see, I am too young to be addressed as you would address my father, God rest his soul." He quickly crossed himself, then placed his hand over his heart and gave her a pitiful look. "Indulge me in this. I promise I will make no further demands." His grin was filled with mischief, his dark eyes dancing, and once more she was reminded of the colonel and his quick and easy smile.

"Very well," she agreed, smiling when the rancher gave an exaggerated sigh of relief.

"Now, we must hurry. I learned at a very early age it is best to please one's grandmother, yes?"

Rebeccah laughed with him. "Yes, indeed it is."

Shortly after the evening meal, Rebeccah was shown to her new residence. "If there is anything you require," Don Fernando said, "it shall be yours." Once more his friendly smile chased away her trepidation. Unlike the stories she'd heard, this particular Mexican was every bit the gentleman. His daughters were well mannered, and she found herself actually looking forward to being their teacher.

"Thank you," she repeated, as he touched a taper to several lamps, then departed. Elegant as the main house, her home was smaller, consisting of only four rooms: a living room with a kiva-style fireplace, a small kitchen equipped with a stove and water pump in a porcelain sink, a study complete with a desk and high-back padded-leather chair, and a bedroom with a canopied bed, bureau and two bedside tables. Her trunk had been placed at the foot of the bed. Taking care to shake the wrinkles out of each gown, she began to unpack.

Rebeccah rose early to finish unpacking the last of her belongings. Just after lunch, she strolled into the study, her arms full of books. The desk she had admired last night sat before a window which, now that the curtain was open, allowed ample light, and, if she chose to daydream, a splendid view. She arranged the books with a few favorite knickknacks on the empty bookcase carved to match the desk.

Only when she heard the children's small dog barking did she go to the living room, pull aside the lacy curtain and peek out. Instantly she recognized the colonel's flashy stallion tied to the hitching post. Her heart picked up its pace, and though she tried to deny it, she was more than a little anxious to see the horse's owner.

Disappointed that her view of the hacienda's front door was blocked by several bushy junipers, she glanced around, wondering how she could step outside without appearing too obvious. Smiling shrewdly, she snatched up a Navajo rug from the floor on the pretense that she wanted to give it a good shaking.

The moment she stepped outside, she felt silly. Squinting against the bright sunlight, she wondered why she had so eagerly sought to get a glimpse of the colonel. Hadn't she decided at the river that he was arrogant and most assuredly too uncivilized to suit her tastes? She gave the rug a fierce shake.

Sure, he was handsome in uniform, but then all men were. However, his did fit more snugly than any other she could remember. But then again, Edward looked dashing in his riding boots and breeches. Edward was everything a woman could want: handsome, wealthy, and, more importantly, civilized, with a safe position in his father's business.

Then why, she wondered, had she rushed out like a silly schoolgirl with the hope of seeing the colonel once more? Perhaps because he was terribly exciting. He was an Indian fighter after all, and he did look utterly irresistible in his dashing uniform. Her revelation startled her. Annoyed with the direction her thoughts had drifted, she finished shaking the rug and went inside, feeling somewhat ashamed that her musings about Edward could be so easily replaced by those of an uncivilized soldier.

Edward. She had been at sea for two weeks, in New York for three weeks, and hoped to have his letter waiting upon her arrival. Before she left, she had made certain to leave him her father's address. Yet when she had questioned her father, he said he hadn't received anything from England. She hurried to the desk, picked up a pen and began to write a letter to her beloved, determined to keep her mind off the colonel.

Two hours later she had successfully related everything that had happened on her journey, taking the time to assure Edward that, although they had been attacked, neither she nor Lydia had been injured. She purposely left out any details about how an army officer had rescued them, or that hostiles were allowed to run about the countryside unchecked. She concluded by saying that any correspondence should be sent to her father. He would forward her mail to Don Fernando's ranch.

When a soft knock drew Rebeccah's attention, she glanced at the clock on the desk, then hurried to the door. Elena and Maria stood there, both with big smiles and laughing brown eyes. Elena held out a piece of folded paper. "Papa told us to give this to you."

"Thank you," Rebeccah replied, quickly reading the invitation to dinner. "Tell your father that I accept." She stepped out onto her small porch and watched as the children darted back toward the main house, the brown-and-white dog yapping as he ran with them. Unwillingly, she wondered if the colonel hadn't been invited to stay and dine, as his horse was no longer tied in front of the house. Once inside, she washed in the sink, then chose a rose-colored gown with tiny white flowers around the neck and on the edge of the short, puffed sleeves.

After she arranged her hair into a tight chignon, she found her knitted shawl, remembering Don Fernando's warning that when the sun sank, so did the temperature. Slipping it on, she opened the door and stepped out to gaze out over rolling hills where the setting sun had turned the sky into a glorious mixture of orange, pink and purple. To her it was a sight as colorful as the men who lived here.

"I'm continually amazed by how beautiful it is out here."

She spun to find the object of her earlier thoughts standing several feet away. He was clad in his typical blue uniform: the formal jacket that hugged his broad chest with the tight high collar and the double rows of shiny brass buttons. A thick black belt was fastened around his waist and a long, sheathed saber hung from its gleaming brass holder. He took off his hat, unaware, she was sure, of how his hair glistened in the dwindling sunlight.

Again she made a mental comparison, only this time she tried to remember if Edward's shoulders were as broad or his waist as slim.

"Do you always sneak up on people?" she asked, trying to hide the fact that he had, indeed, caused her to start. His easy smile and low chuckle baffled her.

"No, ma'am, not unless I've reason to do so." He motioned toward his horse, which, when she looked closer, she realized had been tied in the shelter of the trees where he could munch the wild buffalo grass. "I came to get Rounder and noticed you looking at the sunset." Once more she chanced a quick glance, warming under his gaze.

"Don Fernando has graciously asked me to stay for supper. He also offered a stall for my horse." He touched the brim of his hat and walked toward his stallion.

She felt compelled to follow. "Are we very close to Mexico?" she asked.

"No, ma'am."

She cast him a quick glance, amazed at the way her stomach did a little jump each time she looked at him as they walked toward his horse. "There's no need for such formality, Colonel. You may call me by my name."

"Yes, ma'am, I will endeavor to do so in the future." He looked at her more closely, and she hoped he couldn't see her heart pounding against her breast. "We're in the Territory of New Mexico. Mexico is about three hundred miles south. However, like many Mexicans, Don Fernando's family settled here long before we whites moved in."

"Whites?" she repeated as they slowly strolled toward his horse. "I've heard that idiom before. Is that what we are called out here in the West?"

"To the Indians, yes. To the Mexicans we're *gringos*."

"In England it is assumed that the Mexicans are as uncivilized as the Indians, but Don Fernando appears to be quite the gentleman."

"Depends on what you consider civilized, ma'am."

She raised one fair brow, unsettled by the colonel's statement. "I'm referring to the way they behave—how they conduct themselves in society," she added, hoping to clarify herself.

He seemed casually amused. "I suppose that depends on whose society we are speaking of. To an Apache among Apaches, I'm sure an Apache's conduct is acceptable. In Mexico, a Mexican's conduct is acceptable." He paused and she watched, surprised, as the laughter left his eyes. "It is only when whites invade Indian lands and force our doctrine upon them that they are considered less than civilized . . . by our society." He put on his hat before he untied his horse, then ran his hand down the stallion's sleek neck.

"A savage is a savage in any society," she stated.

"I suppose. Yet sometimes I wonder, in our quest to take what isn't ours, if we are not the savages."

He didn't give her time to respond. Instead, he touched the brim of his hat. "You must excuse me. My horse has been tied for quite some time. I'm sure he'd like some water and a flake of hay." He turned and left her to watch as he led his horse toward the barn at the rear of the main house.

Rebeccah lingered a while outside, thinking about what the colonel had said. As a soldier who had fought in the Indian Wars, she had expected him to be more vindictive. But then, a lot of what the colonel said and did contradicted her preconceived ideas about cavalry officers.

Perhaps what he said was true, that out here there was no difference between men and savages. She pushed the thought aside and took a long, deep breath, pleased that the sage-scented air was as divine as the view. By the time she strolled toward the main house, torches cast their golden warmth on the adobe walls. She reached for the ornate knocker on the double doors, but a maid opened the door before she could knock.

"Come in, come in," Don Fernando called as he hurried up the two steps of the tiled foyer. "You look lovely, *Señorita* Randolph." He took her hand, placed a kiss on the back, and led her into the dining room. "I am so please that you decided to join us tonight."

The colonel was already seated, but stood as they approached. "How nice to see you, Miss Randolph," he said with a polite nod.

"Colonel," she acknowledged formally. She accepted her seat to the left of Fernando's, across from the colonel, noticing that there were only three place settings. "Will the children and your grandmother be joining us?" she asked as Fernando filled their crystal goblets with red wine.

"No. They ate earlier. By now, Maria and Elena are listening to a story, as they get ready for bed. It is a ritual my grandmother looks forward to every evening."

"You should be commended. Your daughters are very well-mannered," she began, taking a sip of wine. "I'm not sure my services are necessary."

"*Al contrario.* Although manners are important, Santa Fe is rapidly changing. Soon the railroad will be there, bringing more and more people. In order for my daughters to be accepted in today's society, they must learn to read and speak English well." Fernando glanced at the colonel. "Don't you agree, *mi amigo?*"

Rebeccah smiled. It seemed New Mexico was no different from England, sharing its views about society. When she glanced at the colonel, he put down his goblet, pausing as if he were thinking about what Fernando had just asked him. When he spoke, it was as if he were speaking directly to her.

"I believe it is safer to comply with what society expects of us."

As usual, his reply conjured up another question. "Safer?" Rebeccah asked, wondering why he chose such a word. "There's no danger in being different."

"Isn't there?" he countered. His expression left her feeling as if he wanted to say more, but he turned to his host. "What do you think, Fernando?"

Fernando smiled, and shook his head as he toyed with a rose he'd plucked from the vase. "The lady directed her question to you, *amigo,* not me."

Two maids appeared with plates piled high with strips of roasted chicken, spicy rice and refried beans, garnished with fresh tomatoes and peppers. Don Fernando warned that the peppers were hot, cutting a small piece and placing it next to the chicken on her plate.

"Well, Colonel, have you forgotten the question?" Don Fernando inquired.

The two men exchanged friendly glances, then the colonel took another sip of wine before he put down his glass.

"Very well, Miss Randolph. I say it is safer to conform to what society expects because I have seen the consequences when we don't."

"Can you elaborate?" she asked, enjoying the conversation as she tasted the rice.

"I will do my best," he said, gliding his knife through a piece of chicken. "If an Indian rides into a white settlement dressed in feathers and buckskin, society assumes he's hostile." He put down the knife, lifted his fork. "He's seen as a threat, and I, as a soldier in the Unites States Army, am called upon to dispatch him as I see fit. Do you agree with me so far?" he asked, taking a bite. "That because I wear a uniform, I'm the man's judge and jury?"

"I-I suppose," she answered, not sure if she agreed or not.

"If this same man rides into a white settlement dressed as a white man, his hair cut short like his white brothers, he is ignored, and my services are not necessary." Her dining partner speared a small pepper and another piece of chicken on his fork. "Therefore, Miss Randolph, it is, as I said before, safer to comply with white men's doctrine."

"Very good, *amigo*," Don Fernando replied with a grin. "I have to admit, I too was wondering where you were leading us, but then I should know better than to underestimate a man of your—how should I put it? Experience."

"How long have you known each other?" Rebeccah asked, turning her attention away from the colonel.

"Only a few weeks, but I find the colonel a most enjoyable opponent."

"Really? I didn't realize the two of you were in competition with each other." Once more her gaze floated toward the colonel's, and she found his eyes riveted to hers.

"*Si*, every chance we get. Am I correct, Colonel?"

"Absolutely." The colonel cut into one of the peppers. Again, he added a small piece of chicken before he placed it in his mouth. After a few moments he commended his host on the excellent taste of the food.

Thinking that perhaps the pepper added to the already wonderful flavor, Rebeccah copied the colonel, smiling at both men as they watched with a sudden intensity that she thought a bit odd. A moment later she knew why. Her mouth felt as if she had just eaten a hot coal. Her first instinct was to spit it out, but they were still watching. Too much of a lady to rid herself of the fiery bite, she forced herself to swallow it, gasping as she snatched up her wine and drained the goblet.

"How is it?" the colonel asked, his vivid blue eyes dancing with mirth.

"Oh, my," she gasped, once she could find her voice. "You made it look so enjoyable." She blinked several times as her eyes watered, then repeated, "Oh, my."

The colonel shrugged his shoulders in innocence, his expression wounded. "Fernando told you they were hot."

"*Si, Señorita.* I did." Her host rang a little bell, and instantly one of his servants appeared. "*Agua fría,* for the lady," he finished in English. His smile was as jovial as the colonel's.

She took a long drink of the cold water the moment it arrived, unmindful that she was the center of their attention. When at last the burning eased, she put down the glass. "Well." She cleared her throat. "I now have a whole new meaning for the word hot. And, in the future, Don Fernando . . ." She smiled at her host. ". . . should you caution me, I shall endeavor to heed your advice."

The rest of the evening passed by pleasantly, the conversation turning to crops and cattle as they enjoyed a dessert of sweetened custard in a delightful caramel sauce. The candles on the table had nearly melted away when Rebeccah covered a yawn. Once more the two men turned their attention to her and she felt her cheeks warm with color.

"My apologies, *Señorita.* We have kept you up too late." Fernando and the colonel stood, but Fernando came around and pulled out her chair.

"May I see you home?" the colonel suggested, stepping around the table and offering his arm before Fernando could let go of the chair.

Vaguely aware of some game the two men where playing, Rebeccah accepted his offer, addressing her host, "Thank you for a lovely evening. My compliments to your chef, I have never tasted food so expertly prepared . . . ah . . . except for the peppers." Her expression brought a smile to Fernando's handsome face. "Those, I assume, are an acquired taste?"

"*Si,* but one I am sure you will come to love." Fernando bowed, then led them to the door. "I promised your papa I would take excellent care of you, but since your *casa* is only a short distance away, *Señorita,* and I will be watching from the window, I will allow the colonel to be your escort." His wink told her he was teasing. "*Buenos noches* to you both."

Outside, Rebeccah pulled her shawl a little tighter. A cool breeze had come up in the night and now rustled the treetops. Too soon they were at her door. Part of her wanted to linger, but another part—a part that only months ago encouraged her to accept Edward's offer of marriage—caused her to stop the handsome officer from opening the latch.

"Thank you, Colonel," she said with a smile as she turned, effectively placing herself between him and her door. His expression was hidden by the shadow of his hat, and although she couldn't see his face, she sensed he felt in no hurry to leave.

"You told me earlier to call you by your name," he said, the deep timbre of his voice strangely disconcerting. "Now I shall ask the same of you. My name is Sayer."

"Sayer," she repeated. "I've never heard that before. Has it a special meaning?"

"None I know of."

"Very well," she said, feeling a little uncomfortable with him standing so close. Before she realized what effect his touch would have, she extended her hand.

When his warm fingers closed over hers, a jolt of excited anticipation shot through her. She had read novels about men in the West and how wild they acted. Most of them were woman-crazy and starved for affection. Would he try to kiss her, she wondered?

Of course not, she answered, quickly banishing the thought. The man was an officer in the army, not nearly as uncivilized as the men she'd read about. And, furthermore, English ladies should not harbor such thoughts, nor allow themselves to become so forward.

Sayer watched her expression in the moonlight, sure that he saw something he couldn't quite name flash briefly in her eyes. Was it doubt?

The moonlight shone upon her hair, and he wondered why she twisted it up into a knot—then wondered what she'd look like with it down and curling around her shoulders. Her hand was cold, and for a moment he wished he could warm her with a kiss.

But, she was a lady, as fine as they came—not the type to fall for an uncivilized man like himself. He let go of her hand and touched the brim of his hat. "Good night, Miss Randolph." Her beguiling smile made him doubt his decision.

"Good night, Colonel MacLaren."

CHAPTER FIVE

Rebeccah soon fell into a pleasant routine and was delighted when not one, but two letters arrived from England. She tore them open and began to read. They were filled with the usual: who was courting whom, the latest styles, and ending with her beloved's undying devotion. A bout of homesickness engulfed her, and for a few moments she had to blink back the tears that blurred her vision. But as time passed and each letter contained much of the same, rather boring, news, she pushed aside her melancholy and became more engrossed in her work.

In the mornings she listened patiently as Don Fernando's daughters recited their lessons in English. During the afternoon meal, she would instruct them on proper etiquette and how to answer when spoken to, and on which topics ladies conversed and which they didn't. After lunch the girls were required by their great-grandmother to take a nap, or what Rebeccah learned, was their customary *siesta*. At three o'clock, they had riding lessons.

It was during one particular windy day, while practicing their penmanship on the table that Fernando placed outdoors, that her papers were whisked away. Before she could gather them, several of the servants' children scooped them up and shyly handed them back to her. "Thank you," she said, but the two little boys and a little girl about the same age as Elena only stared at her. "Elena," Rebeccah called. "Please come here for a moment."

Elena hurried from her place, Maria following behind. "Yes, Miss Randolph," the little girl said in near-perfect English.

"Elena, how do I say thank you in Spanish?"

"Muchas gracias."

"Muchas gracias," Rebeccah repeated, smiling down at the children. They all smiled back, then said something to Elena in Spanish, and giggling, ran off.

"Are they your friends?" Rebeccah asked, once they were back to the table and preparing to continue their lesson.

"Si . . . I mean, yes, Miss Randolph," Elena said. Maria whispered something in her sister's ear. Both girls' eyes lighted up and then Elena spoke again. "Maria wants to know if Miguel, Jorge and Isabel can come to school too."

Rebeccah smiled at their hopeful expressions. "I'll have to ask your father, but if he says yes, then I see no reason why they can't join us."

Soon, instead of two little girls, Rebeccah had four, and three little boys. In an effort to keep things organized, she held school for everyone in the mornings. The afternoons were reserved for private lessons for Fernando's daughters.

Several weeks passed, and when she wasn't writing down her adventures to send to Edward, she found her thoughts drifting to the colonel and wondering if she would ever see him again. Don Fernando was always attentive and polite, seeing to her every need. However, something was missing. A certain excitement. But, at the same time, that excitement was something she didn't want to think too much about either.

It wasn't that she refused to accept the colonel's reputation as an Indian fighter; it just wasn't proper for ladies to think of wars and what happens in them. Those activities were saved for men. Yet one thought led to another, and soon she found herself wondering more and more about the men who had taken this land by force.

It was while she sat in the shade of the veranda on a particularly hot afternoon in July that the colonel rode through the gate, leading another horse. Curious, she put Edward's letter down and turned her attention toward the corral where the colonel stopped and dismounted. Though not as big as his stallion, the smaller animal was just as beautiful. Its dark coat glistened in the sunlight, as did its black mane and long, flowing tail.

"*Buenas tardes, mi amigo,*" called Don Fernando as he climbed down from his perch on the top rail where he watched his daughters ride. "What a beautiful horse." Rebeccah watched as Fernando rubbed the mare's slick neck. "Have you come to sell her to me?" he asked, grinning at the colonel. "I will take her on one condition. You sell your stallion to me too."

Rebeccah heard Sayer's laugh, but couldn't make out his softly spoken reply. Curious, she rose from the bench and walked toward the men. "Good afternoon, Colonel."

He turned, still smiling. Instead of his usual high-necked formal uniform, his faded blue shirt lay open at the neck, and an equally faded yellow scarf was loosely knotted around his throat. Broad suspenders hugged his chest, and his sleeves were rolled up, exposing tanned forearms. His revolver and his long, deadly knife were strapped on his hips, causing her to wonder if they had been used to defeat the savages he fought. When he caught her staring, his eyes twinkled in that way that made her stomach flip-flop as he touched the brim of his dusty navy-blue hat.

"Good afternoon, Miss Randolph," he replied, using her formal name as she had used his. "I've brought you a little present." He nodded toward the mare. "She's gentle enough for a child."

Rebeccah's mouth fell open as she slowly shook her head. "N-no," she stammered, forcing a smile so as not to appear rude. "I can't possibly accept, Colonel—"

"Sayer," he corrected.

"Y-yes. You see, I don't know anything about horses." She cast a frantic glance at Fernando, hoping he would come to her rescue, but he only laughed at her expression, even when she gave him what she thought was her best *help me* look.

"I will teach you along with my daughters," he replied with a cheerful nod. "And then, when you feel more comfortable, I am sure the colonel will be happy to take you riding, yes?"

"No," she answered, shaking her head. She took a calming breath. "He's beautiful, but I can't—"

"She," Sayer corrected with that slow, calculating smile that both pleased and annoyed her. "Her name's Brandy."

"Brandy?" Rebeccah repeated a little desperately. "She's lovely. Really she is, but I simply can't accept such a valuable gift." She looked at the men, but their expressions left no hope that they would relent. When Sayer took her hand and placed the lead rope in her palm, she gave him another stiff smile then turned her slightly frightened gaze to what was on the end of the rope. The mare snorted. Rebeccah jumped and took a step back. The docile mare followed.

"Whoa," Rebeccah urged, taking another step back. Again the mare followed until Rebeccah held up her hand, halting the horse's forward motion. "Nice horse . . . nice Brandy." Rebeccah forced another strained smile as she glanced at Sayer. "I don't know how I will ever be able to repay you."

"Oh, I am sure he will think of a way," Fernando said, coughing to cover his humor. "Come. Let me help you."

Much to her relief, Fernando took the rope and led the mare to the fence, where he tied her. "Renato will take the little mare and put her in the barn with the others." Fernando turned, still grinning. "Let us have a cool drink of lemonade," he said, taking Rebeccah's arm and hooking it over his. "Colonel, I've wanted to talk to you about breeding a couple of my mares to your stallion."

"It's a little late in the season," Sayer said as they entered the shade of the veranda. He took off his hat and placed it on top of the short adobe wall that partially enclosed the patio. Grandmother Gutierrez came out with a silver tray, glasses and a large pitcher. When asked to join them, she replied that she was making tortillas, and it was too hot outside.

Sayer accepted a glass of lemonade from his host and leaned against the wall. "If you breed your mares now, you'll have foals on the ground next June."

"So? That is a good time, no?"

"In these parts, spring comes early. It's better to have them born in April or May. That way, there's plenty of good grass for the mares while the babies suckle." Sayer took a long drink. "Leave it too late, and the grass is dried and withered. If the feed is of poor quality, the mares won't produce enough milk and the foals will suffer for it."

"*Si,*" Fernando agreed. "I have a nephew in Mexico who raises horses, but as you can see, I know very little about it." He offered Sayer another drink, but was waved away. "Perhaps next spring we will talk again."

"I won't be here next spring," the colonel replied casually.

Rebeccah's head snapped up, but before she could speak, Fernando asked why.

"My orders were for Fort Union." He finished his drink and put the glass down on the table before he retrieved his hat. "I'm only here because of the renegades. Hopefully, they won't be a problem when the weather grows cold."

"I see. But then, would that not encourage them to increase their attacks—to steal even more for the long winter?"

"No, I don't believe so. If it snows early, the tribe will be forced to stay in their homes on the reservation."

"Good, then the attacks will soon stop."

The colonel only shrugged. "I'm not so sure all the incidents are connected to the Apaches."

Don Fernando's bark of laughter caused Rebeccah to smile. "No? Then who could be doing them? I do not recall seeing any wanted posters for *hombres* who know how to use bows and arrows."

Sayer brushed at something on his hat. "That's true, but then I don't recall many Indians who shoe their horses, either."

"News of such things frightens me," Fernando added with a feigned shiver. "But I will rest much easier in the knowledge that while the raids continue, you will be here to protect us." Fernando raised one black brow. "You will be here, won't you?"

"Until my orders change."

"Good, good. Then we still have time to finish our game."

"What game is that, if I may ask?" Rebeccah interjected, more curious than she cared to admit.

"The colonel and I play chess. We are presently tied. Friday, after dinner, we will play again, *si?*" Fernando raised one dark brow.

"I'm looking forward to it," Sayer replied as he put on his hat. He nodded toward Rebeccah. "Enjoy the mare." Before she could respond, he turned to Fernando. "I will trust you to see that Miss Randolph learns how to ride." Once more he looked at her over his shoulder.

"I will see to it personally, *mi amigo.*" The two men exchanged a look that left Rebeccah with the distinct impression that Don Fernando had just issued some unspoken challenge.

"Good day," the colonel said, and then strode toward his horse.

She sipped her lemonade as she watched him ride away. The rogue. He'd ridden up with his gift, and now her peaceful afternoons were over. And worse, he left her feeling as if she had to prove herself and become an equestrian. Just the thought of climbing up on the mare's back caused her stomach to twist with dread.

She glanced at the colonel as he disappeared down the road. By the way he sat a horse, any fool could see he was a proud man, his back straight, his long legs relaxed at the stallion's sides. Each time she saw the man, he seemed more alluring, especially today, clad in his more casual uniform. The moment she thought about how well it fit him, she looked away, turning warm as she realized Don Fernando had been watching her watch the colonel.

"I-I must warn you, Fernando," she said, taking a deep breath, "I have no experience with horses. In England there is no need. I simply take a carriage wherever I want to go."

"Then it is good that you learn," her host countered with yet another quick smile. "There are many places that can only be seen from the back of a horse."

He took her glass, then pulled her to her feet. "Come, we will have our first lesson."

"But I am not dressed to ride."

"Who said anything about riding? First you must get to know your horse on the ground. It is the same as with men and women. Once you feel comfortable around her, we will let you get to know her more intimately." When she gasped, he hurried to add, "From her back." He laughed and shook his head. "Ah, *Señorita,* it is easy to bring bright color to your cheeks, but still I am jealous that you do not stare after me as you do the colonel."

Fernando's revelation brought her to a halt. "I was not staring."

Fernando's smile never wavered, nor did the twinkle in his dark eyes. "Of course not," he said, pulling her along. "I remember you telling Elena and Maria that ladies never stare."

"That is correct."

She very nearly stepped on his heels when he stopped abruptly, turned and grinned. "Then enlighten me, *por favor*. What do you call it?"

"Call what?" she countered with a haughty toss of her head.

"What you were doing with the colonel?"

Her attempt to be appalled had no effect. Don Fernando's grin only widened. "Don Fernando," she began in her most formal tone. "I was simply watching him in hopes of learning something that might help me with my riding lessons." She gave a curt nod. "Yes, that was what I was doing. You see—" She cast Fernando a superior smile. "Using ardent perseverance and astute observation, like that you just witnessed, I'm sure I can become as polished an equestrian as you and the colonel." She didn't give Fernando time to respond. She pulled her hand from his gentle grasp, smiled again, then lifted the hem of her skirt and walked toward the corral. "Come along. We mustn't dawdle."

"This really isn't as bad as I thought it would be," Rebeccah said, following Don Fernando's daughters around the fenced-in paddock three days later. Some of her students sat on the fence, watching.

"You are doing so well, too," he confirmed with a bemused smile. "In time, you will even learn how to trot."

Rebeccah ignored Maria and Elena's giggles as they trotted past, turning to smile at their teacher, then waving at their friends. Rebeccah knew she must look foolish, clinging to the saddle horn and the reins both. But she didn't care. One must learn how to crawl before one can walk, and one must learn to walk before one can run—or trot, as Don Fernando put it.

"Try it, Miss Randolph. It is fun," Maria encouraged.

"No thank you," Rebeccah replied, holding on to the horn of

her sidesaddle a little tighter when the mare snorted. "I'm not ready to go any faster. Not yet anyway." Several more giggles came from the direction of the fence.

Fernando finally opened the gate. "It is time that we put the horses away and get ready for supper." His daughters trotted over to him, and after he lifted them down, they waited patiently until Rebeccah guided her mare toward them. "You are progressing nicely," he said, scolding the girls and their friends in Spanish when they burst into giggles. He helped Rebeccah dismount. Once on the ground, she turned and patted the mare's neck before the servants led the horses toward the barn.

"I think you are growing fond of her," Fernando said. "She is a good horse, but you should take my advice and try a regular saddle. I think you will like it much better."

"It is all well and good for the children, but it isn't proper for a lady to sit astride." She walked through the gate while he held it open.

"Then tell me why your skirt is cut like men's pants?"

She laughed and shook her head. "They are not cut like men's pants. This is a riding habit. Lydia insisted I bring several of them. The skirts are split because I suppose there are some women who prefer to ride a regular saddle. But—"

"But, what? Do you think less of them for it?"

"Certainly not. It's just that my grandmother wouldn't approve. She would think it vulgar."

Don Fernando made a wide sweep with his arms. "Am I missing something?"

She gave him a sideways look, aware that he was teasing her.

"Do you see your grandmother here?" He shook his head. "No. She is not here, so there is no reason that you cannot learn to ride like the wind and be comfortable doing so. And, if my memory serves, you yourself said you would heed my advice."

She laughed with him. "Perhaps you are right."

"There is no *perhaps* about it. I am right, and tomorrow I will show you." They were at her front door and, as usual, he took her hand, his glittering dark eyes crafty. "I have invited the colonel to stay at the ranch for a day or two. He will dine with us tomorrow tonight. If you know how to play chess, perhaps you would like to join us and challenge the winner?"

She almost said she'd love to, and then decided it was best to keep her skill with the game a secret. Ladies simply didn't compete with men. She smiled and shook her head again. "I will watch, but I'm afraid I'm not a very good player."

"Good," he said with a wide grin that brought her head up in surprise. "I will look forward to teaching you some tricks that will improve your game."

Rebeccah took special care in arranging her hair and choosing what she would wear. The royal blue of the satin gown accented the dainty sapphire pendant she wore around her neck and the jewel-tipped pins she placed in her hair. She dabbed a little French perfume behind her ear and put on the matching earrings.

The whole time she dressed she didn't think about why she took such pains, only that since Fernando and the colonel dressed for dinner, why shouldn't she? As she touched a match to a lamp, a soft knock sounded on her door. Thinking the children had come to tell her dinner was ready, she called for them to enter. When the door opened, she turned. Her breath caught a moment before she managed a nervous smile.

"Sayer," she began, hating the breathless sound of her voice. She swallowed hard. He filled the doorway, looking splendid in his uniform, his white hat clutched in his gloved hands. "I-I thought you were someone else."

"Don Fernando, perhaps?"

Much to her surprise, she could have sworn his voice held a hint of jealousy. And was it her imagination, or did his smile fade ever so slightly? "No," she said, turning to pick up her shawl. "He never visits. He always sends his daughters. I thought you were Maria and Elena." She brushed past him with a coy smile. "Shall we?"

Dinner was soon over, and Don Fernando left the table to say good night to his daughters. Sayer poured a brandy for himself and a sherry for Rebeccah. Together they strolled out to the garden under the night's splendid sky.

"It amazes me how brilliant the stars are," she said, taking a sip of her drink as she glanced at him. He stood, one hand behind his back, the other holding the snifter, and looked up at the sky.

"I am in awe of ancient sailors," he said, dropping his gaze to look at the amber liquid as he swirled it around his glass. "If I had to depend on the stars to tell in which direction to go—" He paused and cast a lazy grin, before continuing, "I'd be lost for sure."

His smile was contagious. "As would I," she agreed. She sank down onto the bench, surprised when he joined her. It was his usual custom to lean against the wall. This new familiarity made the butterflies in her stomach flutter as if they were awakening from a deep sleep. "Have you ever been on a ship?"

"No, ma'am."

"I thought you weren't going to call me that anymore," she admonished. "Did you forget?"

He stared down into her brilliant eyes. How could he? he wondered. She'd been steadily on his mind for weeks. When he was in town and saw a lady with a particularly fetching hat, he was reminded of Rebeccah Randolph and the day she demanded he replace hers. If he caught a glimpse of lace or ruffles, a whiff of perfume, his thoughts always returned to the dreamy way she had gazed up at the sunset when she didn't know he was watching. Forget? He only wished he could.

"I've been on a stage and a train, but mostly I find that I can get where I want to go on my horse."

"Speaking of horses," she said, feigning a frown. "I rode for several hours today. You should have warned me, Colonel."

"Sayer," he corrected. "It's only fair that you use my name if I'm to use yours, don't you think?"

She matched his smile, still amazed that he could make her feel so relaxed with just a look and one of his delightful smiles.

"Yes, I agree. As I was saying, neither you nor Fernando told me that I would be sore in places I have never been sore before."

He choked on his brandy, causing her to laugh as she patted his back. "Are you all right?" she asked with an innocent lift of her brows.

He nodded, took her hand into his, and looked at her for several long moments. The object of his attention gently pulled her hand free, tucking a wisp of hair behind her ear. He wondered if she knew how feminine her gesture made her appear, or the way it sent a jolt of potent desire straight through him. The torchlight turned her hair a brilliant gold, and he itched to touch it, to see if it was as soft and silky as it appeared. He already knew it smelled good. Each time the breeze wafted over them, he breathed deeply of her sweet scent. Surely if she were more experienced, he thought, she'd be more careful of the cut of her dress—the way the square neckline dipped down to reveal the swell of her breasts.

But she was an innocent, of that he was sure, her experience with men limited to the gently bred nobles of a land he knew nothing about.

At that moment, she looked up at the stars again. In the shadows of the night, her skin appeared smooth and flawless, and he forced himself to look away before she turned and caught him staring.

"Are you ready, *amigo?*" Fernando's voice broke into Sayer's musings. His expression must have revealed his distraction as Fernando added with a knowledgeable grin, "To begin the game?"

"Indeed I am." Sayer grasped Rebeccah's elbow and escorted her back inside. As expected, the chessboard and pieces were arranged on a small table before the window, close to the settee where Rebeccah could sit and watch their game. Sayer took his place while Fernando refilled their glasses.

"You first," Fernando stated, taking his seat.

Sayer moved a pawn. Fernando chose to move his knight. As the evening wore on, the men lingered over their game. Only when Rebeccah yawned did Sayer look up. "I fear we have bored the lady very nearly to death," he said, pushing away from the table. He rose and offered her his hand. "Shall I see you home?"

"I hate ruining your game," she replied.

"Nonsense. I'm sure Fernando will not mind if we finish next time," Sayer said with a sly grin.

"Not at all," Fernando complied. They walked toward the door, but Fernando paused before he opened it. "What say you? Shall we make it a little more exciting?"

Sayer lifted his hat from one of the elaborately carved hooks mounted on the wall. "What exactly do you have in mind?" He held up his hand before Fernando could answer. "I feel the need to remind you that a soldier's pay is nothing to brag about."

Fernando laughed. "*Si,* I understand. However, I, on the other hand, have no need to take your hard-earned wages." He cast Rebeccah a crafty glance. "However, in two weeks, the *señorita* will have learned enough about riding to attempt an outing. I would propose that the winner of our game act as her escort."

Sayer looked at Rebeccah, who was, by her expression, enjoying their friendly challenge. Only when their eyes met did she swallow and quickly look away as if she had done something wrong. The subtle gesture both pleased and annoyed him. Why should she feel guilty? She'd done nothing wrong. He was the one staring. "What would you like to do?" he asked, drawing her beautiful eyes back in his direction.

"Me?" she asked, blinking several times as if trying to think of something to say. "I can't see myself upon a horse for any great length of time."

"I won't take you too far . . . the first time," he assured. "We'll ride into the mountains, catch our lunch and cook it over an open fire."

When she cast a quick glance at Fernando's hurt expression, he tried to look even more pitiful, making her laugh.

"Why don't we all go? I'm sure the children would love an outing. We could have a picnic." Both men shrugged their shoulders, looked at each other for a moment, turned their smiling faces her way then shook their heads.

"I must confess, it sounds delightful, but . . ." Fernando put his hand over his heart. "A bet is a bet. As gentlemen, we must honor it. Perhaps another time." He caught her hand and placed a chaste kiss on the back. "Sleep well." He opened the door, and then caught Sayer by the arm for just a moment. "Until Friday?"

"I wouldn't miss it for the world." Sayer stepped outside and offered his arm to Rebeccah, waiting until Fernando closed the door before he began to walk. "I hope we have not offended you." When she smiled at him, he found his thoughts becoming less than noble. The sweet smells of the evening could not compare to the heady scent of her, nor did the summer breeze make him any less aware of her warm touch through his sleeve.

They were at her door too quickly, but before she could turn to open it, he caught her gently by the shoulders and gazed down into her eyes for a long moment. Innocently, she gazed up at him, her tongue darting out to moisten her lips as if she wanted to speak. That simple gesture was far too inviting, and before he realized what he was doing, he bent his head and claimed her soft mouth. Her hands pressed against his chest, but much to his amazement she didn't resist. Instead, she closed her eyes and melted against him for several enjoyable moments. He deepened the kiss, taking full advantage of her willingness, until she stiffened in his arms and pushed away.

"I-I'm sorry," she stammered, turning abruptly to open her door. Light flooded over them. He thought she would slam the door in his face, but after she stepped inside she turned. "I'm sorry," she repeated, her voice calm, considering how her chin quivered. "I should have told you before that I'm engaged to be married."

Her confession rattled him to the core. "To whom?" he asked, surprising himself with his forward question. Her eyes met his in a most unsettling way.

"His name is Edward Dunlap."

Sayer instantly didn't like the man and nearly said so, but caught himself before he voiced something he'd regret. He watched her closely, wondering why she just didn't close the door. Instead she continued to hold on to it as if she needed it for support. Had their shared kiss affected her as much as it had affected him? He hoped to God it had.

"Well, he's a very lucky man."

"Thank you," she murmured.

"But, he's also very foolish."

"Why do you say that?" she asked, feeling the need to defend her betrothed.

"Because he let you go." Sayer touched the brim of his hat and left, but his abrupt goodbye left her wondering at his meaning. She watched as he disappeared into the darkness, and then finally closed the door. Slowly she turned and leaned back against it, feeling as if she had just done something dreadfully wrong. She closed her eyes to collect her rampant thoughts, but his scent lingered, his handsome face clear as crystal in her mind.

Instantly she opened her eyes and thought of Edward. Poor, dear Edward. How could she behave so wantonly when they were engaged? For heaven's sake. She had promised to be his wife. What was she thinking to let Sayer, a man she hardly knew, kiss her? She yanked the pins from her hair and angrily raked her fingers through the curls to loosen them. She had sent three letters to England in the last few weeks, but still nothing new had come in return.

"Why haven't you written?" she muttered as she pumped some water into the sink. After splashing cool water on her cheeks, she patted them dry, pausing as she pressed her fingertips to her lips. Once more, Sayer's features sprang into her mind, and for an aching moment she relived his kiss. Felt again that strange tingling in the pit of her stomach that spread warmth throughout her body. Groaning, she tossed the towel on the counter then went into the bedroom to undress, blaming the lack of any news from her fiancé for her imprudence.

CHAPTER SIX

Three mornings later, the girls were late in rising. While Rebeccah waited, she strolled over to admire the painting above the fireplace. For three days her indiscretion with the colonel had been a constant in her thoughts, but today she was determined to forget what had happened. Even ladies were entitled to small improprieties.

But she had thoroughly enjoyed his kiss. Found it wildly exciting, and to try and tell herself she hadn't wouldn't be an easy thing to do. Deep in thought, she wandered over to look out the long, narrow window when she glanced down at the chessboard.

Everything was as the men had left it several nights ago. As she studied the position of the pieces, their bet came to mind. The thought of riding out with Sayer made her palms grow moist. Would he try and kiss her again? she wondered. If he acted so brazen with others close by, how would he conduct himself if they were all alone? Glancing around, she caught her lip between her teeth and moved one of Fernando's knights.

"Here we are," came Fernando's deep voice, causing Rebeccah to jump as she turned, smoothing an imaginary wrinkle from her skirt. "Did we keep you waiting long?"

"No, not at all," she answered, hoping she sounded calm and collected when in actuality her stomach was in a nervous knot.

She took a deep breath and forced a smile. "Come, children. We should get started."

By the time Friday arrived, Rebeccah felt secure enough to endure a short ride outside the fenced paddock. If there was one thing she had learned about horseback riding, it was that it gave the riders ample time to converse, and not just on equine subjects. In the last two weeks, Don Fernando had felt compelled to discuss the difficulties of parenthood, raising cattle, and was now on the delicate subject of keeping women happy.

"It can't be done," he stated with a firm nod as he patiently got off his horse for the third time and handed her the rein she had dropped.

Rebeccah glanced down at him and frowned. "You're certain of this?"

"Absolutely. Ask any man." His superior attitude piqued her desire to debate the subject further.

"I'm happy," she countered. She watched him mount then felt his gaze fall on her like the heat of the day.

"Ah, so you say, but are you truly happy, *Señorita?*"

"Of course. I'm here on a very nice horse, having a very nice ride." She paused and gave him a cheerful smile even though she really wanted to clobber him for his arrogance. "With a very nice gentleman. I am the epitome of happiness."

"Ha! You are the epitome of liars," he challenged, grinning as she glared at him. "If you are so happy, tell me this. Why do I see you staring off at the mountains when you think no one is looking, holding one of Edward's letters, hey?"

"I am simply thinking about . . . about Edward and how happy I will be to see him."

"Then explain why you do the same after the colonel has visited?"

"I do no such thing," she defended.

"Ah, but you do. I have seen it with my own eyes."

"Are you spying on me?"

His laughter told her he wasn't. "See, it is like I said. You're not really happy. I think you are confused about your feelings. To love a man an ocean away is a difficult thing to do, *no?*"

"It certainly is not."

Fernando nodded as if he had all the answer he wanted. "You are not happy. You are merely making the best of your situation. It is as I said, women are never happy."

"That's not true," she said with a curt nod. "Men are equally miserable, I'm sure."

His bark of laughter made her smile. His eyes looked wicked, and in that instant she knew he had drawn her into a meaningless conversation only to rile her. "You should be ashamed."

"For what?"

"For choosing such a silly topic." She picked up her horse's reins. "Shall we trot a little?" she asked.

"If it makes you *happy,*" Fernando retorted with a grin.

There was just enough time for a nice hot bath before supper, but even soaking in the tub failed to calm Rebeccah's nerves. Now, as she tried to choose a gown, she thought of the night that lay ahead. What had she been thinking to move their game pieces around in order to assure Fernando's victory? She closed her eyes and groaned. After today's ride, she had her doubts that the handsome rancher was as noble as he professed to be. In fact, both men were equally flirtatious. Perhaps she should dress more conservatively to show them that her heart belonged to Edward and only to Edward.

She glanced at the row of dresses, heaving a despondent sigh. She didn't own anything suitable for dinner that had a high neckline. It simply wasn't the style. She frowned at the clock. In a few more minutes, she'd be late. Glancing at the closet once more, she chose a clean white blouse and blue-and-white striped skirt. When she looked in the mirror, she winced. It was rather severe, especially with the cameo and black velvet ribbon. "It will have to do," she said as she picked up her shawl.

"Let us enjoy a brandy and finish our game," Fernando replied as he pushed away from the long table in the dining room. He paused by Rebeccah's chair. "Unless you wish to teach us a new game," he added with a sly smile. "I could fetch my daughters' boards and chalk."

"Perhaps a lesson in manners?" Rebeccah replied, blinking innocently. She finished her second glass of wine then put the goblet down, hoping she didn't appear as nervous as she felt.

"You wound me," Fernando stated with a smile as he held her chair. "Come. Sit by me tonight for luck." Fernando led her to the settee, placed a sherry in her hand, and then insisted she move more to the left than the right so she could be closer to him. She sipped her sherry, feeling guilty as the two handsome men labored over their game. For a moment she wondered if she had done the right thing, and then once more convinced herself she had.

"Check," Fernando said, drawing her from her less than honorable musings. Again, they fell silent while she watched. Fernando's serious expression gave him an almost sinister look—his dark moustache adding to his good looks. Yet it was Sayer who drew her attention. Though she tried to deny it, his tawny hair made her long to see if it was as soft as it looked. His face was tanned. His dark brows were drawn together over bluer-than-blue eyes focused on the task at hand. She knew men who could keep their expressions expertly controlled no matter what the circumstances, and now, as she gazed at the colonel, she knew exactly what he was doing.

Only when Sayer looked up and gave her one of his lazy smiles did she doubt the wisdom of her treachery. She swallowed her bout of uncertainty, taking several more sips of sherry to reinstate her fortitude.

Another hour drifted slowly by.

When next she looked up, Fernando stood over her, but she realized he had only appeared to refill her glass. When he returned to his seat, she decided not to watch, choosing instead to stare into the cheerful fire while she sipped her drink to console her conscience.

The clock on the mantel chimed ten times, confirming that another half hour had passed.

"Checkmate," Sayer said, and her head snapped up and, wide-eyed, she turned in his direction.

"Are you sure?" she cried before she realized what she'd said. She smiled to hide her outburst. "So-so soon, I mean?" Nervously, she toyed with the pins in her hair, wondering how in heaven's name the colonel could have accomplished such a task.

"Yes, it appears so," Fernando replied with a long, disappointed sigh. He looked up from the board, shaking his head as if he couldn't believe what he saw. "Congratulations, *amigo*. You have won, fair and square."

Rebeccah choked on her sherry.

Chairs scraped on the tiled floor as both men rose. The glass was taken from her fingers and placed on the table as Fernando sat next to her and gently patted her back. "Are you all right?"

"Yes, quite," she managed to say, flashing each man a reassuring smile. "Well then. I suppose . . ." She stared at her hands, trying very hard not to look at Sayer, fully aware that the mere sight of the man caused her more distress than she needed at the moment. ". . . if we are to have our little outing, tomorrow . . ." She finally found the courage to meet his gaze. "I'd best be going home."

"The night is still young," Fernando protested.

"Yes, so it is, but I'm sure that the colonel will want to get an early start in the morning."

"If at all possible," Sayer replied in his deep, velvety voice. "However, I've heard it said English ladies don't often rise before noon." By his tone, she sensed he was teasing.

"I assure you, Colonel," Fernando began, feigning a formality he never used. "In England there is much to keep a lady awake at night." His expression was comical, chasing away her guilt. The rogue deserved to lose. "Why, there is the opera," he continued, "and, I am told, the many *fiestas.*"

Rebeccah giggled, feeling quite merry after two glasses of sherry. "Don't you mean balls?" She made a show of glancing toward the chessboard. "Make fun if you like. However, from what I can see, there is very little to do around here after the sun goes down."

"It all depends on what you find entertaining," Sayer interjected with an arrogant grin.

The men exchanged a glance that made her cheeks heat. "My, it's warm so close to the fire," she said, waving her hand before her face.

She stood, feeling a little lightheaded. She took a small step, but the heel of her shoe caught on the hem of her gown and pitched her forward. She would have fallen if Sayer's arm had not come around her waist. Forced to grab him to steady herself, she gazed up into his eyes, mesmerized by what she saw.

Concern? Was he truly worried about her? The thought was somehow comforting even though his concern was completely unnecessary. Surely two little glasses of wine and two even smaller glasses of sherry couldn't make one inebriated, could it?

"Are you sure you're all right?" Fernando asked, drawing her gaze to his dark one.

"I-I think so. I believe I may have had a little too much sherry," she confessed, trying to pull away from Sayer. "Perhaps I should sit a while longer."

"Nonsense," Sayer replied a moment before he whisked her up into his arms. "What you need is to lie down before you fall down."

"*Si,* I think the colonel is right."

"But . . . but the night is still young," she protested, even though she rather enjoyed the feeling of being in Sayer's arms. "I'm fine . . . just a little dizzy. I'm sure it will pass."

Fernando hurried ahead of Sayer with a wide smile all the while she tried to convince them she could make it home on her own. "*Mañana* you will thank me." He opened the door and, as Sayer carried her out into the cool night air, he added, "I will send one of my maids over in a few moments."

Once outside, the stars seemed to swirl and blend together in a strange and enjoyable way. Unconsciously, Rebeccah put her arms around Sayer's neck and snuggled closer. "Don't you find it odd how quickly it gets cold?" she murmured, listening to his boots crunch on the graveled path. "Yet you're so warm, and smell good too . . . like pine and . . . and leather."

Sayer placed her gently upon her feet as he opened the door to her home. Instantly she leaned against him, and this time she was more than he could resist. When she lifted her chin to gaze into his eyes, he kissed her. Her lips were sweet, tinged with sherry. She gave a little moan and pressed closer, kissing him back. He devoured her willing lips until she was breathless, clinging to him. Slowly, as if it were the hardest thing he had ever done, he reached up and took her arms from around his neck. He wanted her, wanted her badly, but not like this.

"Becky," he said, cupping her cheek as she gazed up at him with a dreamy smile. "Can you stand?"

"Yes, but I don't want to," she said truthfully, leaning against him for support. "I'd much rather you hold me." Her warm fingers inched up his chest, circling each button. "You're very handsome in uniform," she purred.

He steeled himself against the feel of her soft curves, and lifted her in his arms again. He carried her inside to the bed and placed her on top, leaning over her for several long moments. He removed the pins from her hair, aware that it would only make it harder to leave. It felt just as he had imagined it would, as he sank his fingers into the silky locks, spreading them out over the pillows and inhaling the sweet, clean fragrance.

"Someone will be here soon to help you undress," he whispered, placing a kiss on her cheek. At the sound of his voice, her eyes fluttered open. She stretched and smiled a smile that was very nearly his undoing.

"You can help me, if you want," she purred innocently, closing her eyes. The buttons of her blouse strained against her breasts. His gaze slid down the full length of her. If her request wasn't because of too much sherry, he'd surely comply. Even now his trousers felt tight, confining. He stood and moved away, pausing in the doorway for one last look.

The next morning, Rebeccah awoke at the sound of voices outside. She tried to rise then collapsed, pressing her fingertips to her temples. Memories of the previous evening washed over her like the hot breeze from her open bedroom window. She closed her eyes and groaned. How could she possibly face either of those men? Slowly, she rose and shrugged on a light cotton robe. She padded over to the kitchen and looked out the window.

Her stomach twisted into a knot when she saw Sayer leaning back against the hitching post conversing with Fernando. He looked too handsome for his own good with his hat pushed back on his head. Rebeccah groaned again, dragging her fingers through her tangled hair as she turned around and leaned against the counter.

"The picnic," she muttered. The men's laughter drew her back to the window.

"I do not think she will be in any condition to ride." Fernando's voice was filled with humor. "She was well into her cups last night. It is as I said. English ladies do not have the vigor our women have."

Sayer said something, but she couldn't hear it. However, when Fernando laughed again, her shame turned to anger. She pumped some water into the sink and splashed it on her face and neck. Somewhat revived, she hurried to the bedroom and searched through her clothing until she found a light grey riding habit and matching bonnet—both very proper and dignified.

"Vigor," she grumbled as she dressed and pinned her hair up. "I'll show you vigor." She tugged on tall black boots, then, taking one last look in the mirror, grabbed her hat and strode outside.

Instantly the heat of the day slapped her in the face, but she'd die of it before she'd admit that she wasn't well. Her eyes had just adjusted to the light when several of the women who worked for Don Fernando approached. Speaking in Spanish, each woman held out a basket, nodding and encouraging her to take them. Lifting the cloth from the first, Rebeccah was delighted to see it filled with fresh eggs.

"*Muchas gracias,*" she said, a little unsure of her Spanish. In the course of their conversation, most of which she couldn't understand, she realized they were gifts for teaching their children. Smiling, she placed the basket on the bench. The next woman held out her basket. This one was filled with small cakes and cookies. "*Muchas gracias,*" Rebeccah repeated, accepting the basket and placing it next to the first. Finally, the last woman approached. She said something Rebeccah didn't understand, but waited patiently for an answer.

"*Gallina,*" the woman repeated with a wide grin.

"*Si,*" Rebeccah said, having no idea what else to say. Her answer obviously pleased the woman very much. Smiling, she opened her basket and pulled out a live chicken, plopping the squawking bird into Rebeccah's arms. "Ah . . . no, *gracias,*" she said, forcing a smile at the same time trying to give it back. But the happy woman refused, smiled again, and then left with the others.

Rebeccah held the chicken out at arm's length. The young hen continued to squawk and wiggle until one wing was free. Rounder's head came up and his nostrils flared. She shot a frantic glance in Fernando's direction, but he quickly turned his back and burst into laughter. On the other hand, the colonel only had a silly grin on his face until she began to get closer.

The closer she got to him and to his horse, the more terrified the poor animal became. The colonel soon had his hands full trying to calm the stallion down. When Fernando turned to help, Rebeccah shoved the squawking chicken into his arms then dusted off her gloved hands.

"Good morning, gentlemen," she said cheerfully, flashing them both her best smile. "Don Fernando," she began, shouting over the ruckus, "please take care of my chicken while I'm gone. I'd be most grateful." She feigned surprise. "Where is my horse?" She could have laughed at Fernando's expression if her head didn't hurt so much.

"I-I will have her saddled right away." He and her chicken were gone in the next moment, leaving her alone to face Sayer, who finally settled his horse.

A wave of fresh memories washed over her, only this time they were filled with passionate kisses. Dear Lord, had she really tried to seduce him? When she glanced at him, his smile and laughing eyes confirmed it, and a blush crept up her neck and colored her cheeks. "Colonel MacLaren, I would like to apologize—"

"There's nothing to apologize for, Miss Randolph, except that you promised you wouldn't be so formal, remember?"

She gave him a weak nod, deciding it was best to let the matter die a silent death as she flicked a feather from her skirt. "That's very gracious of you." She took out a small handkerchief and pressed it against the tiny beads of perspiration forming on her forehead, just below the brim of her hat.

"I'm sure you'll feel better when we get to the mountains where the air is cool and fresh."

She nodded and gave him what she hoped was an eager smile.

"You've never tasted anything as fine as fresh-roasted trout." As usual, Sayer wasn't as easy to read as Fernando, and for a moment she doubted that he had said anything about her that would have caused Fernando to laugh.

She'd been so sure they were poking fun at her that she had refused to admit her head hurt and her stomach rolled at the mere thought of food. She glanced longingly at her cool, comfortable home, but the deed was done. She had successfully condemned herself to spend the day with the very person she wanted to avoid. It was terribly hot and the outfit she had chosen was dreadfully confining. When would she learn to wear soft, light cottons as Lydia so often suggested?

Angry with herself, she waved the handkerchief to cool her face, causing Rounder to dance and snort in fear once more. She gave the stallion a pitiful look. "I have come to the conclusion that your horse is a coward," she said smugly, ignoring Sayer's soft laughter as he soothed his frightened steed.

Fernando returned, leading her saddled horse. Much to her relief, he'd chosen a regular saddle and not the sidesaddle she dreaded. After he helped her mount, he handed her the reins.

"Now, just remember what I told you and everything will be just fine, *si?*"

"*Si,*" she repeated sarcastically, adjusting her skirts. She frowned when Fernando purposely pulled Sayer aside, whispering something she couldn't hear. "Shall we begin?" she called, irritated with their behavior.

"Have a nice time," Fernando said as Sayer swung up into the saddle and led the way through the gate. "And, remember, *Señorita,* keep tight hold of both reins."

Farther and farther they rode from the ranch, exchanging bits and pieces of polite conversation. Rounder spooked several times, blowing his nose and pricking his ears at things Rebeccah couldn't see, and the more he did it, the hotter and more bothered she became. "Does he always act like this?" she asked after he jumped when a rabbit darted from behind a bush.

As much as she didn't want to, she found Sayer's soft laughter pleasing. "He's just young and inexperienced. I had a lot of paperwork to catch up on and didn't take him out yesterday." Sayer reached down and patted the stallion on the neck. "He's just full of himself. Once he warms up, he'll settle down."

"One would think in this heat, he would already be warm."

"True," her handsome escort agreed with a smile. "It's a figure of speech. It means, once he's burned off some of his excess energy, he'll calm down." Sayer tossed her a sideways glance. "If you're too hot, you could loosen that high collar just a bit or take off that jacket."

"I'm fine, thank you," she lied.

Soon cactus and gravel gave way to grass and pines. They followed a narrow trail that Sayer told her was made by deer and cattle as they traveled up and down the mountain single-file to conserve the grass. Slowly they climbed, following the trail first to the left then switching back to the right several yards above their previous path as the mountain grew too steep to go in a straight line. The higher they rose, the more the heat of the day diminished and the better she began to feel.

A cool, fragrant breeze ruffled the lace at her neck, and she began to relax and enjoy the ride. Brandy, she decided, was a gem, never balking or spooking when they crossed the small, boggy gullies that spilled over from the swollen river. Mountain blue jays scolded from the treetops while squirrels darted in and out of fallen logs and rocky formations.

" 'Tis truly beautiful here," Rebeccah said as she followed her escort deeper and deeper into the forest. Ferns of every shade of green imaginable mingled with the lush mountain grass. Once in a while, when the trees were not so thick, she'd get a peek of the rugged peaks in the distance. She was looking up when she should have been watching the trail, unaware that Sayer had stopped until Brandy refused to move any farther.

Sayer turned in the saddle and put his finger before his mouth to keep her from speaking. Moving very carefully, he motioned for her look between the trees. Her breath stilled and a smile sprang to her lips the moment she did. Three graceful deer were grazing in a small meadow.

Sayer nudged Rounder closer, and leaned over. "See the rack of antlers on the large one?" he whispered. "He's about eight or nine. The little, speckled one was most likely born a month or two ago, and that one, she's the mother." When Rounder snorted impatiently and nipped at Rebeccah's mare, the deer fled.

"Oh, my," Rebeccah breathed. "They were beautiful."

Sayer scolded Rounder, then led the way down a grassy slope where soon she heard the sound of running water. "We'll camp here," he said, swinging down and tying Rounder to a stout branch. He came to her and when he reached up, his gloved hands encircled her waist. She tried not to gaze into his eyes as he lifted her down, but it would have been easier to keep her heart from beating or her lungs from filling with fresh mountain air.

"What shall I do?" she asked, tugging off her gloves as he tied her mare to a different tree. He retrieved his saddlebags, then took her hand and pulled her with him toward the sound of the stream. "Shouldn't we water the horses first?" she asked, pulling her hand free.

"Nope," he answered easily, apparently unaffected by her hesitancy. "They need to cool down a little. I'll see to them in a few minutes."

When he seemed to find the place he was looking for he bade her to sit upon a flat rock while he gathered some sticks and broken branches. After he made a ring out of rocks, he placed the wood in the center and built a fire. He stood and tugged off his gloves before reaching into his saddlebags. He pulled out what looked like several straight sticks with metal tips and hoops along their length. As she watched, he snapped them together, forming a rod to which he attached some line and a hook. He caught her staring and smiled as he removed the ten-inch-long knife from the sheath strapped to his left leg. In a few strokes, the dark, damp soil near the bank was loosened and from that he pulled out a thick, juicy worm. She turned quickly away when he speared it on the hook.

"It's just a worm," she heard him say, his voice filled with boyish amusement. "We need 'em to catch our lunch." Her eyes fused with his when he caught her arm and pulled her to her feet. Her breath stilled in her breast as he carefully removed her bonnet, then the pins before he loosened her hair. His touch was like fire, sending heat to every part of her body, but she dared not give in to her desire to lean toward him.

"Your hair is too pretty to keep it all knotted up under your hat. Come," he said, drawing her away from her wanton thoughts as he hung her bonnet on a branch. "I'm going to teach you how to fish."

"I think you should do it," she protested as he guided her closer to the stream. "I'll just sit and watch."

"You can't catch anything by watching," he said, and she found herself beginning to like his easy manner. He held the rod low, flicking the line into the current of the water with a barely audible plop. Reluctantly, she accepted the pole, nodding as he whispered his instructions then turned to leave.

"Where are you going?" she asked, lowering her voice when he put his finger over his lips. What was she to do if she actually caught something? He came back, standing so close she could feel his warm breath against her ear.

"I'm going to water the horses," he said softly. "I'll be right back." He moved away and gave her a reassuring nod. Her confidence grew with his silent endorsement. No sooner had he disappeared than she felt something tug on the line.

"Oh, my," she whispered, frantically searching the trees for a sign of her teacher. The line jumped again. "Oh, my," she repeated and she took a step back as he had instructed. She gasped her distress over and over again, landing a large fish on the grassy bank.

When Sayer came back, the trout was still jumping and flopping, and she was still gasping, "Oh, my, oh, my."

CHAPTER SEVEN

After Sayer took Rebeccah's trout off the hook, he sent her back to fishing while he went downstream and cleaned her catch. By the time she'd caught two more, he took the rod away, warning her that they had more than they could eat already. She reluctantly agreed, but only after he promised to bring her back to this special place as soon as he could get away from his duties at the fort. Afterwards, he placed the raw fish on sticks, and together they sat on a fallen log and roasted them over the coals.

"That was a feast fit for a king," she said with such a satisfied smile, Sayer laughed.

"Yes, I do believe it was." He stood and began to gather up the remains of their camp.

Rebeccah sighed. "Must we leave so soon?" she asked, unaware that her question filled him with a soft happiness he hadn't felt in a very long time. She accepted his hand and stood, dusting off the back of her skirt, and then picked up what was left of the small loaf of bread he had brought along.

"Let's leave it," he suggested.

"Why?" she asked.

"To feed the birds and the squirrels." He came and took her hand leading her to a large rock formation a little ways away from where they camped. He tore the chunk of bread in two, gave her half, then began to tear his portion into small pieces before scattering them on top of the rock.

"Shall I put mine here?" she asked, motioning to a smooth place that she could reach if she stood on her tiptoes.

"That's as good as any. Even if you drop it on the ground, something will find it and eat it." He caught her hand once more, and for a moment her heart beat a little faster when he hesitated, as if he wanted to take her into his arms. She quickly pulled her hand away and tucked a strand of hair behind her ear. Much to her relief, he glanced over at the horses. "I'd best let them have another drink before we start back." He wasn't gone long. When he appeared with her horse, she accepted his help into her saddle, then remembered her hat.

"Sayer, I left my hat near the river." Once more he walked away, and even though she scolded herself for watching, he was as pleasing to look upon as the rugged mountain peaks. Her thoughts drifted to Edward, but she only had a few moments to wonder what he might be doing when Sayer returned with her bonnet. He held her horse steady while she tied it on.

Before long they were back at Don Fernando's ranch. As a servant led away her mare, Sayer walked her toward her house as she had declined Fernando's dinner invitation, stating that all she wanted to do was take a hot bath and get to bed early. At the door she turned and smiled. "Thank you for a lovely day," she managed to say, staring at her gloves to avoid his gaze.

"It was my pleasure." His deep voice brushed over her like the finest silk.

She couldn't help herself; she had to look up or appear foolishly shy. "I-I hope we can do it again soon, very soon."

His smile was filled with promise. "I had to work real hard for this day," he began, his eyes twinkling with mischief.

"I'm afraid I don't understand."

He pushed his hat off his forehead, a gesture she found most distracting. "I'm usually good at chess—" He paused until she felt her cheeks heat. "But last night I was *brilliant.*"

"You were?" she said, trying to act innocent.

"Yes, ma'am. You see, I had the advantage when I left the game last week. But then something real strange happened. Fernando's knight trotted over all by itself to challenge my queen. That gave me a whole new problem to solve, but lady luck is fickle."

He winked at her as he pulled his hat down, holding the brim a moment before he turned away. "When Fernando left to get you more sherry, that little knight of his trotted clear off the board while he wasn't looking."

It seemed as though time skipped by like little children playing games. Every other Friday, Sayer arrived at the ranch and the threesome shared an elaborate supper. The following Saturday, he took her riding, and so began an enjoyable routine.

Rebeccah peeked out the window. This Saturday she was a little late in rising, and as she expected, Sayer stood patiently outside, holding her horse while she found her hat and gloves, tugged them on and stepped outside. "Good morning," she said, accepting his help to mount her horse.

"It is indeed," he confirmed, handing her the reins. Once he was settled on his own horse, he led the way down the path toward the trail they had used last time. Soon they were riding alongside the river where a cool breeze snatched her bonnet off her head before she could catch it. The next moment, Rounder reared, dislodging his relaxed rider. Sayer hit the ground hard, flat on his back.

"Oh my," Rebeccah cried as she quickly got off of Brandy. "Are you all right?" She watched as he held his breath for a few minutes before he slowly rolled to his feet and dusted off his shirt and pants.

"It's my fault," she hurried on. "You see, I was a little too warm and had loosened the ribbon of my bonnet. The wind . . ."

She inwardly winced when Sayer cast a quick glance at her attire, an outfit she was sure he found too elaborate.

"I'm sure you were a little too warm," he said as he bent stiffly to retrieve his hat. He caught Rounder's reins, then turned and helped her back on her horse. Sayer never said another word. Only when he picked up the bonnet did he mutter something under his breath and, at the same time, gave the stallion a few sharp tugs on the reins. Rounder settled down, cocking an ear as Sayer handed the hat to Rebeccah. Once back in the saddle, Sayer urged his horse to cross the shallow stream.

Rebeccah hesitated. "Oh my, I'm not sure I can do that."

Sayer waited on the other side. "Sure you can. It's not deep, just fast. Let her have her head and she'll walk right on in. Hold on to the horn."

Her fingers tightened around the horn. "You're certain?"

"Yes." His smile was patient, easing some of her guilt for his tumble a few moments ago.

"Very well," she murmured, doing as he instructed. The mare splashed into the water, pausing only to take a drink before she scrambled up the other side. "I did it," Rebeccah cried in joy. "I did it and I didn't fall off."

Sayer's laughter drew her attention. "Trust me," he said, shrugging his shoulder as if it hurt, "it's better to stay on your horse most of the time."

She matched his smile. "Have you fallen before?" she asked as she rode beside him across the lush meadow.

"Anyone who tells you he hasn't is lying to you."

"Really?"

"Absolutely," he said. "However, there's a good way and a bad way to come off a horse." He nodded to where they had crossed the river. "That was a bad way." Again his grin was contagious. "As a boy, my father taught me how to fall from a galloping horse without breaking my neck."

"Really?" she repeated in disbelief. "Why? For what purpose?"

"To stay alive." He reached down and rubbed his horse's neck. "There are other tricks too, like how to ride leaning down by your horse's side, or to dismount and pull him down with you."

"On the ground? Whatever for?"

"To use as cover." Sayer pushed his hat back. "Look around and tell me where you'd hide if someone decided to shoot at us."

Rebeccah glanced around the meadow. "I-I don't know. We're too far from the trees, but then I rather doubt anyone would simply start shooting at us for no good reason."

Her escort's smile bordered on arrogant as he patted his horse's neck. "Think so? Then you've forgotten that this is not our land—that the Indians think we are trespassing, and trespassers are often shot."

"If you're trying to frighten me, you've succeeded," she snapped.

He pulled Rounder to a halt, pushed his hat back off his forehead and turned to look at her. "It's not my intention to frighten you, only to teach you, to make you aware of your surroundings and give you ways to protect yourself." He smiled then, lifting some of the fear from her heart. "Besides, most likely there are no Indians around here. My men have done a pretty good job keeping them on the reservation."

"Exactly where they should be," she confirmed.

"Why do you say that?" he asked, making her feel as if she had said something wrong.

"Be-because they are savages and need to be confined." She wondered why his smile appeared sad. "You don't agree, do you?"

Sayer pushed down his hat and urged Rounder onward. "No ma'am, I do not."

"I will probably regret asking, but why not? Weren't the reservations designed to keep the hostiles from bothering the settlers?"

"Yes, they were, but in order to keep someone in a place not of his choosing, it should be appealing—offer ample hunting, clean water and enough land to graze their animals."

Rebeccah made a wide sweep with her arm. "Isn't this enough? Why, it's simply beautiful every direction you look."

"Yes, yes it is," Sayer said patiently. "But this is not the land the government selected for the Indians. This is the land they took away. What did you see when you left Albuquerque?" he asked, leading her down a small ravine toward a brace of aspens.

"Nothing . . . I can't remember seeing anything special, just desert, rocks and a few stunted trees." She fell quiet, then perked up. "There were more trees by the river, but then as we headed north, I remember seeing some men herding cattle. The dust was so thick I could hardly make them out."

"Exactly," Sayer confirmed with a knowledgeable nod. "It's land like you've described that the government has given to the Indians." He patted Rounder on the neck once more. "Now do you see why they refuse to stay?"

"But you're implying that these . . . these people are civilized when they aren't. They run around in animal skins, hunting with crude weapons, living in crude shelters." She sensed he disapproved of her opinion, but brushed it aside.

"Very well, suppose this meadow that we are in right now is our home, and because we have no need of fancy houses, or fancy clothing, the Indians decided that they are more civilized than us and come and say it is theirs."

"Why, I would refuse to give it to them," she said with a superior nod.

"Suppose they outnumber us and because of that, they force us to leave this place and take us to that place you saw—a place without trees to build a proper shelter, without enough game to feed our children. Imagine how you would feel."

She wanted to speak, but couldn't find anything that would justify such actions. After several quiet moments, she couldn't keep silent any longer. "Isn't it up to your elected officials to deem what is or is not proper?"

"Yes, it is. That's why men vote, but sometimes their trust is placed with the wrong people."

"Then I have discovered the perfect career should you decide to leave the army."

He turned and grinned. "Really? What?"

"You could run for office . . . be in politics." His laughter caused her to giggle. "Why not?"

"I intend to raise horses, not havoc." He turned and pointed at the top of a tree, successfully changing the topic. "Do you see that nest?" he asked, and when she nodded, explained how it belonged to an eagle. As they continued on their way, he pointed out a narrow trail cut in the thick grass, a path used by deer and elk, explaining how they walked single-file to conserve the grass on which they depended for survival.

"Have you ever tasted venison?" When she said she hadn't, he promised that the next time he went hunting, he'd bring her some.

When the sun shone directly overhead, Sayer swung down and tied Rounder to a tree, tossing his saddlebags over his shoulder. He helped Rebeccah to the ground, and then tied the mare to another tree, explaining that to put a mare and a stallion too close to each other was asking for trouble.

"Don't you wish we were more like wild animals?" he asked as he guided her to the shade of a tall aspen tree.

"I'm not sure. I rather like who I am."

His eyes danced with merriment. "As do I, but if we were . . ." He paused, and glanced up at two birds circling overhead. "If we were like those hawks, we'd take only what we need to survive. We wouldn't waste our precious time on this earth trying to acquire what we don't need."

She followed his gaze. "I suppose the freedom to fly about would be nice, too."

He reached into his saddlebags and pulled out a folded cloth, unwrapping two tortillas stuffed with shredded beef and cheese. He gave her one before he leaned back against the trunk of the tree. "You could take off that jacket."

She gave him a firm look, and then turned her attention to the food, wondering how to eat it. "However, we are not animals. We are humans who were given wisdom, and because of it have become civilized." She dropped some cheese into her lap. "Most of the time." She smiled when he laughed.

"You sure do like that word." He held up his tortilla, forcing her to watch as he took a bite. "See, it's easy. Don't they ever eat anything with their fingers in England?" He retrieved a flask of wine and two tin cups.

"Certainly not," she countered with feigned superiority. "Why that wouldn't be civilized, would it?" He laughed again, and the sound gave her a feeling of being appreciated. Of being equally matched.

He gave her a cup, then lifted his own and tapped it to hers. "A toast."

"To what?" she asked, enjoying the wily gleam in his vibrant eyes almost as much as she enjoyed eating with her fingers.

"Why, to you and to the new things you've shown me."

She giggled. "Surely you jest."

"No, I'm serious." And she knew he meant it.

"What could I possibly teach you about the wilderness?" She awaited his answer with more anticipation than she cared to admit, watching while he took a drink.

"It's not so much in teaching as it is in seeing things differently through your eyes." He stuffed the empty cloth back into his bags.

"What things?" she asked.

"Why, everything. Do you know how many times I've pulled a trout out of the water?"

"Many, I'm sure." She finished her wine and gave him back the cup, which he added to the bag.

"Exactly, but not until I watched you do it did I remember the joy in landing my first fish, or the excitement of feeding a squirrel leftover bread." His smile was tender, and as he stood and offered her his hand, she sensed that he had shared something of himself—something he didn't do very often.

His warm fingers closed over hers and he pulled her to her feet before he tossed his saddlebags over his broad shoulder. "It's getting late. If we don't want Don Fernando angry with us, we'd best head back."

The next two weeks quickly flew by, and before Rebeccah was through with the girls' Friday afternoon lessons, Sayer arrived. Rather than interrupt, he simply nodded, touched the brim of his hat and carried a small bundle of clothing and a long box toward the house. For over a month now, Fernando had insisted Sayer use one of the spare rooms on the weekends, as it was half a day's ride back to town. It was an arrangement Rebeccah decided she enjoyed almost as much as she did their Friday night dinners.

"Elena," Rebeccah gently scolded when she noticed that both girls were staring after the colonel with dreamy expressions on their little faces. "Elena, please repeat the last sentence." The child dragged her gaze off the colonel, heaved a long, blissful sigh before glancing at her little sister. "*Tío* Sayer is so, *hermoso, sí?*"

"*Sí*," Maria agreed with an impish smile. "*Muy hermoso.*"

They giggled when Rebeccah scolded them again, softening her reprimand with a smile.

While Elena read aloud, Rebeccah watched as Sayer disappeared into the house. *Yes, indeed,* she agreed silently. *He is very, very handsome.*

The next day, Rebeccah rode beside Sayer as they traveled down the hard-packed road. When she wasn't drinking in the breathtaking scenery, she watched her escort. So intent was she on her inspection, she didn't notice when they rode into a wide meadow until he stopped.

"This looks like a good place," he said, swinging down off his horse.

"Are we going to have a picnic?" she asked, gazing down into his vibrant blue eyes.

"Nope, I'm going to teach you how to shoot a gun."

"A gun?" she repeated in dismay, then gave a small laugh. "Surely you're not serious."

His crafty smile, and the way his eyes twinkled as he lifted her down from her horse, told her he was more than serious. The word that sprang into her mind was *determined.*

She feigned a pout, willing to do anything to get him to change his mind. "I really don't see the need for all these lessons. First you insist that I learn how to ride, then it's fishing, and now you . . . you want me to shoot a gun?"

"That's the idea," he said, his smile as patient as his tone. "You said you didn't like horses, but once you got on Brandy, you liked it. You didn't want to try your hand at fishing, either, but after you landed a few trout, I could hardly drag you away."

He tied Rounder to a stout tree, then came over and took Brandy's reins, leading her to a different tree. He removed his saddlebags and slung them over his shoulder at the same time he slipped his rifle out of the saddle socket.

"Why don't you let the horses graze?" she asked.

"Because, the moment we fire off my gun, they'll both be well on their way back to Santa Fe."

"I thought cavalry horses were used to loud noises."

"They are, but Rounder's not quite a cavalry horse. If I have to go out and do battle with someone," he added, his tone laced with good-natured sarcasm, "I'll be sure to take a different horse. Now, take off your hat."

"My hat? Why?"

"It'll just be in the way," he answered as he began to untie the ribbon. His warm fingers grazed her cheek. A simple touch, but one so delightful and so sensual it caused her to shiver ever so slightly. Apparently he felt something too, as the blue of his eyes deepened and she could have sworn he lingered at the knot. "When are you going to trade in all these fancy clothes for something more comfortable?"

"These are comfortable," she protested, but his expression told her he didn't believe it. When the bonnet was finally removed and hung on a branch, he took her hand and led her to the other end of the meadow toward a group of large pines.

"You ride well," he began, "but what would you do if you came up on a rattlesnake or—"

"Rattlesnake?" she gasped, stopping in her tracks. "You never mentioned that there were snakes up here."

"Well, they usually don't get this high," he replied casually, trying to calm her down. "Come on," he urged until she began to walk alongside him once more. "It's too cold for them, but I'm surprised you haven't seen one on the ranch."

"I spend most of my time indoors with Don Fernando's daughters, not traipsing about in his fields," she countered, still sounding indignant. "You should have warned me before now."

"That's one of the reasons the girls have that little dog. He's not just their pet. Ever notice how he's always running around when he's out with them?"

"I suppose, but I've never thought anything of it."

"I don't think the dog has either, but when he's snooping around like that, he scares off anything that might bother the children."

"Then perhaps I should make better friends with him," she said dryly. "Nevertheless, you still should have told me about the possibility of snakes before now."

"Yes. I should have, but I just didn't think about it." He stopped before they got to the trees and set his saddlebags on the grass, leaning his rifle against them. He lifted his Colt .45 from his holster and placed the pistol in her palm, holding it as he forced her fingers to close around it. At the same time, he moved behind her, one arm on each side, his breath warm against her ear as he instructed her on the proper way to hold, cock, aim, and fire the weapon.

She argued that the gun was far too heavy.

"Yes," he said calmly. "It is for a fact, but not so heavy that you can't hold it."

"I'm afraid of guns," she stated, refusing to give in to his subtle demands that she try.

"I was too, once."

"You're a man," she scoffed. "Men are supposed to know about guns. It's a requirement of being male. On the other hand, I am a woman, and all that is required of me is that I know how to behave like a lady, and ladies do not go about the countryside shooting guns." Sayer's soft laughter nearly caused her to wonder if he really could read her mind. Her amazement evaporated the moment he pointed the weapon at a distant tree.

"What would you do if a bear came up on you while you were fishing?" he asked, and she knew he was trying to frighten her into submission. If he had the power to read her mind, why didn't he realize bears were the farthest things from her thoughts? *He* was the only thing on her mind—his touch burning her skin, his manly scent mingling with the pines and invading every breath, every thought. Did he say something about the truth? The truth of what? That she enjoyed being trapped in his strong arms? Yes, she confirmed, she most definitely liked the way his warm hands held hers in his firm but gentle grasp. Each time his thigh brushed against hers or his muscular body pressed intimately close to hers, he very nearly shattered her composure, and *that* was the *truth* of it.

"Well?" he asked. He repeated his question, drawing her away from her unladylike thoughts. He moved away and she took a long, calming breath, thankful for the reprieve.

"Well what?" she asked, then realized he expected an answer. "Rattlesnakes and bears. Are there any more beasts I should know about that frequent these forests?" she asked, trying to hide the fact that she hadn't paid the slightest attention to his instructions.

"You didn't answer my question."

"Which one?" She tried to look innocent, yet felt just the opposite.

"Any of them," he stated, raising one dark brow. "For starters, you could tell me if it's true ladies fox hunt in England?"

"I-I suppose some do."

"Good. After today, you can go with them."

"We don't use guns, we use dogs," she cried.

He made a face. "You let a defenseless little fox get torn up by a bunch of dogs?"

"It's not as bad as you make it sound. The dogs chase the fox and we chase the dogs."

"Oh," he said with an exaggerated sigh. "That makes it much more civilized." He paused for effect. "Now, I'm only going to repeat this one more time. What would you do if you—"

"Very well," she began, remembering. "If I came upon a bear,

I-I would scream for you to come and save me." She gave him a bright, satisfied smile.

"And I would in a heartbeat," he said, his voice once more like velvet as he moved behind her and resumed his distracting position. The lazy butterflies fluttering in her stomach came fully awake.

"But," he added, close to her ear, "what if I was too far away to hear you . . . and you didn't have a pack of blood-thirsty dogs to scare it away?"

His answer pleased her immensely. She turned. Every time his gaze met hers, her heart did a little dance and she had the undeniable urge to kiss him—knew by the look in his eyes that he wanted to kiss her too. Ashamed that she could so easily brush aside the fact that she was promised to another man, she quickly turned away and focused her attention on the gun in her hands.

"I-I haven't the foggiest idea what I'd do," she said. "If a bear came upon me, and you were not there to shoot him, I suppose I would simply faint away." Her soldier laughed, and the pleasant sound further worked to unravel her already-frayed nerves. He made her take aim on a tree fifty feet away.

"Now, real easy, pull back the hammer," he said.

When she didn't do it, he did it for her, then, adding to her distress, leaned even closer, and bent a little so his head was next to hers. She watched him out the corner of her eyes.

"Keep both eyes open and site down the barrel while you're looking at the tree," he said.

"That's impossible," she countered, wondering if he could feel her heart thudding against her breast. He turned to look at her. She quickly looked at the tree. "How can I look at two things at once?"

"Becky . . ."

"What?" Said like that, in that deep, velvety voice, her

nickname sounded heavenly.

"You need to pay closer attention. Now relax." He moved back into place, carefully repeated his instructions, then put his finger over hers and together they pulled the trigger.

Her scream resounded throughout the mountain.

CHAPTER EIGHT

Had Sayer not been holding the pistol, Rebeccah would have dropped it. A moment later she ducked out from under his arm and would have run to the horses, but he caught her around the wrist and pulled her back, folding her into his arms.

"It's all right," he said, brushing a wisp of hair behind her ear. Slowly her expression changed, replaced with something he scarcely dared to name. For a breath of a moment her gaze slipped from his eyes to pause on his mouth. He doubted she knew what she was doing, but one thing was for sure: if she didn't stop it, he wouldn't be able to resist the urge to kiss her senseless.

"I-I cannot and will not shoot that thing again," she said breathlessly.

He didn't miss the defiant lift of her chin or the rebellious gleam in her eyes. She was a lady through and through, but under all that lace and fancy clothing there was a fire smoldering, and he longed to breathe life into it.

"My ears are ringing, and it's your fault," she snapped, pulling from his gentle grasp.

His smile was beyond patient, but instead of doing as she wished, he moved behind her once more and pressed the revolver back into her hands, supporting its weight. Reluctantly she closed her fingers around the pistol, and this time tried to take aim.

"I'll do it myself, if you don't mind." She took a step forward, aware that it was the only way she would be able to pay attention as she lifted the gun a little higher. Slowly, holding her breath, she pulled back the hammer, checked her target then fired. A small branch snapped in half. "I did it!" she cried, turning with the gun still clutched in her hand. He quickly deflected the barrel.

"Careful," he warned with a proud grin, but she was too excited to realize the danger in what she had done. "You must always remember," he said, taking the weapon from her, "to take care where you point it. Guns are deadly, Becky. Don't point it unless you're going to shoot it."

"Let's do it again."

"All right," he agreed, checking the chamber before giving her back the gun.

While she took aim, he watched her. If she could see herself, how the fresh mountain air had turned her cheeks rosy and made her skin as smooth as the finest china, she'd be more careful—and he didn't mean with the gun. No, she didn't need a pistol. His heart had already willingly surrendered to her. Lost in thought, he jumped when the pistol fired once more.

This time she pointed the gun at the ground when she turned. Her smile was so genuine, he had the urge to pull her close and reward her with a kiss. To hell with the fact that she belonged to another man. "I'd have thought, in England, Edward would have taught you to shoot," Sayer began. "Don't all Englishmen hunt ducks and other game birds?"

Her smile never wavered. "I suppose."

"You don't know?"

"No." She shrugged her shoulders. "I've never asked him."

Sayer nodded, and then directed their conversation away from the man he already didn't like. The rest of the morning was spent teaching her how to load and unload the revolver. By afternoon, he was sure she could handle the weapon safely. It was holstered and the rifle picked up. They moved farther away from the trees as he explained the difference between a rifle and a revolver. "Stand behind me, and I'll show you," he said.

Pretending to be interested, she couldn't help but admire the way the muscles of his arms and shoulders bunched when he lifted the weapon and took aim. She heard him cock the rifle, and aware of what was to come, pressed her fingertips to her ears, turning at the last moment to see a very small branch fly from the tree.

"Lean into it," he said with a grin as he lowered the weapon and motioned for her to come closer. She stepped into his arms and let him show her how to hold the rifle, grateful that he stood behind her as the force of the discharge thrust her back against his chest. When finally she managed to graze a very broad tree, he told her that he'd seen men who didn't shoot as well their first time. When the lesson was done, he slung the rifle over his shoulder then picked up his saddlebags.

"Can we do this again another time?" she asked, sounding like an excited child who has just learned how to play with a new toy.

"Yes, if you'd like," he said, then added, "but there's really no need. You're a natural. Why, I'd bet a week's pay you'll be knocking birds off branches in no time."

"I would never," she gasped indignantly as he helped her into the saddle. She realized he was teasing when he didn't move away. "You are a scoundrel, Colonel MacLaren," she scolded when he finally left to fetch her bonnet and untie Rounder. While she tied the ribbons, he slipped his rifle back in the saddle socket and fastened on his saddlebags.

"I don't know about you, Miss Randolph, but all this shooting has made me hungry." He gave her an ornery smile as he swung up on Rounder's back, turning the stallion north. "Let's go see if you remember what I taught you about fishing."

By the time they had caught, roasted and eaten their lunch, several dark clouds had darkened the sky. A cool wind whipped up the ashes from their fire, but it didn't seem to cause her soldier any concern.

"This has been a most enjoyable day," he said as he rose from the log where they sat. He took off his hat, raked his fingers through his hair, then put the hat back on as he glanced up at the sky. "I'd best get the horses saddled before that storm hits."

She plucked a nearby flower, then stood and brushed off the back of her pale-green riding skirt. Strolling along the bank she twirled the flower and thought about everything that had happened to her since coming to this wild land. She smiled, wondering if Edward would be proud of what she had learned even if it wasn't exactly befitting her status as a lady.

A tiny seed of doubt sprouted in the back of her mind. Edward was a handsome man, sought after by many a fair maiden. Would he be faithful and wait for her?

Of course, she silently confirmed. She glanced at the colonel and her doubt turned to guilt. Was she being faithful? Hadn't she thought of Sayer as *her* soldier only moments ago? She heaved a despondent sigh, tossed the flower into the river, and watched as the current carried it downstream.

"You must be thinking about something pretty serious to be frowning like that."

Rebeccah spun to see Sayer standing directly behind her, holding her mare saddled and ready. When he held out the reins, his fingers brushed against hers and she found his gaze seductive—inviting. "I-I was just thinking, that's all."

"I figured out that much," he said with his usual lazy grin. She watched as he went to Rounder then tossed his saddle blanket and saddle on the horse's back. When he finished and came over to help her mount, she tried to ignore the way his warm hands lingered at her waist, but when he let go she thought that maybe she had imagined it.

"I've been told that July is the rainy season." Sayer climbed up on Rounder and turned him toward the trail, glancing at the angry sky once more. "Maybe we'll beat it home."

When they could, they trotted, but mostly the terrain was too steep and rocky, forcing them to walk. As the forest gave way to scrub cedar and oak, so did the clouds give way to a steady drizzle of rain.

In a very short time they were soaked.

"It's times like this," he said with a lazy grin, "that I bet you wished you'd brought your parasol."

She lifted the droopy brim of her bonnet and gave him a superior nod. "Indeed, but then if I had, your horse would have surely spooked, and you, my heroic colonel, would be on your backside in the mud." Sayer's bark of laughter made her giggle.

"One would think," she continued, "that an army officer would be prepared for anything, including cloud bursts. If I may be so brazen, where is your rain coat?"

"Slicker," he corrected, still grinning.

"Very well, where is your slicker?"

He reached down and patted his wet horse on the neck. "Rounder doesn't much like 'em."

She liked the way he shortened his words when he was being playful. "I see," she said with another superior smile. "I thought as much."

A loud crack of thunder sounded directly overhead, and as she knew he would, Rounder jumped, then danced around, slipping and sliding in the mud. It took Sayer several sharply spoken commands to bring the young stallion under control. The summer storm was over almost as quickly as it began, and much to Rebeccah's delight, the sun pushed its way through the clouds and sent forth a brilliant rainbow. "I simply can't get enough of the beauty of this country," she said in awe.

"Nor can I," Sayer agreed. No sooner had their clothes begun to dry, than the ranch came into view.

"I assume you'll be staying the night?" she asked as they turned down the familiar road.

"Is that an offer?" he teased.

"C-certainly not," she stammered. She felt her cheeks heat up. "I was only wondering . . . I mean, I assumed you'd—"

"Take it easy, Becky. I was just joking. There's no need for you to get your feathers all ruffled." He winked when she found the nerve to meet his gaze. "In answer to your question, yes, I expect Don Fernando will want to play a game or two of chess later on this evening."

"I'm sure he will. However, I'm too tired to stay up very late. I think that I will get out of these wet clothes, get into my robe and spend the evening with a good book."

"What about supper?" Sayer asked. "Surely all that hard work we did shooting and fishing has stirred up an appetite?" His smile and eyes were filled with devilish humor. "How about I ask Rita to send something simple over . . . for both of us? I'll even do the dishes before I go so you can curl up before the fire with your favorite book."

"You'll do the dishes?" she asked, raising her brows as if she doubted him.

He gave her a wounded look. "I swear I will. Every bowl, spoon and saucer."

His suggestion sounded delightful, too delightful to decline. "Well then, Colonel MacLaren, how could I possibly refuse? I believe you have just invited yourself to dine at my home."

Fernando retrieved the package Sayer had brought and went into his study. He placed the box on his desk and after he examined the contents, went to the table by the bookshelf, lifted the stopper from a crystal decanter and poured some whiskey into four small glasses.

"Juan said you wanted to see us, *jefe?*"

"*Si*, come in." Two of the three men were dressed much as their boss, in short coats and long pinstriped trousers. Instead of the short hairstyle Fernando preferred, their hair was longer, tied neatly back with narrow strips of leather. The third man had high cheekbones and looked more Indian than Mexican. He wore a brown-striped shirt with a leather vest adorned with *conchos*, but his long hair was neatly braided. They'd barely had time to take a sip from their glasses when Elena and Maria burst into the room, their eyes dancing with excitement and their cheeks dimpled with smiles.

"Papa, Rita said you are giving Maria a . . . a . . ." her brows knotted together as she practically vibrated with excitement. "I do not know how to say it in English."

"Birthday party," Maria piped up. The child spotted the box on her father's desk. "Is this for me, Papa?" She took a step toward it, but Fernando stopped her.

"What have I told you?" he asked patiently, squatting to look them in the eyes.

"We should always knock," they chimed in unison.

"*Si*," he replied. He gave them both a kiss on the cheek then led them to the door. He smiled at their sad faces. "Go into the kitchen and see if your great-grandmother has any cookies. Tell her I said you could each have two." Their smiles told him he had been forgiven as they dashed off. He watched them go then turned back to his men. "You *hombres* have proved to be loyal and trustworthy." Fernando picked up his own glass. "To a job well done, *si?*"

"*Si, jefe*," they all agreed and took a drink of whiskey. Fernando opened the top drawer of his desk and pulled out a small leather pouch.

"Good jobs must be rewarded, hey, Renato?"

"*Si, jefe.*"

Fernando tossed the pouch to the man in the brown shirt. When he caught it he gave a wide grin then held it up to show the others. "And, Jose, you and Vicente, too, deserve a little bonus for your hard work." Fernando lifted two more pouches and tossed one to each man. "*Muchas gracias, amigos.*" The men thanked their boss, had one more toast to his health, then started to leave.

"Renato," Fernando called, giving the young man the box. "Hide this well, *mi amigo.*" When the man nodded, Fernando smiled. "Soon we will have much to celebrate." Fernando opened the door to his study at the same time Sayer passed by dressed in a clean uniform. The colonel nodded at the men, and they acknowledged him in the same manner before they left.

"Colonel," Fernando called, pulling the door closed behind him as he stepped out into the hall. "What is this?" he asked, flicking his finger across Sayer's chest in a friendly manner. "No fancy coat with shiny buttons? No polished sword? No medals?" Fernando teased.

Sayer matched his grin, only his was full of friendly arrogance. "Not tonight, *amigo.* Just a quiet, informal dinner for two. Now if you'll excuse me—"

"What is your hurry? I have not thanked you for bringing my package to me. Come, let us have a whiskey."

"Thanks, but I've got to check on Rounder. Maybe later."

"I will hold you to that. After all, you saved me a trip to Santa Fe."

"It was no trouble, really. I remembered the last time I was here, you mentioned something about Maria's birthday. I was at the post office when Henry said you had a package. It was that simple."

"Well, you saved me half a day and for that I thank you." Fernando put his hand on Sayer's shoulder and led him toward the kitchen. "I have something I have been saving for just the right occasion. Who knows? Maybe it will be tonight?"

Rebeccah smiled with satisfaction as she stirred the pot on her stove. Rita had been very helpful, starting the wood-burning stove and chopping the meat and vegetables, slipping out almost as quietly has she had come in.

Had Rebeccah known that while she washed and changed her dress, Rita had paused to add salt, pepper, and, to enhance the flavor, a dash of dried red chili powder, perhaps Rebeccah wouldn't have added more. But she didn't know, and by the time she came out of her room, Rita was gone, so, to be on the safe side, Rebeccah gave the pot of stew an extra shake of each, delighted when the stock turned a deeper shade of red. Surely if it tasted as good as it looked, it would be a meal Sayer would never forget.

She had just untied her borrowed apron and checked her appearance when a knock sounded on the door. She added a dab of her favorite perfume, then glanced in the mirror and saw her reflection. Instantly Edward came into mind. The dress she had chosen had been his favorite, and her high spirits sank a little with guilt.

"Sayer and I are just friends," she told her reflection. Another knock drew her away from her melancholy thoughts and she hurried to open it. "Come in," she said with a bright smile.

Sayer filled the doorway. His casual military attire had been brushed and pressed, and his tall black boots were freshly polished. "Don Fernando sent this to go with our dinner," the object of her scrutiny said, holding out a bottle. Instantly her cheeks warmed with color as she realized she'd been caught staring . . . again.

"H-how thoughtful," she said as she decided his smile wasn't the sensual smile of a suitor, but more the honest smile of a good friend. She placed the bottle on the counter and began to search the cupboards for wineglasses. After the third try, she found the cupboard that had some dishes in it, and rather than continue her search, she lifted out two bowls. Sayer was at her side the moment she turned, taking them from her to place on the table. Once more she began to hunt for the glasses.

"I'm sure they're here somewhere." No sooner had she spoken than she spotted them on the top shelf. "Oh, dear," she muttered, unable to reach them.

"Let me," he said, lifting them down and adding them to the table while she searched for spoons and knifes.

"My mother always kept them next to the stove," he said, after she had searched several drawers.

"Why, of course," she replied nervously. "I should have known that. I believe Mildred kept our silver there also." She pulled open the drawer and very nearly sighed in relief as she spotted a corkscrew in the same drawer. "Here," she said cheerfully, holding up the bottle opener. "Would you?" He took it and after a few turns, the wine was opened. Another knock sounded on the door.

"Shall I get that?" he asked.

"No, thank you. I've got it. If my guess is correct, that will be Rita with a fresh loaf of bread." Rebeccah opened the door.

"*Señorita*," Maria began. "Don Fernando told me to tell you that after you eat your supper, you and the Colonel are invited for dessert."

"Why thank you. That will be nice." Rebeccah placed the warm, crusty loaf on the table, next to the small tub of butter and honey, then brought over two bowls filled with stew. "Although Rita did most of the preparation, I added a little touch of my own."

"It sure smells good," Sayer replied as he helped her with her chair. He filled their glasses and took his place across from hers.

"Go on," she encouraged. "I want to know how you like it."

He shook out his napkin and placed it in his lap then lifted his spoon and took a big bite. She frowned a little when he hesitated, but then he nodded, and chewed, then swallowed.

"Well?" she asked as he took a sip of his wine.

"It's . . . it's rather hot . . . not too hot, just hotter than I expected." He couldn't look at her any longer. Instead he looked at his bowl as he took another bite so as not to hurt her feelings.

"Well, of course, silly. It just came off the stove a moment ago." Her expression was so naive as she sliced the bread, he found himself wishing the stew wasn't terrible, that somehow the meal could miraculously turn into the best he'd ever eaten. But, it would take more than a miracle for that to happen. He swallowed his second bite and knew he couldn't take another.

He was just about to warn her when she picked up her spoon and took a small, dainty bite. Her gaze fused with his, her eyes widening a little as she slowly chewed. He expected her to run to the sink, but instead she swallowed with an audible *gulp*. As regal as a queen, she lifted her goblet and took a sip, followed by another and then another, her gaze never wavering from his.

"Would you like some water?" Sayer asked, trying his best to keep even the smallest speck of humor out of his voice. But his best wasn't good enough as it became painfully obvious her distress was far greater than his. Finally she drew in a shaky breath as she placed her glass back down upon the table. He leaned over and quickly put some honey on the slice of bread, holding it out to her. "Take a bite," he urged. When she still didn't obey, he pushed it closer. "Trust me, it'll help."

Cautiously, she leaned over and took a bite of the bread. The moment she lifted it from his fingers to take another, he stood, found a glass and pumped cold water into it. "Here." He gave it to her and after she drank, inwardly winced at the look on her face.

"I-I'm sorry," she said miserably. "I've never . . . I didn't . . . I thought a little of that red pepper Rita's so fond of would enhance the flavor."

"Oh, it did," he confirmed. When she looked up at him, he gave her what he hoped was an understanding smile while he tried his best not to laugh.

"I wanted it to be special," she added.

He put his knuckle under her chin and lifted gently. "It was special . . . very special," he said with a firm nod, relieved when she giggled at his counterfeit concern. "Why, I don't reckon I've ever tasted anything quite like it." He added more wine to her glass then handed it to her before he resumed his seat. "Do you cook for Edward?"

She gave a soft laugh. "No. Thankfully, he has servants to do the cooking."

"I see. Then he's wealthy?" He knew the answer. Knew that he could never give her the things that Edward could give her.

"I suppose you could say he's comfortable."

He found her choice of words amusing. "I'm comfortable on the ground in my bedroll."

"I believe he would prefer a feather mattress to sleeping on the ground."

"How did you meet?" He didn't know why, but he was curious. Perhaps if he found out what kind of man Edward was, he could try to like him for her sake.

"At a ball in London. He's a wonderful dancer, has a delightful sense of humor and the most enticing blue eyes."

He hated her dandy even more by the time she finished. "There's not much dancing out here," he stated for lack of anything better to say. He put down his glass, stood and pulled her to her feet. "Did I hear Rita say something about having dessert over at Fernando's?"

CHAPTER NINE

Rebeccah strolled around the tiled patio with Fernando as he inspected the decorations for Maria's birthday party, nodding his approval, and speaking with the many servants who scurried about to make sure every ribbon and every flower was perfect. His grandmother came out of the kitchen, holding something in a checkered cloth.

Speaking in Spanish, she caught his attention, and gave him the cloth, smiling brightly at Rebeccah. After the old woman accepted his kiss on her wrinkled cheek, she hurried back indoors. Fernando opened the cloth and held it out to Rebeccah. "Taste," he urged as she lifted a warm cookie from the cloth.

"These are heavenly," Rebeccah replied as she followed Fernando through the maze of servants. "What are they?"

"*Biscochitos.* My grandmother makes them every time we have a fiesta. They are good, no?"

"*Si, muy bien.*" Rebeccah laughed at her host's surprised expression. "Your daughters have been teaching me Spanish," she replied with an impish smile.

"They have done well. What else can you say?"

"Oh, just a few things. I'm afraid I don't know much of your language, but they promise me that by the time I leave, I will be able to count to ten and say goodbye to your grandmother."

"So, you are still planning to leave when the year is over?"

"Yes, I am." She finished the cookie then dusted cinnamon off her fingers. "Why are you frowning?" she asked. "That was our arrangement."

"I had thought that perhaps you would change your mind and make New Mexico your home."

"My grandmother wouldn't hear of it."

"Ah, yes, your grandmother." He made a great show of scanning the patio, as if he were looking for someone. "Once again, she influences you, yet I do not see her here." His smile made her laugh.

"You're terrible," she said, shaking her head. "Like it or not, there are other reasons I can't stay."

"Your betrothed is waiting, *si?*"

"Yes." She plucked a flower from one of many in a vase and held it under her nose for a moment. "I can't hurt Edward. As it was, I barely had time to tell him my reasons for leaving."

"And he tells you how much he loves you in his letters?"

She gave Fernando a dark look. "Yes . . . and no."

"Yes and no? How can that be?"

"Well, it's rather difficult to explain. He always ends his letters with an endearment, but mostly he tells me about the family business and some of the social events he thinks will interest me."

"But you are not interested, are you?"

"No. I suppose I should be, but I'm not." She heaved a rather loud sigh.

"Do you write to him and tell him that you can ride a horse and shoot a gun?"

"I told him about Brandy, but I don't think he'd approve my becoming a marksman." Fernando's soft laughter made her smile. "Sayer asked me if Edward hunted, and to be honest, I don't really know." She twirled the flower between her fingers. "In fact, now that I'm here and Edward's in England, I realize that I don't know very much about him."

"Sometimes that is best," Fernando chided.

Elena and Maria came out of the hacienda and dashed up to their father. "Papa?" Elena asked, her eyes wide with excitement. "Will Mama come to Maria's party?"

Fernando's smile faded. "*No, vida mia.* Mama wanted to come, but she could not leave her papa. He is still very sick." The little girl's mouth turned down in a pout, but her sister whispered something in Spanish that turned her frown into a smile. "Maria says Mama sent something for both of us. Did she, Papa, did she?"

Fernando laughed at his daughters' expressions. "*Si,* my darlings, she did."

"Can I—"

"May I," Rebeccah amended with a gentle smile.

"May I have it now, Papa?" Elena asked, barely able to keep still.

"May I, Papa?" Maria added.

"No. Not until it's time." When Elena looked as if she wanted to argue, Fernando raised his finger and shook his head. She nodded politely, then skipped off holding her sister's hand.

"They are darling girls," Rebeccah said, watching as they danced around each post that held up the coyote roof over the circular garden. "I had assumed their mother was dead."

"No," Fernando said with a long sigh. "I brought her here many years ago after we were married. She was very young and very beautiful. She liked it at first, but then she missed her mama and papa. I did not have all that you see back then. In fact, the little house you have now was our first home as husband and wife. After Maria was born, my wife and I had many arguments. I told her that as soon as I could, I would build her a big house and send for her parents, but her mother got sick and died. She left for the funeral and never returned."

"I'm sorry," Rebeccah said. "Does she visit the children?"

"No. I have not allowed it."

"Why not?" Rebeccah asked with a frown. "I can understand that you feel resentful that she chose her parents over you and her children, but it's not the girls' fault that you and your wife couldn't resolve your differences." When Fernando didn't respond, she felt compelled to continue. "I appreciate the fact that you don't want them to leave even for a visit, but consider them and their mother. How would you feel if she had taken them and you were the one who wasn't allowed to see them?"

"Had she cared about us . . . them . . . she would not have left. It is as simple as that."

"No. It is not. I know. My circumstance is very much like your daughters'. I loved my mother dearly, Fernando, and I hated my father for leaving her. I hated him because I was too young to understand his reasons for leaving. Your daughters are too young to understand also, so don't make the same mistake my mother made. Don't let them grow up wondering why their mother never visits. Don't let them grow to hate her without first letting them get to know her." She gave him a sympathetic smile. "Take them for a visit. Let them draw their own conclusions. Had my mother not waited until she died to have Lydia and me know our father, I think that our lives would have been very different."

Fernando nodded, but his features were still very serious. "I will consider it, but I will make no promises."

"Fair enough," she agreed as several servants passed by. Fernando stopped one of the maids as she tied more ribbons around a post. "Go and tell Rita to hang the *piñata* over there." He watched his orders carried out. Rita tied the candy-stuffed papier-mâché *piñata* low enough so that the children could easily reach it with a stick. They continued their walk, and when next he spoke, the anger had left his voice. "I have not seen Consuelo for three years, but that does not mean I do not think about her every day." He heaved a loud sigh, and then forced his usual wide smile. "There will be music and dancing after dinner. You will save a dance for me, *si?*"

"Of course. Why wouldn't I?"

"The colonel will be here tonight."

"Why would that keep me from dancing with you?" she asked a little defensively.

Fernando shrugged his shoulders, but by the crafty smile on his handsome face, she knew exactly what he'd meant. "It is just that I have noticed when he is here you stare at him a lot."

"I do not," she said with a defiant lift of her chin. "I am curious about the medals on his uniform."

Fernando gave a disbelieving snort. "I am to believe that you are more interested in the uniform than the man who wears it?"

"Absolutely. As for the colonel, I assure you, he and I are not romantically involved. We are just friends."

"*Si, Señorita. Amigos.* We are all *amigos.*"

"*Si,*" she repeated, casting him a disapproving glance. "Fernando, you must cease the matchmaking."

"Matchmaking?" he repeated, raising his dark brows innocently as he placed his hand over his heart. "You wound me. How could I possibly do such a dishonorable thing when you constantly remind me that you are betrothed . . . and to a man you know so well?" He paused, but only for a moment, and scratched his head. "However, I am left wondering."

"I know I'm going to regret asking, but what?" she queried impatiently.

"I am confused. Who you are trying to convince? Me? Or yourself?"

Colonel Sayer MacLaren, Rebeccah thought as she peeked out the long, narrow window, was every bit the alluring gentleman. Dressed in his dark uniform, white gloves and gold trim, he stood out among the other men even while he stood back near the wall, sipping a brandy and conversing with Don Fernando and two other men she didn't recognize. She thought about what Fernando had said earlier. Was she fooling herself? Even if what he implied was true, that she and Sayer were more than friends, she had a moral obligation to end things with Edward before beginning them with Sayer.

Pleased with herself for being so honorable, she stepped to the side of the door to check her appearance in the small, framed mirror one last time. She had purposely packed her red satin gown, as it was her favorite, even though at the time she didn't think she'd attend any social function appropriate for it.

But, tonight . . . well, tonight, she admitted as she looped the handle of her matching red-feather fan over her wrist, tonight she wanted to look special. With all the lovely ladies from Santa Fe dressed in their very best attending the celebration, she wanted to stand out just a little.

And she did. Much more than she thought she would. The moment she stepped out of the hacienda, heads turned, and she knew with an excited flutter in the pit of her stomach that Sayer had noticed too. Out of the corner of her eye, she saw him glance past the man he was talking with and look her direction, while she pretended interest in the vase of flowers on the closest table. Taking a deep breath, she raised her head and glanced around, purposely avoiding her soldier's gaze.

Music intertwined with children's laughter, and the smell of spicy food and fragrant flowers filled the evening air with heartwarming cheer. Her father and sister stood across the courtyard conversing with Fernando's grandmother. Rebeccah caught her father's attention and waved as she carefully made her way though the many guests.

"Lydia," Rebeccah exclaimed with a loving smile as her sister met her halfway. "Blue is most definitely your color. Your gown is simply divine."

"I do believe, dear sister," Lydia said with a twinkle in her eyes, "that I shall be forever in your debt."

"Now why do you say that?" asked their father when he joined them.

"Because," Lydia stated, opening her matching fan and waving it slowly before her face, "Rebeccah had the foresight to bring our dresses with her from England."

"I see. Well, you both look ravishing, but I have to ask . . ." He pulled Rebeccah close and whispered in her ear, "Tell me, which of the young men here tonight are you trying to impress?"

"Father, I am engaged, remember?"

"Oh that's right," he teased. "By the way you're dressed, I almost forgot."

"How is that possible when we are *constantly* reminded," Lydia added with a mischievous smile.

James gave a contented sigh. "If I died tonight, I would die happier than I have ever been before." He puffed out his chest and looked at his daughters. "You both make me so proud. Look at yourselves. I'm sure you're the envy of every young woman here."

"Now why would you say that?" Lydia asked, her eyes dancing with humor.

"Because of Don Fernando and the colonel over there," he said, and motioned with a subtle jerk of his head. "I do believe they can't drag their eyes away." James's pride was evident. Slowly, he nodded acknowledgement to several others who openly stared. "Yes, sir," he added with a grin. "The envy of them all." He leaned a little closer to Rebeccah. "Why, I haven't seen Colonel MacLaren look at anyone else since you stepped out of the house."

"Really?" she asked, raising her brows in feigned innocence. "I hadn't noticed."

"*Buenas noches,*" Fernando said with an approving smile.

"Ladies." He first kissed the back of Rebeccah's hand, then lingered a little longer over Lydia's until spots of color stained her cheeks. Finally he looked at their father. "Doctor Randolph. Welcome to my *hacienda*. I hope you are enjoying the festivities?"

"Everything's fine, fine," James said. "And thank you for your generous donation. Someday soon, I hope we will have enough to start on the hospital."

"*De nada*. It is the least I can do. Excuse me. I must greet the mayor and his wife."

Rebeccah knew Sayer had joined them—could feel his presence before he came into view. Her heartbeat quickened and she very nearly forgot to breathe. "Miss Lydia, Miss Rebeccah," he acknowledged with that lazy smile she loved. He offered a handshake to their father, adding, "How are you, James?"

"Fine, fine. Heard there was another incident over at the Winterses' place?"

"Yes, but thankfully it was a false alarm. Some children thought it amusing to turn Mr. Winters's outhouse over."

James laughed. "I'm afraid I have a confession. I did the same thing a time or two when I was a boy."

Sayer grinned. "I expect. But Mr. Winters had just come home from the bank and was indisposed at the time it happened. By the time he got his pants on, the boys had galloped off on their ponies, two of which looked a lot like Indian ponies, according to Mrs. Winters."

"Mrs. Winters has needed spectacles for years," James said, chuckling. "They could have been riding cows and she wouldn't have been able to tell the difference." Someone called to James and when he looked, it was one of his patients. "Excuse me, will you? Lydia, look who's up and about. It's Josh." James took Lydia's elbow and led her toward a young man using a cane.

Rebeccah felt Sayer's gaze turn her way, but could not bring herself to return it, wondering what Lydia and her father would think if she did. Instead she looked slightly past him. "I'm sure the children are delighted you came to Maria's party."

"They're sweet little girls. Fernando's a lucky man to have them."

"Yes, yes, they are, and so polite."

"Are you looking for someone?" he asked.

Her gaze fused with his. "N-no, I-I was just looking at all the lovely dresses," she stammered.

"There's really no need," he said, and she knew by his smile there was more.

"Why do you say that?" she queried.

"Because yours is the most beautiful of all."

"I most certainly agree," Fernando said as he approached.

"Don Fernando," Rebeccah began, giving him a cheerful smile. "The courtyard looks lovely." Her host took her hand, raising it to his lips.

"It pales in comparison to you, *Señorita*." Fernando cast an ornery look at Sayer. "Don't you agree?"

"Absolutely."

Once more the butterflies in Rebeccah's stomach quivered with anticipation when she had no choice but to meet Sayer's gaze. Suddenly the voices and the music faded. The wonderful sights and smells diminished. All she saw was the way his seductive gaze raked boldly over her. Much to her amazement, he plucked a delicate red bud from the vase on the table, leaned intimately close and tucked it in her hair just above her ear.

"It's a Mexican custom for all the unmarried ladies to wear a flower in their hair." His potent gaze prolonged the moment until she heard Don Fernando's deliberate cough. Her head snapped in Fernando's direction.

"Saints," her host said, his voice filled with humor as he looked at something past Sayer. "I believe that is *Señor* and

Señora Winters. If he is here," Fernando said with a wink, "perhaps I should have Renato guard the . . ." he nodded in the direction of the outhouse and grinned.

The flame-roasted chicken was some of the best Rebeccah had ever eaten. Remembering her miserable attempt to prepare a meal the previous evening, she glanced across the table at Sayer. A few moments ago when Fernando had asked about their dinner, her soldier had been most convincing.

"Why, it was a meal I shall never forget," he had said. Then as if nothing were amiss, he expertly changed the subject to the children and how they seemed to live for the moment, without a care in the world. "Look at them," he urged. "They don't care about anything except what they are doing right this minute." He turned to his host. "Don't you wish we could live like that? To live for the moment and not pay any attention to what tomorrow might bring?"

Fernando agreed as Elena dashed up to him and climbed into his lap. "Papa, Maria has finished opening her presents. Can we do the *piñata* now, please, please?"

"Well, then, I suppose we should not keep the other children waiting." Fernando excused himself, calling to all the children. They followed him to a decorated pole in the center of the courtyard. Attached to the pole was a colorful likeness of a cat, bedecked with paper streamers and ribbons.

Fernando tied a blindfold about the first child then lifted the pole and dangled the cat over the boy's head. Before the spectators, each youngster took a turn trying to hit and crack open the *piñata*. Finally, after much laughter, Elena gave it a good whack. Candy rained down upon them and all the boys and girls scrambled to fill their pockets.

"Are you planning to have a large family?" Sayer asked, taking Rebeccah completely by surprise.

"F-family?" she stammered.

"Yes, after you're married, of course." His smile was playful.

"Why . . . I'm not sure." Heavens. She had, only moments ago, decided to examine her decision to marry Edward. Leave it to Sayer to ask perplexing questions. "I-I suppose."

"You don't know?"

"No, not really. Edward and I have never discussed it."

Her soldier's skeptical expression put her immediately on the defensive. "Well, now. I can kind of understand you not wanting to discuss duck hunting, but isn't having a family something two people who are planning to marry should discuss before the wedding?"

"Not necessarily. Children can be discussed after the wedding."

His thoughtful pause increased her distress.

"I reckon you're right," he agreed as he put down his glass. His gaze locked with hers in a most unsettling way. "It's still something I'd be sure to settle before I married. What happens if he doesn't want children and you do?"

She looked at him, fighting the urge to tell him that ever since he came into her life, she wasn't even sure she wanted to marry Edward anymore, but her pride raised its rigid neck.

"What man wouldn't want children?" she said with a small laugh. He was about to say something more when Don Fernando came back to the table at the same time the musicians began to play a lively Mexican tune.

"*Señorita,* come. I will teach you how to dance a two-step." His confident smile, and the fact that she wanted to escape from Sayer's questions, caused her to practically jump into Fernando's arms. He immediately whisked her away, casting Sayer what she thought was a rather arrogant smile. In a few moments she forgot all about Edward and having his children, matching Fernando's steps and thoroughly enjoying herself. Finally the sprightly music gave way to a waltz, but before

Fernando could ask her, Sayer was there, tapping him on the shoulder.

"This one is mine," the colonel stated as he took her hand and pulled her into his arms.

"Of course, Colonel," Fernando said with a feigned salute. "I was only protecting her from all the other eager young men. Look how they hover like hungry wolves as if to eat her alive." Fernando winked, then stepped aside with a graceful bow.

Much to her amazement, Sayer danced as well, if not better, than most of her English suitors. "I have been thinking," he began.

"Not about children, I hope," she countered with a smile. He laughed then, and she knew he was enjoying himself immensely.

"Well, in a way you could say that I was, but this time it's everyone else's children I'm thinking about. Fernando told me that you have acquired a few students besides Maria and Elena."

"Yes," she said, twirling once then coming back into his arms. "Eleven in all, and six more chickens." She smiled when he gave a soft laugh. "They are all wonderful children, so eager to learn."

"Well, since Fernando has donated money for a hospital, why don't you ask him for money for a school?"

She blinked up at him. "Why, that's a wonderful idea. I should have thought about it myself. Thank you."

"You're welcome," he said, his gaze as divine as his dancing. "Now, what are you doing with all those chickens?"

"Don Fernando has graciously built a little henhouse behind my home. So far I have Lydia—you met her on the day we took our first ride, remember?"

He grinned. "Yes, I do."

"Then there's Sarah, Rosa, Rita—though I must say I'm not sure Rita is pleased that I named a chicken after her—and Molly and Mildred. They're sisters." Again his laughter filled her with joy.

"I see, and what does your sister think about having a chicken named after her?"

This time Rebeccah laughed. "I haven't told her."

The music turned a little livelier and he twirled her around. Though each step was bold and precise, he moved with the same manly gracefulness she'd seen each time he mounted his horse or cast a line out over a swiftly running river. Yet when his warm fingers splayed across her back, when she felt the hard muscles of his shoulders where her hand rested, when his laughing blue eyes burned into hers, something happened.

She forgot that she wanted to remain aloof—to just be friends until she had more time to make a decision about Edward.

Sayer twirled her around, his eyes never leaving hers. *Too late,* she admitted with a reluctant sigh. Colonel Sayer MacLaren had become much more than just a friend.

CHAPTER TEN

July melted into August as Rebeccah worked diligently with Fernando's daughters. Friday afternoons were saved for their private lessons. Under her careful guidance, the girls practiced being ladies, learning how to walk, how to dress and how to converse. They learned it was acceptable to speak with other ladies about children or which pretend shops had the best selection of gowns while sipping tea and eating cookies.

Rebeccah pointed her nose in the air and exaggerated her English accent. "However, when in the company of gentlemen," she said in a high, formal voice, "ladies never discuss women's apparel. We keep our subjects simple. We discuss the weather or upcoming outings with friends."

Their session usually ended in giggles as the girls mimicked their teacher.

Now, just barely awake early on Saturday morning, Rebeccah's thoughts turned to Sayer. No matter how much fun she had with the girls, Friday nights were always the best. Her wily soldier always arrived early, saving the cooler late-afternoons for the children. She loved the way he and the girls would play games between the two houses in the shade of the big cottonwood. Their laughter and giggles always drew her to the window.

A smile tugged at her mouth when she recalled that yesterday, he had caught her watching from behind the curtain. It was just like him to add to her embarrassment by pointing at her, then joining in with the girls as they waved. And no wonder the girls loved him. He knew how to win their hearts. He arrived with two adorable dolls, one under each arm, destroying all her lessons on how to act like ladies.

No, she thought smiling; ladies do not throw themselves into the arms of cavalry officers. Nor do they smother their captive with kisses. And, he was certainly no help as he gathered them up and twirled them around until they were breathless and flushed from laughing. Now, as she relived the happy scene, she very nearly envied them their innocent impropriety.

A knock sounded on her door. She sat upright, inwardly scolding herself for lingering too long with her pleasant memories and losing track of time. Or had she? She glanced at the clock. She wasn't late. Sayer was early.

"Becky? Are you awake?"

"Go away. You're an hour early."

"I thought we'd get an early start," he said in a teasing tone. "Come on, it's time to rise and shine."

Groaning, she rose and after a few moments, opened the wardrobe at the same time she grabbed her brush and dragged it through her tangled hair. The doorknob jiggled as she chose an outfit and shrugged out of her nightgown. "There's chicken feed in the barrel behind the house," she shouted so he'd hear. "I'm sure Lydia and the others will be most appreciative if you'd feed them." While he was gone, she dressed in a hurry, smiling when there came another knock on her door.

"Becky," he called again, his voice filled with boyish humor. When he began to whistle reveille, she tugged on her boots and began to pin up her hair.

"I'm coming," she replied impatiently. She quickly arranged her bonnet then threw open the door and returned his smile. "Reveille?"

"It worked, didn't it?" He offered his arm. "The chickens are fed, Brandy is saddled and waiting." His eyes sparkled with humor and his gaze washed over her in a way that made her feel entirely too self-conscious. "You look mighty good for so early in the morning," he said.

"Why do I get the impression you're surprised?" she asked, watching him as he first checked her horse's cinch then helped her to mount.

He shrugged his shoulders. "It's just that some of the married men at the fort have made comments that suggest women don't like to be seen first thing in the morning."

"And why is that?" she inquired, wondering what answer he'd come up with as he swung into the saddle.

"Why, I don't rightly know . . ." He paused and cast a look over his shoulder, and the ornery twinkle in his eyes intensified. "Being that I'm not married."

He escaped too easily, she thought, bemused as he turned Rounder down the drive. "Surely they—the married ones," she said, guiding Brandy alongside, "confide in you as their commander."

"Yes, some do." He turned and smiled, the devil dancing in his eyes, goading her on.

"Well?" she prodded.

"Some of their wives, I'm told, tie their hair up in rags and whatnot." He turned Rounder on the path that would take them into the mountains.

"Whatnot? What is that, exactly?" she asked.

"Hats, I think."

"Oh, I believe you're referring to nightcaps."

"That's it, nightcaps."

She relaxed a little, sure he couldn't turn something so simple as a nightcap into something sinful. "Some women wear them to bed to keep their hair from getting tangled."

Again the corners of his mouth twitched and his expression

was downright scandalous. "Really?" he asked with feigned naïveté. "Why, what on earth do ladies do in bed to tangle up their hair?"

She matched his smile and his virtuous expression. "I haven't the foggiest."

Although they invariably went up into the mountains, he always found something different to show her. This time, he took her to a crooked log that jutted out over the river several miles away from where they had camped that very first day. Again he made a fire, and while the small logs burned down to coals, they fished. After the fire was doused and they were full of roasted trout, he took her hand and urged her to sit with him upon the log, even though she told him she didn't like the idea of dangling over the water.

Nervous at first, she soon relaxed with his exaggerated promise of how he would risk his own life to save hers, adding that in reality, the water wasn't deep enough to drown in.

"Why did you choose to join the army?" she asked once he was sitting next to her.

"I didn't choose it. In fact, my mother wanted me to go to a fancy boarding school somewhere in New York."

"Why didn't you?"

"My father was a colonel in the Civil War, and when it ended, he was promoted to general then transferred. We moved out west to Nebraska. I was just a boy."

"How exciting it must have been to be able to see so much of the country at such a young age."

He jumped down from their perch, and much to her amazement, began to gather late summer flowers, returning with a handful of colorful buds. "I grew up in a fort full of Indian fighters," he said, and as he twisted their stems together, he told her stories about his childhood and what a good mother he had. "My mother was beautiful," he said, glancing over at

Rebeccah. "She had long, blond hair, a lot like yours."

"Really? Does she still live in Nebraska?"

"No," he said softly, turning back to his task. "She was killed when a couple of Pawnee warriors attacked our home while my father and I were out hunting." He paused for a long time, all the while working with the flowers. "When I was seventeen, I enlisted. I served with my father until he died fighting the Sioux a couple of years ago."

"I'm sorry," she murmured. "You must miss him."

"I miss him . . . when it's quiet like this. He was a good husband." Sayer's smile was forced, and a tiny muscle jumped above his jaw as he placed the delicate crown on her head. "But after my mother died, he focused his full attention on his career."

Sayer stared at the water, but she sensed he was seeing something far different. "He drove his men hard, and as the general's son, he drove me hard too. I suppose I have him to thank for the man I am today."

He stood and jumped down from the log, then reached up to help her. She placed her hands on his shoulders and he lifted her down, but he didn't immediately let her go. He held her for several moments, his gaze locked with hers, then slowly, reluctantly, he released her, bending to pick up his hat and saddlebags. "We'd best be heading back."

On their journey home, he was not as talkative. When she expressed a desire to ride out more often, he grew somber. He stressed how she should never ride alone, that until the trouble with the renegades was settled, it wasn't safe to do so.

"It's easy to forget," he said, "that as beautiful as this country is, it's still untamed and very dangerous. As I have mentioned before, there are Apache warriors who refuse to stay on the reservation, and with good reason." He turned and once more their eyes locked, but instead of the usual humor she'd grown to love, something different flickered in his. "Never forget that all you see was theirs before the white settlers decided to take it."

"You are a perplexing man," she began, guiding her mare around a fallen log. "At times you sound as if you think the Indians were treated unfairly, yet I should think you would hate them after what they did to your mother and father."

"How can I hate a man for fighting for what he thinks is his, whether his skin is white or red?"

"I'm glad that there are laws governing such things. If not, there would be chaos."

He gave her a patient smile. "Indians don't believe in our laws, nor do they believe men, any man, can own the land. They have no deeds, yet they lived here long before the white man came. Did that not give them ownership?"

"I-I suppose. As I said, there are laws regarding squatters' rights." She caught sight of a squirrel as it dashed behind some rocks. "Men have been fighting over land for centuries. It's all part of progress—of becoming a civilized society."

"There's that word again," he said, shaking his head.

His cynical mood disturbed her. "Which word?" she asked. "Civilized?"

"Society." He gave her a doubtful smile. "Let me ask you this. Who determines what is civilized and what is not?"

"The more advanced race," she said with a nod, confident that he would agree. "I, for one, am glad that we do not walk around in animal skins, killing our food with clubs." He smiled, but she knew he was still very serious. "I'm here because it was my mother's dying wish that I visit my father, but I think, had I come to make my home here, I would expect to be able to do so without the threat of being attacked by savages."

"That is a very civilized statement. Now, answer this if you can. Would you kill to protect what is yours?" he asked without emphasis.

His question startled her—filled her with uncertainty. "Would you?" she countered, annoyed that he had put her on the spot.

"Yes, I would. It's the same with any man who wants to keep what's his."

His confession turned her cold.

"That is the difference between you and me," she said, avoiding her soldier's gaze. "I do not believe there is anything more valuable than a human life."

"Even if the human you speak of is, in the eyes of society, considered uncivilized?" His expression changed. Gone was the sparkle in his eyes, replaced with what she had first seen a little while ago when they were at the river, but now she recognized it as remorse. "I don't condone murder or the random butchery I've seen. Many men have died on both sides—tortured and mutilated by the savages who captured them, and you must believe me when I tell you the savages I speak of weren't always Pawnee or Sioux. Sometimes they were generals from Missouri who settled in Nebraska."

He paused, and although she felt the need to offer some words of comfort, she couldn't speak. She was too stunned by his testimony.

"However," he began, this time with a note of contempt in his voice. "We must never forget that people settled these parts because men like my father gave their lives to make it safe to do so."

Again the trail narrowed, and since she had to follow behind, they could no longer speak comfortably to one another for almost an hour. When at last she urged her mare to ride alongside him, she heaved a sigh of relief when he stopped his horse, leaned over and took her hand in his.

"It wasn't my intent to spend the day discussing Indians when we began our ride this morning. But there is something you must know. I have taught the men in my command that there are other ways than senseless slaughter to procure peace."

She felt wretched the moment she looked at him, but again she couldn't think of anything to say that wouldn't reveal the fears and uncertainty his disclosures had aroused in her. When she thought she couldn't bear another moment of his silence, he turned in the saddle and pushed his hat back from his forehead with a smile. "Someday, when the trouble is over," he teased, "and after you've married your English dandy—"

"He is not a dandy," she protested, relieved that he was back to being the arrogant soldier she was so fond off.

"No? Can he shoot a gun or skin a deer?"

She laughed, shaking her head. "I doubt he has ever found the need to do either. There aren't many deer roaming about in the city."

Sayer gave a nod then urged Rounder down the trail. "As I was saying, I've bought a small parcel of land near Fernando's ranch. Assuming I'm able to build a house suitable for guests, you could come for a visit. You and he could ride out to these mountains. You could show him the things I have shown you, and you could teach your English gentleman how to fish."

She laughed at his earnest expression, but inside she almost felt like crying. Never could she share these mountains with another man. They were hers and Sayer's special place.

"I shall hold you to your invitation," she replied, thankful that her voice didn't betray her feelings. They were on the path toward Don Fernando's ranch, and in the pasture cattle grazed. "Is the land you bought good for farming?" she asked, trying to take her mind off her melancholy thoughts.

"Who said anything about farming?" He reached down and patted his stallion affectionately on the neck. "Rounder is mine, not the army's. It's only because of my clean record and the fact that I'm General MacLaren's son that I've been allowed to keep him. I've also been able to purchase several good mares. A man can make a good living raising horses and running a few head of cattle. Who knows," he added with a wink. "Maybe someday I'll find the right woman and settle down with a bunch of kids." He turned and winked. "And maybe some chickens."

Though she smiled, instead of admiring how handsome he looked in his uniform, his words were a reminder of who he was, what he had done, and, worse, what he was capable of doing. Regardless of the fact that it was his duty to protect people like her and her sister, could she ever believe that killing could be justified?

"I won't be able to take you riding for a few weeks."

The sound of his voice drew her back to the present. Much to her disappointment, they were already at the ranch. "I've got to check out a few Indian sightings near the village of Mora," he explained, reaching up to help her down. He held her hand longer than usual, gazing into her eyes as if trying to gauge her reaction to his news.

Reluctantly, she slipped her hand from his and smoothed her skirt. "Duty calls?" she said, for lack of something better to say.

"For a while longer," he added, drawing her eyes back to his. He was leaving for a few weeks. To chase after hostile savages. To possibly shoot at them and . . . and be shot at. Her sister's words crept into the dark places of her mind. *Cavalry officers don't usually live long enough to grow old with their wives.* This is what it must be like, Rebeccah thought bleakly, for the wives at the fort each time their men rode away. Did their stomachs knot painfully with the knowledge that their husbands may never return? She shivered, grateful when he didn't notice.

"I promise we'll ride again the first Saturday I'm back."

She had to force herself to return his smile, lost in her morbid thoughts. His patient expression didn't help. In fact, it had the opposite effect. Didn't he realize that each time his warm hand closed over hers, or that every time he looked at her, his gaze filled her with doubt—doubt that returning to England was what she really wanted—doubt that Edward was the man she really wanted? And now, could she give her heart to a man who, in the line of duty, might ride away someday and never return?

"We'll ride as long as the weather holds, I promise." Sayer's statement stabbed into her heart, adding more weight to the uncertainty resting on her shoulders.

"I-I will hold you to that promise," she said with more conviction then she felt.

"Becky? Is something—?"

She only had a moment to see the concern in his eyes before Don Fernando came up to them, drawing Sayer's attention. "Colonel. I am glad you are back. Your sergeant was here looking for you. He gave me this note." He waited until Sayer finished reading, frowning at his friend's expression. "Will you be able to stay for supper?"

"Thank you, but I can't. There's been another Indian attack. I'd better check it out." Fernando didn't miss the way Sayer paused, as if he wanted to say something more to Rebeccah. Instead, he mounted his flashy stallion, touched the brim of his hat, then rode away.

"Be careful . . ." Rebeccah's voice faded away into a long, despondent sigh.

"How was your day?" Don Fernando asked. "Instead of coming home all smiles, you are frowning this time."

Together they walked toward her house, but she sensed he wasn't going to leave her alone. "I think that over the past few months we have become good friends, *si?*" When she still didn't answer, he added, "You said so yourself at Maria's party, remember?"

She gave him a small smile. "You have a very good memory, and in answer to your question, yes, we are very good friends."

"*Bien.* Good friends confide in each other." He grinned when she cast him a suspicious look before she leaned on the wooden fence next to her horse. "Do not fear, *Señorita*. I am a man who can be trusted."

Again she smiled, but it didn't brighten her eyes. "I'm troubled."

"That I can tell. Now, tell me why," he persisted.

"There are many reasons." She heaved a long sigh. "First, I'm spending a great deal of time with a man whose beliefs are contrary to my own. Yet, I can't bear the thought of never seeing him again." She pushed away from the fence to leave, but Fernando caught her hand and pulled her around to face him.

"I see. But there is more, *si?*"

"Yes, there is more. I'm enjoying one man's company while I'm engaged to another."

"Yes, that is a problem," Fernando confirmed, but before he could say it was easily resolved, she spoke.

"However inappropriate, it's trivial compared to what I learned when I asked Sayer about his father, and even though he didn't come out and say it, he implied that during the course of his father's career, he killed without remorse." She paused to swallow. "Perhaps even innocent women and children."

Fernando nodded. "So I have heard."

"How can you sanction such ghastly conduct?"

"Terrible things happen in war, *Señorita*." Fernando's voice was soft and laced with understanding, causing tears to pool in her eyes.

"Really? Well that's not the worst part, Don Fernando," she cried, jerking off her riding gloves. "I suspect Sayer, following his father's orders of course, has done the same." She glanced down at her hands, even more distressed as Fernando shook his head in denial.

"You have seen him with my little ones. Do you honestly believe he could take the life of a child?"

"I could never forgive him if he did."

"The man is a soldier." Fernando squeezed her hand. "Surely you know he is very good at it because of his ability to—how should I say it—protect others and defend himself?"

"Killing, even in self-defense is horrible, Fernando." She headed down the gravel path toward her house.

"Perhaps in England where you are from. But here . . ." Fernando shook his head, then hurried to catch up with her. "Here it is much different. I have seen many men lose their lives protecting their families from the Indians and dangerous outlaws. If I or my daughters were in danger, I would not hesitate for one moment to protect them, using whatever force is necessary to do so."

Rebeccah heaved a disheartened sigh. "That is almost word for word what Sayer said."

"Then how can you fault him for his beliefs? From what I know of him and what I have heard about his past, he is more forgiving than I would be under the same circumstances. I have come to believe he is an honorable man. To assume he has not killed would be to assume the sun will not rise *mañana*. The colonel is, after all, a soldier. But to assume he has killed without reason . . ." Fernando shook his head again. "That would be an unfair assumption."

They were before her door, but he put his hand on it, stopping her from entering. "I have seen how you look at the colonel and how he looks at you, so please listen to what I say. I lost the woman I loved because I did not know how much I loved her until she was gone. Do not make the same mistake."

"I shan't. I am engaged to a very nice man who I'm sure has never killed anyone or anything in his entire life."

"Ah, yes. *Señor* Edward, the accountant. How exciting his life must be. I can see why you are in a hurry to return to it." Fernando gave her a sympathetic smile, then moved out of her way, shaking his head. "As your friend, I ask you to heed my warning. It is my belief that the man who truly desires you is spending every free moment he has with you."

"You don't understand. A promise is a promise. I promised Edward I would return."

Fernando frowned. "Then do so if you must, but not to keep a promise that we both know is dead in your heart. Do so to ask that it be annulled."

"It's not just my promise . . ." she began. "Edward's life may not be very exciting, but Sayer is a soldier—"

"*Si*, for now. But not forever. I think he has grown to hate it as much as you do." Fernando shook his head. "It is unfair of you to judge him by his past. Do you know Edward's past?"

"His family is very well-to-do."

"Perhaps, but do you know how they acquired their fortune? No? I did not think so. Now, answer this if you can. Are you willing to destroy a true love for one that only exists on paper and, for all you know, may not even exist at all when you return?"

Her expression tore into Fernando's heart. Though tears pooled in her eyes, she held her head high. "Since you and I are friends, I will carefully consider your advice." She turned and pushed aside the door, pausing in the opening. "But do not ask me to compromise my beliefs because I can't. They have been too long a part of me to so easily cast them aside."

CHAPTER ELEVEN

The three weeks Sayer said he'd be gone multiplied into six. The same happened to Rebeccah's chickens. She acquired four more hens and a fine red rooster, which helped her hens produce twelve fluffy chicks. She was finally forced to ask Don Fernando to add them to his flock as the little fenced-in coop he'd constructed behind her house was overcrowded and much too noisy. When Fernando tried to encourage her to talk about her feelings, she politely refused, assuring him she was capable of making her own decisions.

Every day that passed, Rebeccah threw herself into her work, refusing to admit that she missed Sayer far more than she'd ever missed Edward, even though she and Sayer had only known each other for about the same amount of time. In the evenings she sat at her desk and tried to find something to say to Edward, but the words didn't come easily. When all she could do was tell him about the children and her chickens, she'd end it with a cordial endearment.

At night, she climbed into bed with a book and read until she finally fell asleep. In the morning she'd meet Rita at the door and ask if there was any mail from England, then sometimes, even though she thought it wasn't proper, she'd ask if there had been any word from Sayer.

However hard she tried not to think about the truths Don Fernando pointed out, it was even harder to deny that what he said made sense. She consoled herself with the knowledge that

151

time would dull her unhappiness, and that by the time Sayer returned, he'd be none the wiser that his confession had shaken her to the core.

To make waiting easier when she wasn't teaching, she decided to ask *Señora* Gutierrez to teach her how to knit. The kindly old lady was patient, giving encouragement in broken English, that if Rebeccah tried hard, someday she would be making blankets instead of scarves. When knitting became bothersome, she would spend a few hours in the kitchen, watching Rita cook. In a very short time, she had learned how to make bread and a stew that was savory and delicious—with only a hint of red chili powder.

September brought warm days and chilly nights, casting the countryside into a bounty of brilliant colors. The vines on Fernando's walls turned scarlet, a beautiful contrast with the yellows and golds of the cottonwood trees, and the blue-green of the pines. Now, when she strolled around the courtyard or out to the barn to visit her horse, Rebeccah needed a woolen shall to stay warm.

"*Señorita*," Don Fernando called as she sat on the swings with the children. "News has finally arrived from Sayer. He will be able to come for a visit this Friday." Fernando's excited smile only added fuel to her own excitement as he waved at her to join him. "Come have coffee with me while I tell you of my plans."

Rita placed a plate of cookies on the table as Fernando helped Rebeccah with her chair. "I have decided to have a special feast," he began, explaining to Rebeccah that it was a Mexican custom to roast a whole pig in a pit and have music and dancing.

"We will celebrate the colonel's return," he said with a smile that meant he was up to his old tricks and matchmaking again. "I will bring out a keg of beer and some of my best wine, and we will sing and dance until the rooster crows, *si?*"

"I doubt I shall be able to stay awake that long," Rebeccah teased as she sipped her coffee. In the distance, Elena and Maria's laughter could be heard, adding a festive mood to their conversation.

"Then no more lessons until after," Fernando said with a firm nod.

"After what?" she inquired.

"After the *matanza, Señorita*. I insist that you take a nap every afternoon and go to bed early every night. Come Saturday, you will be well rested and able to dance all night long."

She smiled at his expression. "I assume these *matanzas* are held outdoors?"

"*Si, si.* Trust me. You have never experienced anything quite like it. The food, the wine, the music."

"In case you haven't noticed," she said with a skeptical smile. "It's quite chilly at night."

"That is why we will have a big fire with lots and lots of wood. That and lots of wine and dancing will keep you warm." He leaned a little closer and lowered his voice. "I proposed to Consuelo at such an occasion. And—" His smile was smug. "—after she accepted, we didn't need the fire to keep us warm."

"I think you're the one in need of a few lessons in what is and what is not appropriate to discuss in public, not your daughters." She smiled to soften her reprimand and shook her head, trying hard not to laugh at his wounded expression.

"It is good that I am a married man," he said. His eyes crinkled at the corners with amusement.

"Really?" She feigned in her most formal tone, enjoying his company. "Pray tell, enlighten me."

"I . . ." Fernando placed his hand over his heart. ". . . am not as patient as the colonel. I would have insisted you marry me the first time I kissed you."

Her cheeks grew warm and Fernando laughed again. "Oh

no," he laughed. "He has kissed you, no?"

"Of course not," she lied. "I have not allowed it."

"And he has honored your wishes?" Fernando shook his head in disbelief.

"Yes. He's a gentleman."

"*Ay caramba*," Fernando exclaimed. "He is more than a gentleman, the man is a saint."

She tried hard to look angry, but failed miserably. "I do not think he is a saint, precisely, but more a man who is—"

"Patient beyond anything I could imagine," Fernando finished.

"You aren't going to let this rest, are you?" she asked firmly. His teasing grin was his answer. She gave him a scornful look even though she enjoyed his banter. "I shan't have you thinking he's not capable."

Fernando tried to look contrite. "I would never think such a thing."

"Somehow, I don't believe you," she challenged, sipping her coffee.

"Tell me, *Señorita*," Fernando began, trying to be more serious. "Have you wanted him to kiss you?"

She choked.

Fernando stood and patted her back. "I see," he said with a very confident nod.

"You see what?" she demanded once she could catch her breath.

Fernando returned to his seat and gave her a wide smile, looking even more the rogue. "That you wish the colonel . . . how should I put it?"

"Put what?" she cried in exasperation.

"That perhaps you wish the colonel wasn't such a gentleman."

She would have rebuked him for his insinuation had his

grandmother not walked in at just that moment. She smiled sweetly at Rebeccah, who smiled sweetly back, then frowned at Fernando.

Fernando spoke to his grandmother in Spanish for several moments, then they both smiled what Rebeccah thought looked very much like meaningful smiles. Though her understanding of Spanish was sparse, she managed to make out the word *love*, and most definitely heard the word *colonel* in the old woman's thick accent. Finally Fernando's grandmother patted his cheek and hobbled over to where the children were playing.

"What did you tell her?" Rebeccah demanded.

Fernando feigned innocence. "Nothing. Nothing at all."

"Oh, yes you did. I could tell by the way she looked at me."

Fernando shrugged his shoulders. "I might have let a little something slip out."

"What? What did you let slip out?"

"Nothing . . . nothing to be so upset about, I assure you. My grandmother, she is a very wise woman. I do not think I told her anything that she did not already know. Come," Fernando encouraged. "I want you to have something special to wear for my party."

Rebeccah accepted his hand, curious but unwilling to let him have his way so easily. "I have gowns aplenty."

"*Si*, you do, and beautiful gowns they are, too, but not like the gowns women in Mexico wear."

She followed him into the kitchen where Rita was chopping vegetables. Much to her distress, they conversed in Spanish, and this time she had no inkling as to what was said. Once more her cheeks grew warm as Rita nodded, then glanced at Rebeccah as she listened to Fernando. When he was through, the pretty little Mexican maid nodded happily. "*Si, jefe,* it will be my pleasure."

★ ★ ★ ★ ★

Rebeccah stood on a chair as Rita and Fernando's grandmother made the final touches on her new dress. Though she was sure her own grandmother back in England would have fainted at the sight of her granddaughter, Rebeccah was pleasantly surprised. Instead of the smooth lines and conservative colors she usually preferred, the teal-blue, many-layered skirt was full, and each ruffle hemmed with white lace and decorative red and green ribbons. The seductive bodice had been designed to be worn off the shoulders, making her feel as if it wouldn't stay up if she moved. Each time she tugged it higher, Fernando's grandmother pulled it back down.

"*No, no, no,*" the old woman scolded, smiling when she had Rebeccah's shoulders bare once more. Once Fernando's grandmother felt satisfied with their work, Rebeccah was allowed to step down from the chair and ushered over to the old woman's vanity, where Rita took special care arranging her hair. After a few tokens of advice from *Señora* Gutierrez, a yellow sunflower was pinned in her hair. A soft knock sounded on the door, and Rebeccah instantly recognized Fernando's voice. Before she could stop them, both women invited him in. His stunned expression was compliment enough.

"Magnificent," Fernando said softly, walking around as if he inspected a valuable statue. He picked up her hand, bowed formally, then placed a chaste kiss on the back. "You are more beautiful than even my Consuelo was that night so long ago." His wink brought a smile to her lips. "Let us hope you are as . . . shall I say, successful?"

Rebeccah pulled her hand away. "Don't start that nonsense with me. Must I constantly remind you that I am already—"

"Ah, yes . . . engaged." Fernando smiled sinfully. "Perhaps, but until there is a gold band on your finger, you are still . . . obtainable." He glanced at her hand. "What is this? You are not wearing your beloved's ring?"

Rebeccah snatched her hand from Fernando's and tucked it in the folds of her gown. "I have made a decision," she confessed. "But you must keep it a secret for now."

He put his hand over his heart. "I swear."

"I have decided to break my engagement."

"That is wonderful news."

"Fernando," she said, pausing to choose just the right words. "If I were to write Edward a letter explaining how I feel, do you suppose that would suffice?"

Fernando's brows snapped together and his usual laughing eyes grew serious. "You mean you no longer wish to go back to England?"

She nodded. "I mean, if you think it isn't too cowardly of me, I'd just as soon send a letter as see him in person."

"That is the best news I have heard all week," Fernando said with an understanding smile. "Now there is even more to celebrate."

Rebeccah trembled more from nervousness than the chilly night air. As Don Fernando had promised, the heat from the huge fire kept them all warm. Much to her surprise, instead of the townsfolk, his men and his servants were their only guests, laughing and enjoying their overlord's hospitality. Once more she glanced toward the front of the hacienda, but still there was no sign of the showy stallion or his handsome master.

"He will be here soon. I am sure of it." Fernando's softly spoken words caused her to jump—his laughter caused her to smile. When she turned, he handed her a glass of wine, then draped an embroidered shawl the same color as her gown over her shoulders. "The shawl is only until the colonel arrives. The wine will help pass the time."

Rebeccah took a sip, watching her host over the rim of her

glass. He was dressed in black, the silver trim on his short jacket sparkling in the fire's light. Like the other men conversing with their wives and sweethearts, he wore a wide-brimmed hat, elaborately decorated in silver. All the women wore colorful dresses like hers, their hair adorned with fall flowers.

The children had long ago been fed and taken inside with the elders to share milk and cookies and then listen to bedtime stories. More wood was added to the heaping pile, drawing Rebeccah's attention away from the road. Someone called out that the meat was ready. She watched intently as they uncovered the roasted pig, slicing off hunks of savory-smelling pork to be divided among the hungry guests.

"You sure look good at night," came Sayer's deep voice, causing her to spin around. "But then, I haven't quite decided what time of day you look best." His lazy smile warmed her more than the wine, and she couldn't quite tell if the sparkle in his eyes was just from the fire. He held his white hat in his hands, and like Fernando, had dressed in his very best. "I like the dress," he added, his gaze raking sensuously over her. "I don't think it's one you had hidden in that trunk of yours, is it?"

She gave a soft laugh. "No. Fernando had it made for me." Though his smile never wavered, she thought she saw something flicker in the depths of his eyes. It was dark and she couldn't be sure, but the thought that Sayer might be jealous caused her heart to beat a little faster.

"*Amigo,*" Fernando called, extending his hand. "You have arrived just in time. Come, both of you, come and sit down and let us enjoy the feast."

More wine was poured into Rebeccah's glass the moment she sat down on one of the benches that had been placed near the fire. While they ate, music played and singers sang in Spanish, but she knew by the way the women looked at their men and the men sat ever so close to their women that they were songs of love.

Sayer served her, cut her meat and sat so close she could feel his warmth. The food smelled savory, but not as enticing as his heady scent, or as rich as his deep voice. They ate and talked and when they weren't talking, she was trying to think of how to tell him she planned to break her promise to Edward. But nothing came to mind. How could she think clearly with Sayer so close that his leg occasionally brushed against hers?

When she'd eaten all she could hold, and the food was cleared away, the music became livelier. Couple after couple began to dance, and much to her surprise, the women lifted the hems of their skirts and waved them around in time with the seductive music, exposing ankles and calves in their promenade.

"Come and dance with me," Fernando pleaded.

She would have refused, but Sayer gave her an encouraging smile. "You've got to try it. It's something I'll bet you'll never do with your English dandy."

She gasped when Fernando pulled her tightly against his chest and grinned sinfully down at her. After several embarrassing moments, she learned the steps, and as the music intensified, so did her courage.

"You are having a good time, *si?*"

"*Si,* a very good time," she answered, waving her skirt like the other women and laughing with the pure wanton pleasure of it.

Fernando's grin widened as he glanced over at Sayer. "I think he is jealous. Have you told him you are breaking your engagement?"

"No."

"Why not?" he asked with a displeased frown. "What are you waiting for?"

"I don't know," she snapped. "I'm . . . I'm still not convinced that I can forget the things Sayer has done in his past."

Fernando gave a disbelieving groan and purposely guided her past the colonel. "Look at him, *Señorita*. Look at how he watches us . . . watches you. That is the look of a man in love. Now, when this dance is over, you must tell him how you feel."

"I'll try," Rebeccah said breathlessly.

"No, do not try. Do it. None of us know what happened when his father was killed, or why the colonel asked to be transferred. Ask him. Give him the chance to tell you the real story."

"What if I can't bear it?" she asked, trying to smile for the sake of Sayer and the other dancers.

Fernando spun her around then pulled her back and looked deeply into her eyes. "Is forgiveness something you only teach my daughters?"

Before she could answer, the music ended and the dancers dispersed for a cool drink. Fernando led her back to Sayer, who stood the moment they arrived.

"*Muchas gracias, Señorita*," Fernando replied, a little winded himself. "Forgive me for not staying, but I promised Rita a dance."

He lifted Rebeccah's hand and placed a chaste kiss on it before he strode away.

Sayer held his hat in his hand, but put it on, caught her hand and tucked it in the crook of his arm before she could sit down. "Don't you think it's a bit too warm this close to the fire?"

"Yes, now that you mention it. When I first saw this gown, I thought I'd freeze, but I should have known Fernando knew what he was talking about." Once more she thought she saw a spark of something enticing in Sayer's eyes.

"You dance well," he said as they strolled away from the others. In the shadows, the stars brightened up the night's sky. He stopped abruptly and turned her to face him. "I missed you, Becky."

"I missed you too," she confessed. Would he kiss her now? she wondered. She had no sooner thought it than it became a reality. Sayer pulled her closer, and she felt safe in his embrace. The kiss was gentle at first, but the moment she leaned against his chest, it became more demanding, filling her with the need to give back some of the pleasure he gave her. Her hand slipped up from his chest to encircle his neck as she pulled him even closer, liberated by her decision to end her engagement. His kisses intensified until she was breathless and clinging to him. Slowly, he pulled back and gazed down into her eyes, his own hooded—the moisture from her mouth glistening on his lips.

"I think you missed me more," he teased, his voice deep and husky.

"You're still a scoundrel, I see."

"I brought you something." He pulled her arms down from his neck, but didn't let go of her hand.

She smiled up at him, pleased that while they were apart he had been thinking about her. "You shouldn't have," she lied, secretly wondering what it was.

"I've got it down in the barn."

She hesitated for a moment. "Not another horse."

He grinned then shook his head. "Better."

"Better than Brandy?" she scoffed. "Then whatever it is, it must truly be a prize worth having."

"Just wait until you see him . . . it," he quickly corrected.

She gave him a skeptical look, but they were at the barn and he let go of her arm to light a lamp. Rounder nickered a greeting as did Brandy and some of the other horses. "Where is it?" she asked as Sayer led her over to a stack of straw. He hung the lantern on a nail, and then walked into the shadows where several bales formed a makeshift wall. He reached over and lifted out what looked like a ball of fur.

"I haven't named him yet." Sayer cradled the puppy in his arm, scratching his little pointed ears. "Before you say anything, I know you're still thinking you're going back to England, so all I want you to do is keep him for me until I'm out of the army."

Rebeccah melted at the sight of the pup. "Oh my," she crooned as she took the puppy from Sayer, forgetting to tell her soldier that she'd changed her mind about Edward and England. "He's adorable. What kind is he?"

"Well, he's not really a dog."

Rebeccah laughed. "He's certainly not a cat," she countered with a small laugh. "Now, tell me. What kind of dog is he?"

"He's a wolf pup." When her head snapped up, Sayer nodded. "I found him wandering around in the forest all alone. I suspect his mother was killed, as they don't usually leave their young ones to fend for themselves." Sayer moved a little closer, rubbing the pup's fuzzy head. "I couldn't leave him, but I don't have a place to keep him either, not yet."

"Yes," Rebeccah said without a moment's hesitation. "I'll be delighted to keep him for you, but he'll have to have a name." When she looked at Sayer, he smiled.

"You choose one."

"Very well, how about Kaiser?" She waited as Sayer thought about it for a moment. "It's German for king."

Sayer took the pup then held him up to look at his face. "I think he'll look like a king . . . when he's grown a little more. Right now he looks kind of sleepy, don't you think?"

Rebeccah nodded. "Sleepy and cold. He's shivering. Let's take him over to my house. We'll make him a bed by the fire and give him some warm milk."

Sayer tucked the ends of the woolen throw around the sleeping pup, then placed another log on the fire. Rebeccah came over to stand next to him, disappointed that he was preparing to leave. He reached over and lifted his hat off the nearby wooden rocker, then plucked the flower from her hair and carefully tucked it in his hatband. "I did a little fishing while I was gone, but . . ." He paused and his eyes twinkled with humor. ". . . absolutely none of them tasted as good as those you caught."

She shook her head. "Are you ever serious?" she scolded.

"More than you realize," he said as he pulled her to him. He placed his knuckle under her chin and lifted ever so gently. And even though propriety dictated that she resist, she couldn't. She leaned against him, reveling in the barely audible groan that rumbled from his chest as he kissed her. His hands left her waist, slipping around her back, pressing her even closer as he deepened the kiss. When he was through, he lifted his head, but he didn't let her go. "Did I tell you how lovely you look tonight?" he asked, his gaze so seductive her heart turned over.

"Y-yes, more than once."

His eyes searched hers, then fell once more to her mouth. Slowly, as if savoring every delicious moment, he kissed her again, and her feelings for him deepened and intensified. Edward was forgotten as Sayer kissed a path down her neck and across one bare shoulder.

"Will you ride with me next Saturday?" he whispered near her ear, his voice soft and a little huskier than usual.

"Yes, if you'd like," she replied.

"Good." He smiled, but his eyes held a glint of sadness that threatened her happiness. "There's one last place I'd like to show you before the weather changes."

"You make it sound so final," she said, distressed that what he said was true. Winter would surely spoil their outings, and then, by the time it warmed enough to begin again, he'd be gone. No matter, she told herself, and instantly felt brighter. She'd wait for him.

"Fernando will be wondering where I am." Sayer turned and retrieved his hat, rearranging the flower. "I told him we'd play a game of chess." She walked with him to the door. When he turned, she caught her breath with anticipation, but instead of pulling her back into his arms, he nodded to where the puppy still slept. "Take good care of him for me, will you?"

"Yes," she promised, hating the breathy sound of her voice. He hesitated for a long moment, then put on his hat and walked out into the darkness. She watched as his image faded away into the darkness, then quickly closed the door before she gave in to the urge to call him back.

CHAPTER TWELVE

Sayer listened patiently while the Mexican farmer ranted on about how it was his duty to rescue his cow so that his six children could enjoy her milk. Although he agreed at the right times, his mind was not on the farmer's cow. Apaches had attacked another stage, wounding the driver and four guards, taking the hefty payroll intended for the miners in Silver City. In all his days of fighting Indians, never had they shown so much interest in gold. Their needs were usually basic: horses, clothing, and guns to hunt for food.

"Are you sure she just didn't wander away?" Sayer asked.

The Mexican farmer shook his head at the same time Sayer heaved a long, impatient sigh. Chasing after a cow was the last thing he wanted to do. In fact, he had nearly decided it was a perfect job for Lieutenant Williams when the farmer's next sentence reluctantly changed his mind. "I did not believe her at first, but my wife told me that you are an honorable man, and that you take care of important matters yourself. Now I see that she was right."

Those simple words weighed heavily upon Sayer. Before he realized what he was doing, he accepted the man's hand, shook it, and promised he would do his very best to return his cow. While several of his men prepared for the ride, he and Fergus walked over to the cantina to have a cold beer. Just as they were about to enter, the three men he'd seen at Don Fernando's rode up.

The tallest of the three lifted his horse's front leg and examined the hoof for a moment before he joined the others. In passing, Sayer glanced at the ground, noticing that the animal had a broken shoe. Then he looked at the animal's rider. If he didn't know him to be one of Fernando's men, the man, with his long, braided hair, could pass for an Indian.

"Are you comin', Colonel?" Fergus asked impatiently, obviously anxious to quench his thirst. They sat at the bar paying no attention as Fernando's men sat at a nearby table.

"What is your pleasure, Colonel?" the proprietor asked with a thick Spanish accent.

"Two beers," Sayer replied, tossing a couple of coins on the counter. When their drinks came, Fergus lifted his glass and admired it.

"Ah, a brew fit for a king," Fergus said, taking a long drink. He let out a contented sigh. "Now, I've been thinkin' 'bout what that man said about his cow." The sergeant took another drink, and then dragged the back of his hand across his mouth. "If'n it were the same bunch that's been causin' so much trouble, why did they only take the cow?"

"It's not the same bunch," Sayer replied, sipping his beer as he pushed his hat off his forehead. "Do you remember when the doctor's daughters arrived?"

"Sure I do. In fact, that reminds me, did you ever decide which one is the prettiest?"

Sayer grinned as he shook his head. "You have a one-track mind, don't you?"

"Me?" Fergus finished his beer and put the glass down on the bar. "I'm no' the one who's been staying at Don Fernando's ranch every other weekend pretendin' tae like chess." He gave his commander a sly grin. "My money's still on Miss Rebeccah. Now, back tae your question. I remember it as if it were yesterday. Never in my life have I ever seen two more beautiful lassies, that—"

"Sergeant," Sayer said impatiently. "Don't you find it odd that when we inspected the place where they were attacked, most of the tracks were of shod horses?"

Fergus frowned. "Now that you mention it, I do."

Sayer continued, telling the sergeant his theory, unaware that Fernando's men listened.

"Colonel MacLaren," a young corporal called as he came through the door and stood at attention. "The men are ready, sir."

Sayer returned the man's salute. "Good, thank you, Corporal, that will be all." He drank the last of his beer before turning to leave. "I'll be heading north toward Pecos."

"Yes, sir," Fergus acknowledged, following Sayer outside. "How long do you think it'll take?"

"I reckon it depends on how fast a few braves can run a cow."

Fifteen minutes later, Sayer sat at his desk and picked up a pen. He wrote a hasty note to Rebeccah, explaining that he would be gone longer than the usual two weeks because he had to go look for a cow. He smiled once more when he added that it wasn't just any old cow, but a very important cow. He folded the note, picked up his rifle and walked outside.

"Did you pack my rod, Sergeant?" Sayer asked as he slipped his Sharps carbine into the saddle socket before he mounted.

"Aye, sir, that I did."

Sayer pulled an envelope from his inside pocket. "See that Miss Randolph gets this note." He gathered up his reins. As usual, for military business outside the fort, Rounder was decked out like the other horses in a black halter and cotton lead under his bridle. The leads had been neatly knotted around the horses' necks. Full canteens were tied to the pommel, while clothing and rations for several days had been packed in the men's saddlebags, and bedrolls secured to the cantles.

"I will for sure," Fergus answered, saluting his commanding officer. No sooner had Sayer disappeared down the road toward the north, than Sergeant Carmichael cleared his throat and hollered so the other soldiers could hear. "Listen up, lads. I've money here for the takin'. All you've got tae do is guess which of the Randolph lassies the colonel thinks is the prettiest." Several men nodded to each other then pulled out their wallets. "Now, now, don't be shy. I've got a hundred dollars that it's Miss Rebeccah. Take part of it or all of it, it's your choice, lads."

Sayer and his troops chased the renegades high into the mountains. Their tracks skirted around the small village of Pecos and headed up the rugged trail toward Jack's Creek. On the morning of the third day, they found the cow grazing in a small, grassy meadow surround by tall pines. Obviously too slow for the warriors who took her, she'd been milked, and other than a few scratches on her spotted hide, she appeared none the worse for her adventure. After searching the surrounding area, Sayer was satisfied that there had only been two warriors on unshod ponies.

"Corporal Rogers," Sayer called. "You and the others take her back."

"Yes, sir, but aren't you coming too, sir?"

Sayer pushed his hat back on his head and glanced at the fast moving Pecos River. His chances of getting this high again before being transferred to Fort Union were slim. The river was tempting, deep, with lots of grassy bank. The perfect hiding place for trout. "After I do a little fishing, Corporal. You won't be able to travel fast. I'll catch up to you tomorrow."

The young man nodded and rode over to the others. Soon

the three of them were driving the cow down the narrow deer trail.

Rebeccah helped Rita carry out a basket of freshly washed clothes, smiling as Kaiser lumbered after her. A gentle breeze wafted through the treetops, and in the bright sun the wash would dry quickly. The first week after the *matanza* had passed quickly, and Sayer would be arriving soon to take her out riding. Though she had never thought herself an equestrian, she did so now with pride.

"So," Rita said with a knowing smile. "Has the colonel asked you to be his woman?"

"I beg your pardon?" Rebeccah asked with a disbelieving laugh as she took her stocking out of Kaiser's mouth. "Bad dog," she scolded.

"His woman," Rita repeated. "You know, has he asked you to marry him yet?" Rita shook out a wet shirt and pinned it to the line. "He is very handsome. If you marry, I am sure you will have many pretty babies."

Again Rebeccah gave a small laugh at Rita's hypothesis, but secretly her heart soared. "Rita, I am still engaged, and until I can settle things back home in England—"

"This man, the one in England, he loves you very much?"

"I'm not sure. We've only known each other for a few months."

"I see many letters come at first, but now I don't see so many."

"Yes. It seems we've run out of things to say to each other. I'm not sure what I'll do when the time comes to leave."

"You are not leaving us?" Rita asked with a worried frown.

"No . . . possibly. I haven't decided. I'll just have to wait until I can ask the advice of my sister. She'll know if breaking an engagement by letter is acceptable or not."

"That is a very smart thing to do," Rita said, her words

muffled by the clothespin she held between her teeth. "My sister is wise too. But I do not see why you are so upset."

"I'm upset because I don't want to hurt Edward."

Rita frowned. "Oh, the man in England."

"Yes. You see, I promised him I'd return, and now I've got to break that promise and I'm not looking forward to it."

"The colonel will chase away your unhappiness."

"Do you think so?"

"Oh, *si*. Even a blind woman could tell that the colonel loves you."

Again Rebeccah's heart took flight—just as Kaiser took off with another stocking. She ran a few steps and brought it back, shaking off bits of dirt and leaves. "This will have to be washed again."

"So, if your sister says it's all right to send a letter, you will stay?"

"Yes, I believe I will," Rebeccah replied as she tried to stop the pup from stealing a wet towel from the basket.

"And if the colonel asks you to be his woman, you would say yes?" Rita asked with a smile.

"Kaiser, drop that." Rebeccah threw up her arms in exasperation, then caught the pup, plunked him in the basket and picked it up. "Come, Rita, I've got to wash these things over again." Somewhere in the distance an owl hooted and Rebeccah stopped to enjoy the sound.

"*Oh Dios mia*," Rita whispered, crossing herself.

Rebeccah glanced over at Rita and frowned. "What's the matter? You look as if you've seen a ghost."

"*Si, Señorita*, did you not hear that sound?"

"The owl? Of course. It's beautiful, but not often heard during the day. Owls are nocturnal. It must be nesting nearby." The owl called again. "There. I think it came from those trees. Shall we try and find the nest?"

Rita shook her head and crossed herself again. "No, it is not beautiful. It is very bad to hear such a sound. I am sorry we did not finish sooner." Rita grasped Rebeccah's arm and pulled her along, trying to hurry her. "Come, let us go inside before it happens again."

"Why on earth are you so upset?" Rebeccah asked as she reluctantly followed. Once more the owl's cry was heard in the distance.

Rita stopped, her eyes wide. "To hear it in the daytime means someone will die."

The afternoon was warm, and the trout were elusive. Over the noise of the river, Sayer thought he heard a branch snap in the direction where he'd tied Rounder. When he turned, he saw three Apache warriors scouting the area. While two carried rifles, only one carried a bow and a quiver of arrows. At first he thought they'd be satisfied with stealing Rounder, but then they began to search the trampled grass, following his tracks to the river. Sayer dropped his rod, crouched down behind the dense foliage and quietly lifted his Colt .45 from its holster.

The next morning, Rebeccah read Sayer's note while Sergeant Carmichael waited. "Thank you, Sergeant," she said, trying to hide her disappointment. It was Friday and now, from his note, it would be at least a few more days before she saw Sayer again. "Would you like a cup of coffee before you return to the fort?" she asked, tucking the note into the pocket of her gown.

"Why, that's mighty nice of you, lass. I'd love one."

Rebeccah served them both then took a seat across the table from Sayer's friend. "You've known the colonel a long time, haven't you?"

"Aye, since before he enlisted. His father was my commander, and I kind of took tae the lad."

She added some sugar to her cup and listened as the rugged old man told her stories of Sayer's childhood. She realized that he was probably with Sayer when his father was killed. For a moment she thought to ask, and then decided against it. Some things were better left in the past. But the kindly sergeant loved to talk, and when he finished with Sayer's childhood, he began on his career in the army.

"Sayer told me he's going to be out of the army soon," she interjected, trying to turn the topic to something other than Indian fighting.

"Aye, we both are."

"Really?" she asked with a small sigh of relief. "Are you looking forward to it?"

"I don't know. I've been a soldier my whole life, but the colonel wants me tae go inta business with 'im. Says we can get rich raising horses." The sergeant took a sip of his coffee. "He's more like my son than my commander, so I reckon I'll try my hand at ranchin'. He's awful gude with horses. There was a time when we were surrounded by hostiles, and the only way out was to cross a deep, fast-moving river. Some horses balked, but after Sayer urged his horse in the water, the others followed."

Rebeccah tried a new subject. "He told me a little about his mother, but I don't remember him mentioning any brothers or sisters."

"Nope, the lad's an only child. Sad thing it was for 'im tae lose his mother. Katherine was her name. She kind of softened his father's strict ways, if'n you know what I mean. When we came back from huntin' that day . . ." the sergeant shook his head. "I'll never forget the look on the boy's face—seeing his mother on the floor, her beautiful hair cut from her head."

Rebeccah's throat closed and for several seconds, she felt as if she couldn't breathe. "They scalped her?"

The sergeant's features grew stern. "Aye."

She rose and went to the stove. It took several moments before she felt composed enough to return with the coffeepot. "So now I understand why he asked for the transfer . . . to get away."

"It weren't 'cause he's a coward, that's for sure." Though the sergeant's tone sounded gruff, she knew it wasn't directed at her. He nodded his thanks when she refilled his cup. "I wanted to tell those men at Bonnie's that they had no right tae say what they did. The colonel's a proud man." Sergeant Carmichael raised his gaze to lock with hers. "When his father was killed, I thought he'd never get over it."

Rebeccah sank down in her chair, praying the old warrior would find something else to speak of.

"Sayer was with him when he died, you know."

"I only suspected he was," she said softly, her heart sinking with the knowledge that her worst fear was about to become reality.

"Aye, he was. It was early, just after dawn nearly two years ago. There were forty men in our detail. We'd had an early melt and the river ran high. General MacLaren ordered me tae take the supply wagon and half the men ahead."

Fergus fell quiet for a long time, toying with the spoon and staring into his cup. "When the others never showed, me and some of the men went back. The only one we found alive was Sayer. He'd been staked out on the bank by the river—an arrow through each arm and two more through each leg, pinnin' 'im tae the ground so he couldna move while they tortured the others."

Rebeccah closed her eyes, trying to block out the picture, clutching her cup. "Why . . . why was he spared?"

"He told me later, after we got 'im back tae camp, what happened. He said that fifty or so Sioux warriors came out of the trees with their women and children. By the looks on their faces, they were as surprised tae see the soldiers as the soldiers were tae see a bunch of Indians. He swears tae this day that all they wanted was tae pass by without any trouble. But his father wouldna have any part of that—not after what happened to his wife."

Fergus shook his head and the frown on his brow grew deeper as he stared into his cup for a moment, then raised his eyes to hers. "I'm no' makin' any excuses, but he was never the same after she died. Sayer said the general pulled out his revolver and began to shoot at anythin' that moved, includin' the women and children. The lad tried tae stop him and, I suspect, that's why in the end the Sioux let him live." The sergeant heaved a long sigh.

"What did they do to his father?" she asked, her voice sounding as if someone else had asked the question.

The kindly sergeant shook his head. " 'Tis better that you don't know, lassie."

Sayer came awake with a start. Somehow he was on his back, lying in the tall grass under the shelter of a tree with no memory of getting there. His head throbbed, but that was nothing compared to the agony in his chest and leg. Slowly, gritting his teeth against the pain, he crawled to the closest tree and pulled himself to a sitting position, feeling sick when he saw an arrow protruding from his thigh. In his confusion, he reached for his revolver, unnerved when it wasn't there.

"Ah, God," he whispered, leaning his head back against the rough bark. His chest felt as if it were on fire and when he glanced down, blood oozed from a small hole in his shirt. He pulled his knife from its scabbard and forced himself more upright, thankful that it didn't take long to cut through the slender shaft of the arrow.

He closed his eyes, trying to remember what had happened. He saw himself running toward Rounder when he was hit in the leg. Collapsing, he fired three shots, killing one of the warriors. Again he tried to make it to his horse, but the other two men were gaining on him. He fired twice more before he was tackled and his gun was wrestled from his grasp. The muddled, painted features of a warrior, furious at having been wounded, hovered before him only a second before Sayer felt the barrel of his own gun pressed against his chest.

Sayer's eyes snapped open and he very nearly cried out as he jumped once more—feeling the impact of the bullet all over again. After a few moments, his breathing became more normal, and with trembling fingers, he touched the gash above his eye where the warrior must have hit him with the Colt before riding away. He tried to focus on the calming sounds of birds and the rush of the nearby river, but in his mind he heard the sickening click of his pistol as the warrior fired again and again, only to growl in rage when it ran out of bullets.

"I am against you riding out alone," Don Fernando scolded. "It will only take a few moments for me to saddle my horse."

"You don't understand," Rebeccah replied while she gathered up her reins. But before she could step into the stirrup, Fernando lifted her to the saddle. "I want to ride alone. I need some quiet time to think."

"Is it not quiet in your house?" he challenged.

Her smile was patient. "Yes, very, but it's also indoors, and I need some fresh air. I shan't go far. Just to the river and back."

"Can it not wait until the colonel returns? I am sure he will take you riding."

"No. He's part of the problem." She shook her head before Fernando could speak. "I found out why he transferred, and I am much relieved, but there are still some things I need to work out. Now, please, let go of my horse."

"If you insist," he said, still frowning. "Wait a moment," he ordered. She watched him disappear into the house then return with a small-caliber pistol, smaller than the one Sayer had used when he taught her how to shoot. "Take this," Fernando urged, slipping it into her saddlebags.

"What ever for?"

"Just to please me, hey?"

She knew it was futile to argue. "Very well. Is it loaded?" She asked with a smile, hoping to alleviate his concern with her newly acquired knowledge.

"Of course," Fernando snapped.

A blue jay called from the treetops, and Sayer's eyes snapped open. He had no idea how long he'd slept, only that his wounds had stopped bleeding. Now, if he could muster the strength, he had to see if he still had his horse. The thought that his stallion might have been taken deepened his despair, but nevertheless, he gave a loud, shrill whistle. The result was worth the effort as Rounder trotted out of the trees, his coat matted with dried sweat. He stopped several yards away, his nostrils flaring, his eyes wide with fright.

"Easy, boy," Sayer murmured as he dragged himself closer. When his fingers brushed against the cold metal of his revolver lying in the grass, he grabbed it, but before he shoved it back into his holster he noticed a print in the soil. He knew it should mean something, but he couldn't remember why. Using the stirrup, he pulled himself upright, leaning heavily against Rounder for several long moments. Slowly, the pain almost overwhelming, he climbed into the saddle. After another rest, he reached into his saddlebags and pulled out his last clean shirt. Taking his knife, he sliced it into strips, stuffing a wadded sleeve inside his shirt. He tied the rest around his thigh, cursing when he pulled it tight. Gritting his teeth, he urged his horse down the mountain.

Rebeccah turned her mare down the grassy path adjacent to the river. After Sergeant Carmichael left, she had felt confined, restless. Now, in the fresh mountain air, she was determined to think things through. Sayer's life had been so different from hers—so frightening. Even now, miles away from the ranch, she doubted she could have ever survived the pain and suffering he had endured.

"Ignorance is truly bliss," she muttered as she urged the mare deeper into the forest. Although she tried not to think about it, the sergeant's recounting of Sayer's past followed her, until all she wanted to do was lose herself in the beauty of the mountain for an hour or two. Soon she passed the small pool where Sayer had showed her the dam, teaching her about beavers. Half an hour passed and next came the clearing where they had seen the deer. The more familiar the terrain became, the more she relaxed, and the more she remembered the good times they'd shared.

By the time the sun rested on the treetops, Sayer was out of water, and now as he followed the river down the mountain, all he could think about was a cold drink.

"Easy, son," he said gruffly as he eased out of the saddle. He clung to the horn a long while until the pain subsided and the earth stopped spinning. His hands shook as he untied his canteen. Though the river was only a few steps away, he stumbled, catching himself on a rock as he slid to the ground. He tried to rise, but he didn't have the strength. Groaning, he leaned back against the rock and closed his eyes. He thought about Becky, and soon the pain diminished as her image invaded his dreams.

★ ★ ★ ★ ★

Rebeccah looked for the crooked tree that jutted out over the stream, remembering the day that Sayer had made her a wildflower crown. Had she not been lost in her sweet memories, she would have noticed how her mare's ears pricked forward and her nostrils flared as the horse stared at something Rebeccah couldn't see.

The rock formation where she had placed some bread for the squirrels was next, and she knew that just around the bend was the rock circle Sayer had made to contain the fire over which they had roasted their catch. It was only when her mare wandered off the trail and nickered softly that Rebeccah caught a glimpse of Sayer's stallion through the copse of trees. Her heart beat a little faster in anticipation that she would not have to return to the ranch alone. She rode toward Rounder, frowning when his master was nowhere to be found.

"Sayer?" she called. But she knew that, if he were fishing, the noisy little stream would drown out the sound of her voice. She dismounted and tied Brandy to a tree. Rounder lifted his head, his reins dangling—the whites of his eyes visible as he blew hard through his nostrils. Odd, she thought as spider legs of fear trickled up her spine. Sayer would never leave his beloved horse unattended.

"Nice horse," she crooned, but still he shied away when she reached for the reins. "Steady," she said softly, catching sight of dried blood smeared over the stallion's shoulder. *If I have to go out and do battle with someone, I'll be sure to take a different horse.* Sayer's words didn't ease the terror that dried Rebeccah's mouth and moistened her palms. Hoping the blood was from a scratch on the horse, her fingers closed around the reins as she glanced cautiously around. She tied the stallion away from her mare, then hurried to her saddlebags, and just to be safe, withdrew the little pistol.

CHAPTER THIRTEEN

"Sayer? Can you hear me?" Rebeccah called, her voice carrying out over the stream. She searched the ground for footprints, but the only prints she could find were her own and those of his horse. She was just about to return to the horses when she decided to check the river on the other side of the rocky formation. Holding the pistol tightly in her hand, she stepped around.

"Oh, no," she whispered, her breath catching as she ran to Sayer's side. If it weren't for the broken shaft of an arrow protruding from a makeshift bandage on his thigh, he would have looked as if he were napping. He sat on the ground, his back braced by the rock, his head bent, and the late afternoon breeze ruffling his hair. With trembling fingers she touched his arm, gasping when he lifted his head and opened his eyes. It was then that she noticed more blood on his shirt. "Oh, no," she repeated in despair.

"I-I must be dreaming again," he said, his usually strong voice barely audible. His statement frightened her even more than the ashen color of his skin. She tore a long strip of cloth from her petticoat, ran to the water, and after wetting it, came back and bathed the sweat and blood from his face. Her touch partially revived him.

"Becky," he began, wincing when he shifted his weight. Fresh blood soaked his shirt, and raw panic clawed at her insides. She had to swallow back the urge to scream for help, knowing full well there was none to be had.

"You mustn't move," she ordered, tearing more cloth to add to the bandage he'd made for his shoulder. She untied the silk scarf around his neck, but when her fingers touched something sticky behind his back, she realized that the bullet had gone through. She ripped more of her petticoat off then pressed it against his back, using the scarf to secure it in place.

"I-I can't protect you like this," he said.

"Then I shall protect you," she countered. "See, I have brought my gun." Remembering that he always carried a small tin cup in his saddlebags, she hurried to fetch it. She filled it with water and returned to his side, holding it as he drank. When finally he pushed it away, his voice sounded a little stronger.

"If they come—"

"No one's coming. We're alone, and we're safe here."

"No, listen to me," he ground out. "You can't let them take us alive." His warning terrified her almost as much as his expression.

"You must stop this nonsense," she demanded in a shaky voice. "You're scaring me."

Instantly his tone filled with regret. "I'm sorry. I-I didn't mean to frighten you." He leaned his head back against the rock and his eyes drifted closed. She left him then, found his canteen, and after she filled it, hurried to his horse and tied it to the saddle.

"Sayer, please. I can't do this alone," she pleaded, holding Rounder's reins. She knelt and tried once more to revive him. "Colonel MacLaren," she said in her most formal tone. "As a soldier, 'tis your duty to protect me and act as my escort. I want to go home."

His eyes fluttered open. "Yes," he replied, and she knew her ruse had worked. He clenched his jaw, and with her help, he stood, leaning against the rock a moment before he slowly climbed into the saddle. Surprisingly, Rounder settled down the moment Sayer took the reins. She hurried to untie the rope around the stallion's neck then led him closer to her horse so she could mount.

With each torturous mile, the stain on Sayer's shirt grew larger. Though he managed to stay in the saddle, they stopped frequently when he asked for a drink. Often he listed so badly she feared he would fall, but she'd ask questions, pressing him to answer, knowing that it helped to keep him awake.

"You never told me your age," she said, trying to think of anything to keep his mind alert.

"Tw-twenty-seven."

When she glanced over at him, he was trembling. She stopped and retrieved his blanket from his bedroll. It was no easy task to find something upon which she could stand, but finally she spotted a small rock formation, and after leading Rounder to it, managed to climb up and drape the blanket over Sayer's shoulders. "How long have you been a soldier?"

"Eight . . . no . . . ten . . . ten years," he replied as she scrambled back on her mare. More and more she had to repeat her questions, urging him to answer. Initially, he was coherent, but then he began to drift from reality to places he'd been. For the most part, she ignored his rambling, finding it odd that time after time he would mention unshod ponies and broken horseshoes.

It was dark and cold by the time the faint light from the ranch came into sight. As she rode closer, she saw mounted men holding torches, preparing to search for her.

"There," one man shouted, and soon Don Fernando was alongside Sayer, slipping from his horse and mounting Rounder to ride behind his friend.

"Come, we must hurry and get him inside." Wrapping his

arm around Sayer's waist, Fernando spurred Rounder into a gallop, sliding to a stop at the hitching post.

"I thought you were lost." Fernando turned before she could reply, and in Spanish told one of his men to get more help. Two more men appeared, and working together, they carried Sayer to a room down a long hall.

"How . . . where did you find him?" Fernando asked.

"On the trail by the river," she said, stifling a sob.

Sayer groaned when the men placed him on the bed. *"Dios mio,"* Fernando exclaimed, his dark brows pulled tightly together as he noted the blood on Sayer's chest. He touched the back of his hand to Sayer's flushed cheek. "He trembles, yet he is burning up." Without being asked, one of the servants hurried to build a fire. Fernando turned to the other man. *"Agua y vendas."* When the man left, Fernando stood and put his arm around Rebeccah. "Are you all right?" he asked, but before she could answer, he called to the maid. "Get *Señorita* Randolph something hot to drink, and bring some warmed brandy for the colonel."

"Please don't worry about me. We must help him," Rebeccah answered in a rush of words as her soldier's grave condition hit her full-force.

"Shush, calm down. Come and warm yourself." Fernando led her to the chair nearest the fire. "I will take care of him." Rita came in with a basin of water and several clean cloths tucked under her arm and placed them on the table by the bed. The other maid returned with a tray on which sat a steaming cup of tea and a small glass of brandy. Fernando insisted Rebeccah take the tea, then carried the brandy over and sat on the edge of the bed. *"Amigo.* You must drink." He lifted Sayer, bracing him as he forced some of the brandy down his throat.

Slowly, Sayer opened his eyes. "Becky . . . is she all right?"

Relief surged through her at the sound of his voice. But when she came to the bedside, his appearance shattered her hopes. In the light from the lamps and fire he looked even paler, his wounds appearing even more ghastly. The gouge on the left side of his forehead was badly bruised, and his left eye was nearly swollen shut.

"See," Fernando said with an encouraging smile. "He rests easier, knowing you are here." Fernando took Sayer's knife from his belt and cut away the bloody bandage around his leg, then cut away his shirt. "This is not good. He was shot at very close range."

Though the bullet hole still oozed blood, high on Sayer's left arm was a puckered, jagged scar. His right arm bore a similar scar, and once more the sergeant's stories came back to haunt her. Fernando spoke so softly to his maid, Rebeccah could barely hear, but she heard her father's name, then the word *pronto*.

By the time she and Fernando had washed and bandaged Sayer's wounds, he was held tightly in the throes of his dreams. He muttered orders, then warnings, sometimes using names she recognized and sometimes not. More than once he asked where he was and how he came to be there, but he'd drift back into the fitful sleep of the sick before anyone could answer him. More time passed and Fernando urged her to rest, but she feared to leave Sayer's side.

"Then sit here in this chair while I get more water," Fernando said as he pushed the chair closer to the bed before leaving. In the hall he motioned to Rita. "Find Renato. I wish to speak with him. Afterward take the *señorita* an extra blanket."

A few moments later Renato and Jose came into Fernando's study. Furious, their overlord raked his fingers through his dark hair, then turned and grabbed Renato, releasing him the next moment when the man cried out in pain. "You are injured?"

Fernando asked, his frown growing even fiercer.

"*Si, jefe,*" Renato answered, holding his arm, "but it's not serious."

"Not serious, hey?" Fernando purposely grabbed Renato's arm again, ignoring his pained expression as he jerked him closer. "Tell me, Renato, how did you hurt your arm? And where is Vicente?" He didn't wait for Renato to answer. He turned and pinned Jose with his angry gaze, then shoved Renato away. "Where were you two days ago? Perhaps in the mountains?"

"*Si, jefe* . . . I mean, *no.*" Jose swallowed audibly and cast a desperate glance at Renato.

"He killed Vicente," Renato ground out.

"Vicente is dead?" Fernando gave an anguished groan, dragging his hands down his face. "What am I to tell his wife?" Fernando grabbed Renato by his shirt. "Where is his body?"

"We have it hidden. We don't know what to do, *jefe.* We could not leave him there."

"Where?" Fernando glared at the younger man. "Well?"

"I forget," Renato muttered, scowling.

"You forget? Well, perhaps I can help you remember." Fernando sloshed some whiskey into a glass and took a drink before turning to face Renato. "I think you followed the colonel up into the mountains, ambushed him, and left him for dead. That's what I think. And I think the colonel had no choice. I think he killed Vicente in self-defense." Fernando closed his eyes for a moment to collect his thoughts. "In the morning, take the body to Father Sanchez. Tell him Vicente was cleaning his pistol and it accidentally went off. He has no reason not to believe us."

Jose stepped forward. "*Jefe,* please listen to us. We overheard the colonel talking to his sergeant in the cantina. He thinks that someone other than the Apaches are robbing the stages. He said he had evidence to prove it. When we learned that he was going to look for some stupid *vaca*, we followed. We thought we could make it look like Indians as we always do, but then he saw our faces."

"He knows," Renato added, still holding his injured arm. "He knows it is us."

"Where were his men? Have you killed them all too?" Fernando demanded.

Jose shook his head. "No, no. Fortune was on our side. He told the others to leave so he could do some fishing. We waited many hours until we were sure he was alone."

"Listen to me," Renato began anxiously. "The colonel must pay for what he has done. If you take the *señorita* out for a short walk, I will finish—"

Fernando backhanded Renato. "*Silencio!* I will not have you commit murder in my home. I never wanted anyone to die, *cabron*. I am sorry your brother is dead, but it is not because of the colonel. No. It is because you acted foolishly."

"The colonel knows," Renato repeated tightly, wiping away the trickle of blood from his cut lip. "Refuse to believe me if you wish, but mark my words, he knows. When he is strong enough, he will go back and get his men, and they will hunt us down like animals."

Once more Fernando raked his fingers angrily through his hair. "*Idioto.* We have . . . had nothing to fear. Until now, no one had died." Fernando turned after a long pause. His gaze stabbed into Renato's. "You told me he saw your faces?"

"*Si.* That is why he must die."

"How were you dressed?" Fernando demanded.

"As Apaches."

"Then you cannot be sure he knows it was you, hey?"

"We cannot be sure, *jefe*," Renato agreed, shaking his head as if he were using a great deal of restraint.

"You want revenge?" Fernando asked with a savage smile.

"I want him as dead as my brother," Renato ground out.

"You are forgetting something very important, *cabron*. The colonel is like a brother to me. Touch him again, and I will kill you myself." Fernando stormed out of his study.

Renato swore under his breath turning his rebellious gaze to his friend. "*El jefe* is the fool, not I." Renato rubbed his sore arm, shaking his head. "We put our lives in danger time and again for him, and this is how he repays us?"

"You told me the colonel was dead," Jose replied desperately.

"How was I to know he would survive? *Dios mio,* I shot the *bastardo* in the heart."

Jose began to pace. "If he wakes he could identify us. Then what will we do?"

Renato stopped his friend. "Then it is up to us to make sure that does not happen, hey?"

"N-no," Jose stammered, shaking his head. "Did you not see the look in Don Fernando's eyes? He and the colonel are *amigos.*"

"Perhaps, but is their friendship worth hanging for?" Renato went to the table and poured himself a drink, gulping it down. "I say it is better that the colonel dies peacefully in his sleep."

James Randolph tied his horse to the rail next to Sergeant Carmichael's, helped Lydia out of the buggy, then grabbed his medical bag. They hurried inside to Sayer's room. The moment Rebeccah saw her father and sister, she burst into tears.

"Now, honey, get hold of yourself," James murmured, patting her back. He gave her a hug, passed her to Lydia, and then placed his bag down on the bedside table. Rebeccah clung to her sister while Don Fernando told her father the extent of Sayer's wounds. Her father lifted the cloth off Sayer's forehead, and then examined Sayer's shoulder. "You've stopped the bleeding. We'll leave this alone for the time being."

Next he looked at Sayer's leg, shaking his head. "This is the one we'll do first." James sat down, then patted Sayer none too gently on the cheek. "Colonel? Can you hear me, son?"

Sayer stirred, but didn't come fully awake. James reached into his bag and took out a dark bottle, pouring a small amount of a clear liquid into an empty glass. He lifted his patient and forced him to drink. Sayer choked, and tried to push her father's hand away with surprising strength.

"Father, please be gentle," Rebeccah protested, ignoring her sire's frown.

"Becky," Lydia said softly. "If Papa can't get Sayer to take the laudanum, it'll only make it more difficult to remove the arrow."

"Then give it to me." Rebeccah waited until her father stood, then took the glass and sat on the side of Sayer's bed. Beads of sweat dampened his forehead as he tried hard to focus on her face. "Colonel MacLaren," she admonished. "You must take your medicine and stop behaving like a naughty child."

"Becky?" he murmured, barely able to lift his hand. She caught it between her own. Fernando came around and lifted Sayer while she coaxed him to drink. When he was finished, Fernando eased him down and stepped aside. He relaxed a little, yet the pressure of his fingers increased when he shifted his weight. "I-I put you and your sister in danger," Sayer began. "I'm sorry . . . I should have left to escort you back sooner." His eyes drifted closed. "I-I shouldn't have tossed your parasol into the river."

"It's quite all right, Colonel," she said softly as it dawned on her he was speaking about the time they first met—when the stage bogged down in the river. "We're safe now."

"No . . . you are not," he said, his expression as well as the tone of his voice filling her with dread. "It's not safe out here. You must go back . . . back to your dandy."

"What in the hell is he talking about?" her father asked as he handed his daughter a wet cloth for his patient's forehead.

"I believe he is referring to Edward," Rebeccah whispered, trying hard to be strong. When Sayer's gaze focused on her, she forced a smile even though she felt like crying at the emptiness in his gaze.

"You are the prettiest, Becky . . . I'm sure of it now," he murmured before he fell asleep.

Sergeant Carmichael's low chuckle broke through the stark silence. "Finally, I win a bet, and he's too sick tae even know it." He grinned again as he scratched the stubble on his chin.

"Do you care to explain?" James asked, laying his medical instruments on the table.

Sergeant Carmichael's sad smile never wavered. "No disrespect tae your daughters, Doctor, but when our company first arrived in Santa Fe, there were rumors floatin' about concernin' Miss Lydia's charm and beauty. When she left tae fetch you, Miss Rebeccah, we all thought you were just a wee little girl, but then at the river, we all learned differently." He gave a small, uncomfortable cough. "Well, as it was, I asked the colonel who he thought was the prettiest."

"And did he tell you?" James asked as he took off his glasses, cleaned them, and put them back on, smiling.

"Well, not exactly, sir. But, then, the colonel began tae spend a great deal of his time here . . . at Don Fernando's, playin' chess . . . or at least that's what he told us, but we all knew it was because of Miss Rebeccah."

"You did?" James asked, rolling up his sleeves.

"Aye, sir, we did. Everyone knows the colonel isn't that fond of chess. And, beggin' your pardon, Miss Rebeccah, I, being a poor Scotsman, doin' my best tae scratch a meager livin' in the army, decided tae try and improve my lot by placin' a few bets with the men."

"A few bets?" Lydia asked, pouring hot water into a bowl next to some bandages.

"Aye. On which one of you ladies our colonel thought was prettier." The sergeant coughed again. "And, being that I'm a wee bit more fond of blondes, I chose you, Miss Rebeccah, and I'm a richer man for it today than I was yesterday."

Her father chuckled, then washed his hands and reached for a towel. "Let's get that arrow out of his leg." Her father's voice broke into her reverie. "Rebeccah, you'd best get some air." His formal tone and dark expression left no room for argument.

"Y-yes, of course," she answered as she stood. Don Fernando came to her, placing his arm around her shoulders.

"Come. I will sit with you until it's over."

"The next twenty-four hours will be critical," Rebeccah's father stated as he took off his spectacles and rubbed his eyes. "His wounds are serious, and he's lost a lot of blood. Luckily, the bullet went through clean, missing his heart. For a day or two, he's going to be in a lot of pain. And, by the looks of the bump on his head, he's going to have one hell of a headache when he wakes up, so I've left some laudanum on the table. A teaspoon in some water should help."

Although her father's words caused her insides to twist into a painful knot, Rebeccah remained silent as Fernando motioned for her father to sit, pouring him a cup of steaming coffee.

"It's crucial he remain quiet," James continued. "I don't care if the whole Apache Nation attacks, he can't hear of it, do you both understand?" he asked, adding a spoonful of sugar.

"*Sí*," Fernando replied, his expression as grim as her father's.

"And, Fernando, I hate to impose, but he can't be moved for a couple of weeks, either."

"That is not a problem. I insist he stay here until he is completely healed. I will not have it any other way." Fernando shook his head, and then looked at her father with a forced smile. "Since it is late, I have had Rita prepare rooms for you and your daughter. I do not think I can get the sergeant to leave for longer than a few moments, so I have sent for more pillows and blankets. If there is anything you need, ask and it is yours."

James nodded his thanks, then stood and pulled Rebeccah to her feet. "You look tired. Lydia will stay with the colonel while you get some rest."

"But what if he needs me?" she protested.

"He's sleeping, and he'll continue to sleep until the laudanum wears off. When he wakes . . . that's when he'll need you to take his mind off of the pain. But you need to be rested. I'm thinking tomorrow's going to be a long day." James reached down, drank the last of his coffee, then took her hand. "Come on, honey. I'll walk you home." James nodded at Fernando. "I'll be back in a little while to check on the colonel, and then I'll take you up on that bed."

Once outside, her father put his arm around Rebeccah's shoulders. Together they walked down the path toward her home, pausing as she and Sayer had done so many times to look up at the multitude of stars. "If there's any change . . . I mean . . . if you go back and he's worse, or—"

"I'll send Lydia for you right away."

She blinked against the sting of tears. "It's just that we've become friends . . . good friends . . . and he looked so wretched when I found him."

"You did everything right, Becky. Neither Lydia or I could have done more." He kissed her cheek. "If you decide you don't want to be a teacher any longer, I could always use another nurse." He put his knuckles under her trembling chin. "Hey, have you heard from . . . just a moment, I'll think of it . . . Edmund?" he asked.

"Edward," she corrected, and even though Edward was the

last person she wanted to speak about, she knew her father was trying to make her think of more pleasant things.

"Ah, young love. I suppose he writes to you every day?"

"Almost," she sniffed. "I haven't been as diligent."

Her father's expression filled with sympathy.

"Well, you know, if he loves you, he'll understand."

Suddenly, Rebeccah couldn't hold back her tears. She turned, and when her father folded her in his embrace, she wept. Not for herself, but because she was terribly confused and frightened that she still might lose Sayer.

"Hey, don't cry. He'll wait, I know he will," her father murmured, placing a fatherly kiss in her hair. "As long as his letters keep coming, you've nothing to worry about. I wrote to your mother every week, and every week I'd wait for the mail, but I never got one single letter. No, sir, not once, and it still pains me to think about it."

Rebeccah lifted her head, realizing that her father thought she was upset because she missed Edward. "W-what did you say?"

"I said, if he loves you, he'll wait. But I have to tell you, it hurts when you love someone and they don't love you back."

"No, not that . . . about writing to Mother?" Even in the dark, her father looked haggard. "You said you wrote to her, didn't you?"

He nodded. "Every week for sixteen years, up until I got the letter telling me she'd died. It was the first time I'd ever received a letter from England, and I remember for a moment I felt so happy. But it wasn't from your mother. It was from your grandmother." He turned away, looking up at the stars again as he dragged his hand across his eyes. "It sure is pretty out tonight."

"Yes, yes it is," Rebeccah replied ever so softly. Memories of her mother waiting for the post, then turning away with tear-bright eyes, swam in Rebeccah's head. If her father had written, what had happened to his letters? With a sad smile, she hooked her arm through her father's and leaned her head on his shoulder, aware for the first time in her life the sacrifice he'd made when he sent his wife and children back to England.

CHAPTER FOURTEEN

The following morning, Rebeccah heated some water on the stove. All night her dreams had been plagued with images of Sayer when he had recognized her by the river—his tormented expression when he had told her not to let *them* take him alive. She didn't know how long the teapot had been whistling, only that when someone knocked on the door, she had to hastily remove the pot before she could answer.

"Did I wake you?" Lydia asked.

"No, not really." Rebeccah tucked a strand of hair behind her ear and stepped aside. Dressed in her robe and slippers, Rebeccah knew she looked terrible, her usually bright eyes red and puffy from crying.

"The mail came." Lydia held out an envelope. "I thought you might want this." She gave her sister a bright smile. "It's from England. Is that the teapot I hear?"

"Yes, please come in." Rebeccah took the letter, glanced at it before dropping it on the side table. "Would you like a cup of tea?"

"Yes, thank you." Lydia took off her shawl, draping it over the rocker near the door. "I don't believe we've shared a cup of tea in months."

"Is Father with Sayer?" Rebeccah asked, her voice unusually soft.

"Yes. He's having a nice visit with Sergeant Carmichael. There's no need to worry. I'm sure the colonel will sleep most of the day." Lydia watched as her sister prepared the tea. Perhaps what Don Fernando said was true—that he suspected the colonel and her sister were very much in love. Lydia cast a curious glance at the letter on the table, wondering about her sister's lack of interest before she turned her attention back on Becky. "How is Edmund these days?"

Her sister looked haggard, but managed to shrug her shoulders. "Well."

"That's all? Well? I should have thought he'd be counting the days until your return." When Becky didn't answer, Lydia frowned. Perhaps Don Fernando was just jumping to conclusions. The colonel wasn't at all her sister's type. The handsome Mexican rancher had only known her sister for a few months. He didn't know Becky had always been the one to play it safe. He couldn't know that she never ventured too far from the ordinary. Never wanted more than a quiet, peaceful home in the English countryside, with a quiet, peaceful husband and well-mannered children. In fact, when Lydia had learned about the engagement, she realized the man was perfect for her sister—secure in his father's business with a small estate in Colchester. But why, Lydia wondered, if that were so, did Becky ignore her fiancé's letter and look so utterly wretched?

Lydia sat down at the table when her sister carried over the little pot and two cups. "You look tired. Didn't you sleep well?" she began, intent on getting some answers.

"Not very," her sister confessed, still standing.

Lydia frowned as she poured a little cream into her cup. "Something's bothering you, and it's not just lack of sleep. What is it?"

"Nothing."

Nothing, Lydia thought suspiciously. Perhaps she was wrong. Perhaps it was the colonel's condition that had her sister so distraught. Perhaps Fernando was right. With that assumption,

Lydia hurried to ease her sister's fears. "If you're worried about the colonel, Papa is confident that he will—"

"Oh, Lydia," Rebeccah sobbed. "What am I to do?"

Lydia blinked back her confusion as she stood and wrapped her arms around her sister. "Poor dear," she managed to say as her sister wept on her shoulder. "Come now, let's sit down." Lydia guided Rebeccah to the settee, and when they sat, she pulled out a clean handkerchief from her pocket and pressed it in her sister's palm. "Here, dry your eyes, Beebee."

Rebeccah's head snapped up. "Y-you haven't called me that since . . . since—"

"Since you were a very little girl." Lydia waited patiently while her sister composed herself. "Now, tell me why you're so unhappy."

"Well," Rebeccah began, her voice catching a little. "As you know, I didn't want to come to America."

"That's putting it rather gently," Lydia confirmed.

"I was very happy back in England, Lydie. I was looking forward to my marriage and . . . and I was looking forward to being free from Grandmama's control." Rebeccah sniffed and dabbed at her eyes. "Then Mother died." More tears trickled down Rebeccah's cheeks. "And . . . although I know she wouldn't have done it on purpose . . . she r-ruined my life."

Once more, Lydia consoled her sister, patting her back and offering gentle support. "Has it really been that bad?" Their eyes met and for the first time, Lydia actually saw her sister's pain. "Oh dear, my poor little Beebee. The year will be over soon, I promise. We'll both sail for England, and I'll help you plan your wedding. We'll have a wonderful time."

"No," her sister cried. "That's not what I want anymore."

Lydia frowned. "You've told me time and time again that you're engaged. I thought you were counting the days until you could return to Edmund and be married."

"His name is Edward, and will you stop speaking about him?" Rebeccah asked a little hopelessly. "This isn't about Edward, it's about Sayer and . . . and me."

Lydia started to speak, then closed her mouth for a moment to ponder what her sister just said. When the silence stretched out uncomfortably, she finally found her voice. "Rebeccah, did you just imply that you and Sayer are romantically involved?"

"Yes . . . no . . . not intimately, but certainly I care deeply for him, and I believe he feels the same way about me."

Lydia stifled a relieved sigh. "Then I don't see a problem. Of course, you'll have to break things off with Edmund—"

"Edward."

Lydia blinked at her sister's impatience. "Yes, I meant Edward. You can't let the poor man wait forever. You'll have to send him word right away, and of course, you'll have to send him back his ring." Lydia glanced at her sister's bare finger. "You haven't gone and lost it, have you?"

Rebeccah shook her head. "Do you think I could just send it back with a letter? That doing so wouldn't be considered imprudent?"

"I don't believe it would. And the sooner the better," Lydia countered. She stood and brought over their tea. "Now, tell me, when did you realize you were attracted to the colonel?"

Her sister dabbed at her eyes and shrugged her shoulders. "I-I'm not quite sure. I suppose it was that very first time we went riding and . . . and he taught me how to fish."

"Really?" Lydia exclaimed. "I don't believe it. Did you actually touch a worm?" She smiled when her sister gave a wobbly grin.

"Heavens, no. He baited my hook for me, but I did catch a fish all by myself." The expression on her younger sibling's face matched the one she'd get when she was a very little girl and managed to button her own dress or comb her own hair. Lydia was just about to speak when Rebeccah began again. "Then there was the time when he taught me how to shoot—"

"Shoot? A gun?" Once more Lydia couldn't believe what she was hearing as Rebeccah told her about the day Sayer and she had spent in the meadow, and afterwards, when they had just talked quietly around the fire after lunch. On and on Rebeccah talked, as if a dam had been opened, and all of a sudden Lydia's passive little sister was telling her how she was suddenly, sometimes reluctantly experiencing life.

"My goodness," Lydia said when Rebecca finally paused. "It sounds as if you've had a wonderful time together. Has he asked you to marry him yet?" Lydia nearly spilled her tea when her sister broke into tears all over again. "Oh, dear," she muttered, taking her sister's cup before it toppled. "Now what's the problem?" she asked as she placed the cups on the side table.

"I'm afraid, Lydie . . . terribly afraid." Rebeccah stared at her hands, huge tears pooling in her eyes.

"That he will . . . or won't?"

"Please, don't confuse the issue." Rebeccah wouldn't look at her. "Do you remember when we first arrived at Father's house?"

Lydia nodded, trying to make sense out of what her sister was saying.

"You said that soldiers don't live long enough to grow old with their wives, and," Rebeccah said, her voice growing more and more pathetic, "now I believe you."

It was several moments before Lydia could persuade Rebeccah to stop weeping. Finally, after retrieving another handkerchief from her sister's bureau, Lydia had Rebeccah calmed down. "Rebeccah Randolph, I'm ashamed of you." Her sister's head snapped up and when she saw her haggard appearance, Lydia very nearly lost the courage to continue. "You have never listened to me, and now you're telling me that you did once, and worse, you believed me."

Lydia gave her sister an exasperated look. "It was rubbish, pure rubbish. I made it up to avoid answering your questions, as I knew you were attracted to him the moment you laid eyes on him. I only said it to keep you from thinking I wanted him for myself. Why, look at Sergeant Carmichael," she hurried to add. "He's at least as old as Papa . . . and . . . and what about Papa? He was a soldier for many years, remember?"

Rebeccah nodded, gazing up with red-rimmed eyes, making Lydia feel as if she were her mother rather than her sister. "Colonel MacLaren is a strong man. Although he's gravely injured, he won't be down forever, Becky. You should stop worrying."

"I'm trying," Rebeccah said in a small voice, standing to warm her hands near the fire. "Really I am. You don't understand. I was just getting used to his being a soldier, counting the days until he was released from the army, and now this happened." She turned and wrapped her arms around herself. "I'm not strong like you. I'm weak and selfish. I couldn't bear it if I lost him. What if I hadn't found him by the river? He'd . . . he'd be dead, Lydie."

Lydia heaved an impatient sigh. "Becky, you don't know that for sure. He was on his way back—might have made it back nonetheless. We don't know the future or why things happen the way they do. We must simply take each day as it comes and hope for the best. If what Don Fernando says is true, Colonel MacLaren is very much in love with you. And, from what you've told me and the way you're acting, I think you care a little more than you're willing to admit." Lydia crossed over and put her arms around her sister and gave her a little squeeze. "Surely the times you've shared and will share . . . surely that's enough for now . . . until you sort out your feelings."

"Sometime I think it is enough, then other times I'm not so

certain." Rebeccah turned and stared into the fire once more. "I have always wondered why Mother just didn't pack our things and bring us back to be with Father, but now I think I know." She took a calming breath. "I think, although she dearly loved our father, a part of her was afraid . . . just like me. I think she hated the thought that as a soldier, Father would kill to protect us, just as I hate knowing Sayer has killed and would do so again if necessary. I think she worried that one day he would ride away and she'd never see him alive again."

"Becky, don't punish yourself like this. You said yourself that Sayer won't always be a soldier. From what Sergeant Carmichael has told me, as well as Fernando, Sayer wants to settle close by and raise horses."

"Yes, he mentioned it to me also."

Lydia heaved an impatient sigh. "This isn't England and it never will be. This is the American West, Becky. It's as wild and untamed as the colonel himself, and I rather doubt that you'd be happy even if you convinced yourself to return to Edward."

Lydia shook her head. "You may spend your days with Edward on his comfortable, safe estate, but your heart will always be here . . . in these mountains . . . with Sayer."

Lydia stayed with her sister the rest of the morning. By noon, she left briefly to inquire about the colonel's welfare. On the way she snapped the stems of half a dozen wild sunflowers and carried them inside. Rita found a vase and after Lydia arranged them, she entered the colonel's room and placed the cheerful flowers on the table.

"How is he?" she asked, peeking over her father's shoulder while he snipped at the bandage on the colonel's leg. The colonel, she decided, was a boldly handsome man, even ill. No wonder her sister fell in love so easily.

"He's holding his own, but his blasted fever isn't letting up any," her father said. "Don't tell Becky, but I half expected to find him dead this morning." Her father shook his head. "But he fooled me. He's a lot tougher than I thought. Fetch me some hot water, hon."

"Wouldn't it be best just to leave him be for another day?" she asked.

Her father shook his head and continued snipping at the bandage. "Not this one, hon. Arrow wounds aren't like gunshot wounds. Though I'm pretty sure I got the arrow out nice and clean, there's always the risk of missing something."

"Like what?"

"Well, like a chip or a splinter off the arrow itself, or a tiny piece of cloth torn from the colonel's breeches when it when through into his leg." She inwardly shuddered at the pictures her father had conjured in her mind as she helped him remove the old padding of cloth.

"Well?" she asked with a worried frown.

"Looks good," he confirmed. He cleaned the wound before he dressed it, then pulled the covers over the colonel and tucked them around his chest. "In fact, it looks a lot better than I expected."

By the time they finished, the colonel stirred and slowly opened his eyes. It was painfully obvious that he was still very sick, muttering his displeasure and trying to get more comfortable.

"Rest easy, son," her father crooned in a soft and gentle voice, bathing the colonel's face with a cool cloth. All business one moment and all kindness the next, her father's bedside manner impressed Lydia. The next moment the door opened and Don Fernando stepped inside.

"Dr. Randolph, Rita has made a fresh pot of coffee and some biscuits. There's butter and honey."

Lydia took the cloth. "Here," she said, sitting on the edge of the bed. "You go. I'll stay with him."

"Well, maybe I will," James said, washing his hands and drying them before he pulled down his shirtsleeves. After he left, Lydia gazed down at her sister's soldier and continued to bathe his face with cool water. He felt hot to the touch, and when his eyes slowly opened they were glazed with fever and pain.

"Becky?" he asked hoarsely.

Lydia gave him a sympathetic smile. "No, Colonel. I'm Lydia." She wasn't sure if he understood at first, but then he gave a very slight nod.

"Yes, ma'am." Again he was quiet for a long time, but she knew he wasn't asleep. "If I could trouble you for some water."

"Oh, it's no trouble," she hurried to reply. She quickly filled a cup and carried it to the bed. Doing the best she could to support his back, she helped him hold the cup while he drank his fill. When he was through, he gave a soft groan when she eased him back down.

"I can give you something for the pain," she said, dabbing at the beads of sweat on his forehead.

"No . . . ma'am. I'm fine," he said, his gaze steady under heavy lids. Again a long time passed before he spoke. "Where's Becky?" he asked, and she knew he was disappointed that she wasn't there. "Is she safe?"

"Yes, of course. We all are. She's resting right now, but she's been very concerned about you."

"You, Becky and James, you must go, and take the women and children with you." The urgent edge to his voice gave her cause for alarm.

"Colonel, please, calm down. There are no savages here." She tried to say the right things, but he grew increasingly restless.

"You must believe me . . . deep down inside we are all savages."

It was then that she knew he was still seeing things that didn't exist. When he tried to toss aside the covers, Lydia caught his hand. "Colonel MacLaren, you're sick. You mustn't get out of bed."

"No," he argued, trying to push her aside, but too weak to be much of a threat to her. "There are women and children in danger. For God's sake, let me go. Can't you see them?"

"You're dreaming," she replied in an authoritative tone. "I shan't have you falling out of bed. Now lie down." She pushed against his chest.

"I-I've got to—" He squeezed his eyes tightly closed, then pressed his fingers against the bandage on his head as he collapsed against the pillows. "No, Pa, not the children . . ." His breathing was fast and shallow, as if he were running. Then a moment later his voice dropped to a contemptuous whisper. "Y-you bastard. You . . . killed the little children . . . you killed them all."

Lydia stifled a gasp, realizing that as he swore several more times, he was lost in a dream. A muscle jumped in his jaw at the same time his eyes snapped open, and she very nearly cried out in pain from his grip on her hand. As the pressure eased, his eyes cleared as he focused once more on her face. Sensing he was suffering from two kinds of pain, she started to rise to get some laudanum, but he wouldn't let go. "Please . . . don't leave me," he whispered.

"I won't," she promised, patting the back of his hand, but still he held her tightly. "Just rest. I'll stay right here."

And she did, holding his hand and bathing his face until the fever broke and he finally drifted into a deep, healing sleep. When his fingers went slack, she slipped free and moved to the chair, thinking about what he had said. When she could make no sense of it, she strolled to the fire and added a few more logs. It wouldn't do to have him catch a chill now that his fever was so much better. A soft knock sounded on the door and when she turned, Sergeant Carmichael stood in the opening, his hat crunched in his big meaty hand.

"I was just comin' tae see if you'd like a breather," Fergus said with a warm smile.

"Come in, Sergeant. He's asleep, but if you don't mind, I'd like to talk with you for a while."

Several hours later, Lydia found herself standing on the veranda gazing out at the sunset, deep in thought. In England, she'd read many stories about Indians and the wars fought between them and the United States Army, but until now, she'd never put real people and real faces to the men who were involved. She pulled her shawl a little tighter. No wonder her poor sister was in such turmoil. The man she loved had been and was still a very brave soldier, and according to Sergeant Carmichael, this wasn't the colonel's first brush with death.

"*Buenos noches, Señorita* Randolph."

Lydia glanced over her shoulder to see Don Fernando walking toward her. "Good evening," she replied with a smile. "It's a glorious evening, isn't it?"

The rancher gazed out at the horizon and nodded. "Indeed." He turned and leaned back against the waist-high wall. "I have asked your father, but like the good doctor he is, he gives me no valid answer."

"What do you mean?" she asked.

"I mean, I want to know if the colonel will live?"

Lydia nodded with understanding. "Yes," she said with firm conviction. "He's a very strong man, and while I sat with him this afternoon, his fever broke. Now it's only a matter of time. We should see some improvement every day, I assure you." She returned Fernando's smile. "Now, for my father. You must remember he's a doctor, and doctors and nurses learn very quickly how to skirt around certain questions."

"And why is that?" Fernando asked.

"Well, first, we're only human. Secondly, it's as difficult for us to predict whether a patient will do well or do poorly as it is for anyone. I personally see no benefit in telling someone the worst, so we use half-truths to keep hope alive."

"Ah, I see." Fernando twisted the edges of his moustache. "You and your papa are very wise. Without hope, we have nothing." He heaved a long sigh. "So tell me, what is it you hope for?"

Lydia gave a small laugh. "I'm not sure. What about you?"

"Me?"

She nodded.

"I hope to see my daughters grow up to be very beautiful and successful young ladies, like you and your sister."

Lydia felt the heat of a blush. "Why thank you, Don Fernando. As for me . . . I hope—"

Fernando's daughter burst through the door and ran into her father's arms with a big smile. "Papa, come quickly," the little girl said breathlessly. "Doctor Randolph says *Tio* is better, and the doctor wants to play a game of chess."

"Well then," Fernando agreed, kissing his giggling little girl. "We had better not keep the good doctor waiting."

Lydia watched them go inside then glanced in the direction of her sister's cottage. Heaving a contented sigh, she walked down the gravel path, all the while thinking about how excited Fernando's daughter was and how easily she got her father to follow her inside. Lydia knocked on the door, smiling as a plan formed.

"Rebeccah?" she called. "It's me, Lydie. Hurry, open the door. The colonel is better and he's asking for you."

Chapter Fifteen

By the time Rebeccah changed her dress and arranged her hair, her spirits were much lighter. Lydia sat on the bed, chatting about various things, but always, it seemed to Rebeccah, her sister especially liked telling her how much Sergeant Carmichael and Don Fernando liked the colonel.

"Why, even the little girls seem to love him," Lydia added. "The older one, Elena, she called him *tío*. Do you know what that means?"

"Uncle," Rebeccah stated as she smoothed the folds of her gown. "When he visits, he brings them presents."

"They say men who are kind to little children make wonderful husbands."

Rebeccah cast her sister a skeptical glance. "Really. I don't recall ever hearing that, but . . ." She picked up her shawl and slipped it on. ". . . I'll give you the benefit of the doubt, as I happen to agree." Rebeccah led the way to the door, glancing at the vase of flowers Rita had brought over earlier. "Do you think these will brighten up his room?"

"Why, of course. What a wonderful idea." Lydia's smile was almost too bright.

Rebeccah entered Sayer's room carrying the vase of colorful wild flowers. Only after she nodded to Fergus and approached the table by the window, did she see another vase full of sunflowers. Instantly she realized why her sister had seemed so jovial as they walked to the main house. "Wonderful idea, indeed," Rebeccah muttered under her breath.

"Well now," Fergus said, casting a glance over his shoulder. "Maybe now that you're here, he'll settle down and mind his manners." The weathered old soldier was coaxing Sayer to take a glass containing a small amount of liquid. "Take this and drink it," the Scotsman ordered as she carried her flowers to the bedside table.

"I don't want it." Sayer was propped up against the pillows, and by his appearance, he'd been shaved, and as her father had mentioned in the hall, his bandages had been freshly changed.

"It will ease your pain and—"

"That it does, but it clouds my mind, and I'd like to remember what happened," Sayer said, gritting his teeth as he tried to get more comfortable. He swore under his breath, and she knew the moment she looked at him that he was using every ounce he could muster to keep from yelling at the kindly sergeant, who still stubbornly held out the glass. Rebeccah hurried over and lifted it from his hand, speaking so that only he could hear.

"I'll see he takes it later." She placed the glass on the table next to the flowers, then forced a bright smile as she inquired about her soldier's health.

"I'm fine," Sayer said a little tersely. She knew he wasn't annoyed with her, but the fact that Fergus still stood behind her, glaring at him.

"He's not either," Fergus countered. "His leg is—"

"Is just fine," Sayer finished.

"If you'd take the laudanum—"

"Damn it, Sergeant. I told you, I'm not taking—" He moved a little, and again he swore, only louder this time. "Don't you have something to do?" Sayer demanded, placing his hand over the thick bandage on his shoulder.

Fergus matched Sayer's dark look. The angrier the sergeant became, the more pronounced his brogue. "I'm tellin' you, lad. If'n the pain isna better tomorrow, I'm no' waitin'. I'll be sendin' for the gude doctor, and he'll be tellin' you what tae do, no' me."

"Now, now, *mis amigos,*" Fernando said, stepping into the room with a cup of steaming broth. He placed the broth on the table by the flowers, and then put his hand on the sergeant's shoulder. "Sergeant Carmichael, Rita has baked a fresh apple pie for our dessert. I suggest we go and have some, so that *Señorita* Rebeccah can spend a few quiet moments with the colonel while he has some soup. Don't you agree?"

"Yes," Rebeccah encouraged. "I think that you'd enjoy a cup of coffee and some pie." Fergus gave a disgusted snort before Don Fernando coaxed him out of the room, winking at her as he pulled the door closed.

"You look better," she began, standing to retrieve the soup. "How are you feeling . . ." She glanced at him over her shoulder, noticing in the lamplight the beads of sweat that dotted his brow. "And don't lie to me."

"I would never lie to you," he said, his voice softer than normal. "I'm just tired." He rested his head wearily back against the pillows and closed his eyes, but she could tell he was too uncomfortable to sleep. Shielding his view with her back, she poured the laudanum into the soup then carried it over to the bedside.

"Here, I think Rita sent this with strict orders to finish it . . . all of it."

Sayer clenched his jaw when he moved to accept the cup. "I'd rather have pie," he said, taking several sips of the broth before he had to rest. His eyes drifted closed, but she could tell he wasn't asleep by the way he held the cup.

"Sergeant Carmichael only wants to help. He doesn't mean

to be so annoying."

"Yes. I know." Sayer opened his eyes and she felt a little uncomfortable by the intensity of his gaze. "Becky, I-I can't remember. Where did you find me?"

"If you drink more broth, I'll tell you." After he took several more sips, she continued. "Do you remember where you first taught me how to fish?" His tired nod told her he knew. Again she coaxed him to take more nourishment, and again he complied, resting the near-empty cup in his lap.

"My men . . . what happened to them?" he asked, his voice edged with despair. "Fergus won't talk to me. He just tells me to rest."

"Father told him not to say anything to upset you. He's just trying to obey orders."

"I need to know."

"Very well. Sergeant Carmichael told me that you sent them on ahead after you found the farmer's cow. Nearly all of your men were getting ready to go back for you when they heard that you'd been hurt and that I had brought you here."

He seemed to be overcome with relief, closing his eyes and sinking deeper into the mound of pillows. He lay quiet for several long moments, then gazed up at her from under heavy lids. "Had you not come along—"

She pressed her fingertips against his mouth. "Shush. Please, don't. I couldn't bear it if anything happened to you. That's why you must do everything you can to get better." She took the soup cup and placed it on the table, then took hold of his hand once more. He pulled her closer.

"Becky," he whispered. "Promise . . . promise you won't leave quite yet."

"I-I promise." His eyes drifted closed, and a moment later he fell sound asleep. She didn't know how long she sat motionless, holding his hand, concentrating on the steady rise and fall of his chest as she willed herself to be strong. He would live, and in time make a full recovery, but would she? Later, when she went to bed and it was dark and quiet, would she see his face, hear his desperate plea? She took a ragged breath.

"I'm not strong like Lydia," she murmured, brushing a lock of hair from Sayer's forehead. "I've never craved adventure. All I ever wanted was a modest home with a good man and children—lots of children."

Are you planning to have a large family? Sayer's voice whispered in her head. *After you're married, of course.* She closed her eyes remembering that day at the party—his teasing expression—his lazy smile. *Isn't having a family something two people who are planning to marry discuss before the wedding?*

She opened her eyes and smiled sadly. "I'm not sure there will be a wedding."

After you've married your English dandy. . . . A picture of Sayer grinning at her from the back of his horse warmed her, yet at the same time chilled her to the bone. "I suppose he is a dandy compared to you," she answered aloud. *You could come for a visit . . . show him the things I have shown you.* Hot tears stung her eyes as she leaned closer and placed a kiss on Sayer's mouth, then gently caressed his cheek. "I could never share those things with another man."

After a while, she rose and crossed the short distance to the big leather chair Fergus had pushed close to the hearth. Sinking down into it, she closed her eyes, and with the feel of Sayer's lips lingering on her own, she remembered another time.

Rebeccah had no way of knowing how long she dozed. She only knew that she thought she had heard the door open and close. Curious about who could have come in, she peeked over the chair. Much to her surprise, Renato stood by the bed holding a pillow.

"Is there something wrong?" Rebeccah asked as she came to her feet and stepped around the chair.

"Begging your pardon, *Señorita*." Renato placed the extra pillow on the bed then snatched up the water pitcher. "Rita sent me to get fresh water for the colonel for the night, but then when I saw him, I thought that he looked uncomfortable with all those pillows, so I took one away. See, he rests easier for it, *no?*"

Rebeccah walked over and sat on the edge of the bed, agreeing that Sayer did indeed look more comfortable. "Thank you," she said, "for your kindness."

"If there is anything I can do for you, *Señorita*, please, do not hesitate to ask." He left before she could reply.

The next day, while her father changed Sayer's bandages, Rebeccah decided to take a little walk. Inhaling a deep breath of fresh fall air, she headed in the direction of the stables. She pulled her shawl a little tighter as she leaned against the railing, watching as Brandy munched hay in her stall. Her gaze roamed over the other horses, then down to the dirt floor as she remembered how Sayer had taught her to track, saying that if they ever got separated she'd be able to find him if she followed Rounder's tracks.

"Here, see this mark?" he'd asked as he knelt by the path. "That's Rounder's hoofprint. You can tell his from Brandy's because of this." He pointed to a small US indentation in the soft soil. "Property of the United States Government, just like me."

Now as she gazed idly at the many tracks inside the barn, she found Rounder's prints. There were others too, but only Rounder's stood out.

"I have been looking for you," came Don Fernando's deep

voice, drawing her away from the tracks. She turned with a smile.

"Your father is a good doctor. The colonel is getting better, and you and he will soon be riding into the mountains again. This I know, because I am a very wise man." His expression made her laugh. "Come. I told him I would find you. If we take too long in returning, I fear he will grow even more jealous and send the sergeant after us."

She gave Fernando an admonishing smile. "Why should he be jealous? We are only good friends, remember?" Fernando's soft laughter warmed her heart. Together they walked toward the house.

"*Si*, I tried to tell him that myself, but when a man is in love, he does not always listen to what another man says." Fernando urged her on. "Come. We must not keep him waiting. He is the type who will come for you himself if he thinks I am taking too long."

On the third day, Lydia and their father prepared to leave. Rebeccah stood patiently as her father told her how and when to change the bandages. "If you see any redness, or if the swelling doesn't go down, send for me. He's been complaining that he can't remember what happened. I'm worried he'll try to get up too soon, just to go back and see if he can find any clues that will help his memory."

"That's not possible," Rebeccah replied fearfully.

"Of course it isn't. Furthermore, Don Fernando isn't about to let him. I only told you so you could steer him away from such foolishness." James put his medical bag behind the seat. "I've left you some salve and a small bottle of laudanum. If he tries to do too much or the pain gets bad, give him a little in some soup or some tea. It'll have him sleeping like a baby for several hours."

Lydia gave her sister a hug and a kiss on the cheek. "When all of this is over, you'll come for a visit? And, who knows? Perhaps we can start to plan a military wedding?" Lydia accepted her father's help into the buggy, missing her father's baffled expression.

"I didn't know Edward was in the military," James stated, turning to Rebeccah.

"He's not, Father."

"Then what's this about a military wedding?"

"Lydia was just teasing, Father. A lady must first be asked to be married before she plans a wedding."

"Yes, of course," her father said as if he knew exactly what she meant. But he didn't, and that alone gave her a reason to smile as he scratched his head then climbed in beside Lydia. "Just remember, Becky. He isn't going to be up to doing much for a few weeks, and if he thinks he is, don't let him. Take my word for it, these young fellas can be mighty stubborn."

The moment Rebeccah entered Sayer's room, Rita gave her a big smile and hurried out the door. "She's either afraid of you or has something very important to do," Sayer said, his voice husky from sleeping. "Come here and help me with these danged pillows."

Rebeccah returned his smile as she sat on the side of the bed, and after fluffing and rearranging the pillows behind his back, took his hand. "Father says you should rest."

Sayer heaved a despondent sigh. "I don't want to sleep anymore."

"And why not? It's the only way you're going to get back your strength." She stood and filled a glass with some water.

His eyes closed for a moment, then slowly opened. "When I sleep, I see things in my dreams."

"What kind of things?" she asked, hoping if he told her she

might be able to help. She sat and gave him the glass, waiting while he took a drink.

"I see a man holding my pistol pointed at my chest." He paused, and she knew he was trying to sort through his thoughts. "I feel the impact, but there's no pain. I hear him shouting, but he has no face and I can't make out his words." He took another sip, and this time she noticed that his hand shook ever so slightly.

"Maybe you're trying too hard to remember," she said, aching to help him. "My father told me that people who've experienced a serious injury as you did . . . well, sometimes they choose to forget."

He looked at her, his expression growing even more somber. "But I want to remember. If what you say is true, and I'm doing this to myself, then why can't I stop?"

"I wish I knew, but I don't." She took his glass and placed it on the table. She would have stood, but Sayer caught her hand. "If I never remember what happened up on the mountain," he began, his voice almost distant, "it's all right as long as I always remember the times we've spent together. It's those memories that sustained me when I thought no help was coming."

She brushed her fingertips softly over his cheek. "I think you should stop worrying about your dreams and try to rest." When she stood, his hold on her hand tightened.

"Don't go, not yet." His smile didn't quite reach his eyes. "Have you seen Rounder?"

"Yes. He's doing well."

"None the worse for . . ." Sayer's voice fell away, but by the way his eyes grew darker, she knew he was immersed in thought.

"What is it?" she asked, almost afraid to break the silence.

"I-I was trying to get to Rounder when they found me. I was worried they'd take him." Sayer's voice was vague, his expression fathomless.

"They?" she repeated. "How many were there?" she heard herself ask, even though she didn't really want to know.

"Two . . . no . . . three. I think I shot one, but . . . but . . ." He heaved a tired sigh. "I can't remember." He was silent for a long time, then, as if he had to force himself away from his morbid thoughts, he turned his attention back to her with a strained smile. "Rounder's a good horse. The next time you go down to the barn, take him an apple. He loves them."

"I'll be sure to do that," she said, uncomfortable under the intensity of his gaze. She resisted the urge to kiss him goodbye, telling herself that once things were settled with Edward and her grandmother, she would be free to tell him how much she loved him. She had no sooner made her decision than he caressed the back of her hand with his thumb. His small, simple touch brought her to him immediately, and before she realized what she was doing, she leaned closer and accepted his kiss.

CHAPTER SIXTEEN

Rebeccah smoothed a strand of hair back into her chignon and took a step back from the mirror to inspect the fit of her gown. Her father had left a week ago, and since then almost every soldier from Fort Marcy had stopped by to see how their commander fared. Sometimes whole patrols would show up to share refreshments and stories.

Although she knew they were genuinely concerned, Sergeant Carmichael always followed them back to their horses, collecting his due from their bet. By the end of the second week, the sergeant left only after he promised Don Fernando that he'd be back in a few days to see if they needed anything.

Now, as she added the finishing touches to her hair, she smiled in anticipation. It had been nearly three weeks since she dressed for dinner and tonight, Don Fernando had made plans for the three of them to have a very special evening together. She found the matching green shawl and after one last look in the mirror, added a splash of perfume and stepped outside.

"*Señorita,*" Fernando called, drawing her attention. He came down the gravel path and took her hand into his warm one. "Ah, you look especially beautiful tonight, but," he said, putting his hand over his heart, "I suspect it is not for me, but the colonel, *si?*"

"I am simply setting the example," she countered, raising her chin and giving him a sweet smile.

"The example?" he inquired.

"Yes, an example. You see, I have taught your daughters that a lady always dresses for dinner. It simply wouldn't do if I didn't look my best, don't you agree?"

"Ah, I see. So, it is not for the colonel that you look so beautiful, but for the sake of my daughters?"

"Precisely."

His laughter made her smile. "I think I am having a little difficulty believing that. But if you say so, who am I to disagree?" He opened the door for her to enter his house. "Come, the colonel is waiting."

Rebeccah entered wondering if Fernando could hear the increased pounding of her heart. Clad in a long velvet robe, Sayer sat in an overstuffed leather chair, his right leg resting on a matching ottoman with his knee braced by a fluffy pillow, his left arm cradled in a sling. Rita had just finished covering him with a colorful blanket, smiling at the handsome soldier as he thanked her.

"Look who I have brought," Fernando stated, drawing Sayer's attention. He never looked at his host, only at her, and she felt the warmth of a blush creep up her neck into her cheeks at the intensity of his vivid blue eyes.

"I'd stand, as a gentleman should, but I'm—"

"Oh, no, don't," she interrupted, coming to his side. When he offered his good hand, she took it, her stomach giving a little flip as he brushed his thumb back and forth over her fingers.

"You look beautiful, as usual," he said, giving her a lazy grin.

"And you still look pale. You should be in bed, not wasting your strength like this."

"Surely, he must eat." Fernando filled a glass from the decanter. "Here, *amigo*," he said with a grin. "For the pain." He filled one for himself and poured a sherry for her, handing her the dainty glass. "A toast, to good friends, *si?*" They all touched glasses and in unison, repeated the toast then drank.

After dinner, Fernando had Rita move a small table close to Sayer's chair, where they placed the chessboard. In a short time it became obvious that Sayer's mind wasn't on the game. Though he had been talkative at dinner, he was now unusually quiet, and soon Fernando had him in checkmate.

Rebeccah stood and took the throw from Sayer's lap. "Come. You've been too sick to stay up any longer."

Don Fernando tossed the last of his brandy down this throat and stood. "I think the *señorita* is right. You would never have lost so easily if you weren't still recovering."

"Rita," Fernando called, and she instantly appeared. He told her something in Spanish and a few moments later, Jose stepped into the room. "Come, the colonel needs help back to his bed."

Rebeccah inwardly winced when Sayer clenched his jaw as Fernando took a gentle hold of his injured arm while Jose took hold of the other to assist him to his feet.

"Good night," she said, placing a chaste kiss on Sayer's cheek.

"I will see you home next time," he promised. She watched as they disappeared down the dimly lit hall. A few moments later, Jose and Fernando came back. Fernando thanked Jose, and then showed him to the door.

"I thought it was too soon," she said, twisting her hands into a knot as she turned back to Fernando. "Now I'm sure of it."

"Do not frown at me," Fernando said lifting his brows innocently. "It was his idea, not mine. I tried to talk him out of it, but he insisted."

"You should have refused," she admonished, pacing before the fire. "What if he has a relapse?"

Fernando heaved an impatient sigh. "The last time your papa was here, he said he could get up for short periods." Fernando threw up his arms. "You know the colonel as well as I. He is as stubborn as an ox. I could not dissuade him." Fernando refilled his glass. "When will you believe me, hey?"

"Believe you? About what?" she challenged, accepting another sherry.

"The man would endure more than just a little pain to be with the woman he loves."

Rebeccah spun around. "Will you stop insisting that he is in love with me? You are giving me a headache."

Fernando shrugged. "I am merely stating the obvious. And you, as you have been doing for weeks now, are refusing to accept it. Why, I do not know. I suspect that by denying the truth, you think it will make it easier to leave him when the time comes."

"I am not leaving him," she countered, growing angry. "Sayer may have deep feelings for me, but he has never said he loves me."

"Aha, that is it, isn't it?"

"I don't know what you're talking about." She crossed her arms over her breast. "Once again, you are jumping to conclusions."

"Am I? I think not. You, my little dove, are unwilling to admit the colonel loves you because he has not said so himself." Fernando gave a satisfied nod. "Now I see your predicament. It is a matter of pride, is it not?"

"No, it is not. Pride is a man's weakness, not a woman's."

The next week went by quickly. A visit from her father confirmed that Sayer was indeed well on the road to recovery. James stayed at Fernando's ranch for a few hours, then, stating that he had other, more needy patients, climbed into his buggy and drove away. No sooner had he disappeared than Sergeant Carmichael rode up.

"I've brought his mail," the sergeant proclaimed as he swung off the giant horse he always rode. He patted the roan affectionately, and then, pushing his hat off his head, heaved a long sigh. "The air's a wee bit fresher out here. Why, I bet the colonel is itchin' tae be outside."

It was those words that started Rebeccah thinking. While the sergeant visited with Sayer, she sought out Fernando with what she thought was a reasonable request.

"I am not the one to take him for a drive," Fernando argued. "You should do it." He scratched the wolf's ears. "This fellow should go, too."

"But I don't know how to drive a buggy," Rebeccah protested, trying her best to convince Fernando that the fresh air would be good for Sayer as she dodged a lick from the pup.

"*Si,* it will do him good. But it will do him more good if you take him, not I."

"You are impossible," she finally cried. "Perhaps I can convince the sergeant to take him outside." She lifted her chin defiantly and headed down the hall toward Sayer's room. Knocking before she entered, she gave both men a smile. This time, instead of finding Sayer in bed, she discovered him clad in his borrowed robe, sitting in the overstuffed leather chair that the sergeant had pushed closer to the window.

"How are you feeling today?" she asked as she came over and sat on the arm of the chair, placing the pup in his lap. Sayer dodged several licks but wasn't as successful on the last one. Laughing, he wiped his chin, then took her hand and placed a kiss on the back.

"Better, now that you're here."

"I'd best be gettin' back, Colonel," the sergeant said as he got up from the window seat. He bent and scratched the pup's fuzzy head.

"Oh, please. Don't let me chase you away," Rebeccah hurried to say, her hopes that the sergeant would take Sayer outdoors dying a miserable death.

"I'd stay if I could," Fergus said, "but there's things tae do that canna wait." He saluted his commander, more for her sake than Sayer's, she felt sure, then jammed his hat on his head and left.

"You look like someone just took away your doll," Sayer said.

"Do I?" she asked, forcing a bright smile. "I thought you'd enjoy Kaiser's company for a little while. He's not too heavy on your leg, is he?"

"No, not at all. In fact, I missed him."

"Good, then you two have a nice visit. I've got something I need to do too."

Sayer heard the door open and close. When he felt sure he was alone, he tucked the pup in the crook of his arm and lifted the folded paper from his lap. Once more he read it through, and once more he heaved a disgruntled sigh. As soon as he was fully recovered, he had to report for duty at Fort Riley. Although he'd known that eventually he would have to leave, he had hoped for more time. He tucked his orders into his pocket and sank his fingers into the pup's silky fur. "You're nice and fat," he murmured to the pup as it grew sleepy. The wolf pup yawned and snuggled close to Sayer and fell asleep.

Rebeccah leaned on the railing near the barn as she watched Fernando drive a horse and buggy around the paddock after her first attempt failed. "See, it is easy. Now come." He waved her over and helped her up onto the seat next to him.

"I'm really not dressed for this," she complained.

"I promise. You will not get dirty." He waited until she smoothed her ruffled skirt. "Here, hold the reins in both hands. Pull right, turn right, pull left, and turn left, pull back to stop. It is simple, *si?*"

"Yes, I think I can do it."

Fernando laughed. "I remember not so long ago that you didn't think you could ride, and now you are a confident horse-woman. I am proud of you."

"Thank you," she said. Reluctantly, she grabbed the reins and slapped them on the horse's rump, catching her breath when the buggy lurched forward.

"Not so hard next time," Fernando scolded. "I do not want the colonel scared to death."

"Would you like for me to help you back to bed?" came Rita's voice.

"I'll be fine for a little while longer," Sayer replied, unwilling to disturb the pup. The window offered him a generous view. In the distance, the rugged peaks of the mountains beckoned to him, as if they were as anxious as he to have him remember what had happened on the day he was injured. Only when something moved did he realize that someone was driving a buggy in the paddock to the right of the window. By the way the horse stopped often, started with a jolt and nearly ran into the fence, it was obvious that the driver was just learning. Squinting against the sun, Sayer leaned a little closer. His amused smile grew when he saw pink skirts and ruffles.

Fernando took hold of Rebeccah's hands and while she held the reins, he showed her how hard to pull to stop and how hard to tap to begin. Around and around the arena they went until she did it all by herself. By the end of the two hours, she drove the horse down the road and back without a bit of trouble.

"That was very good," Fernando commended as he helped her down. "I will have Rita cook something special for your picnic tomorrow."

Stubborn orange and gold leaves clung hopelessly to the trees while others covered the paths and trails. Though early November had many warm days, cold winds and pelting rains plagued the nights. A gentle breeze ruffled Rebeccah's hair as she hurried outside with a colorful Navajo blanket over her arm.

She placed the blanket behind the seat with a basket filled with food. These past few weeks she had learned that in the Territory of New Mexico the weather changed quickly and often violently. One moment it could be blowing dust, and the next a drenching rain could fill the arroyos with swiftly flowing rivers of muddy water that could wash away anything that dared to be in its path.

She looked up to see Sayer stepping out of the hacienda, leaning on a cane. Much to her surprise, he wore a clean uniform and freshly polished black boots. A yellow scarf was knotted loosely around his neck, adding to his masculine appeal. Except for the cane and a slight limp, he looked as if he'd never been injured. Fernando followed him with a rifle.

"Thanks," her soldier said as he accepted Fernando's help into the buggy. Sayer took the rifle and slipped it behind the seat. Rebeccah was by his side the next moment, taking the reins before he could. "Are you sure?" he asked, making her wonder why he would doubt her ability.

"Do not worry, *amigo*. While you slept like a baby, I taught the *señorita* how to drive." He gave them both a wide smile, brushing the ends of his moustache. "Just remember to hold on tight," he hollered as she urged the horse into a lively trot.

"It's a beautiful day," Sayer said, taking a long, deep breath. "It feels good to be out for a while."

Rebeccah flashed him a smile. "Where shall we go?"

Sayer contemplated her question, and then motioned toward the right fork in the road instead of their usual left. "Let's go this way." He leaned back and at the same time draped his arm on the back of the seat behind her.

They drove for several more miles, each content with the other's company. They passed a large rocky formation and the terrain grew a little more rugged, the road narrowing to two tracks with grass growing in the center. Scrubby junipers gave way to taller pines, and it seemed to Rebeccah that the air smelled a little fresher, the breeze felt a little crisper. "Shall I get the blanket for your legs?" she asked, her brow furrowed with concern.

Once more his smile warmed her all over. "No, thanks. I'm fine. When we get to that pile of stones, turn right."

She gave him another quick look. "Then you know this road?"

"Yes, ma'am. I do."

It had been so long since he used that expression, it dampened her high spirits. Had his long sickness and the fact that they hadn't been able to spend very much time alone destroyed the closeness they had shared? She turned the horse, speaking softly as Fernando had done to urge the animal back into its comfortable pace. Another hour passed—Sayer with his half smile, Rebeccah wondering if they could pick up where they left off.

"Here," he said, drawing her away from her gloomy thoughts. "Stop here."

She glanced around, spotting a run-down shack. Windows were broken and the door hung askew. The chimney was missing a few stones and there was a large hole in the roof. The front porch had a broken step and one post was missing, causing that portion of the roof to sag.

"Are you sure you want to stop here? I can hear running water. Perhaps we could drive a bit farther and eat by the river?" She quickly set the brake and tied the reins when Sayer began to get down. "Wait a moment and I'll help," she said, but he seemed to ignore her. She came around the buggy and slipped her arm under his, hoping to help keep his full weight off his leg.

"Well? What do you think?" His breath was warm against her ear as he tucked her closer to his side.

She frowned. "About the house?"

"Yes. What to you think about the house . . . my house?"

She cleared her throat. "Well," she said, trying very hard to be tactful. "Well, it's . . . certainly unique." His soft laughter caused a warm glow to spread through her body.

"Yes," she amended, feeling a little braver. "I believe with a little work and a little—" she ducked out from under his arm, giggling. "And a lot of prayer, it could be repaired." When he reached for her, she dashed away, regretting the moment he stepped wrong on his leg and fell onto the withered grass.

"Oh, my," she cried as she came to his aid, sinking down. She yelped when his strong arms came around and he rolled over, pinning her to the ground.

"A lot of prayer?" he repeated. His smile faded as his gaze slipped from her eyes to pause on her mouth. "I'm a believer," he murmured a moment before he bent his head and kissed her.

His lips were cool, persistent, and before she realized what she was doing, her arms encircled his neck and she kissed him back, basking in the knowledge that everything Don Fernando said was true. The way Sayer looked at her, the way his knuckles grazed her cheek as he gazed down at her, was all the proof she needed, and it both frightened her and delighted her at the same time.

"Sayer," she whispered, pushing him back ever so gently. "I-I—" His warm fingers stroked her lips.

"Shush, don't talk." He kissed her again, then stood and pulled her up with him. He took her hand, reached into the buggy and retrieved his cane and the basket. "I don't know about you, but I'm starving. What's in the basket?"

"Fried chicken." She frowned when he gave her a wounded look. "What's wrong?"

"It isn't Lydia, is it?" he asked with a horrified expression made comical by the twinkling in his eyes. "Tell me it's not."

She threw the blanket at him.

CHAPTER SEVENTEEN

They spread the blanket on the grass, and while they ate, Sayer shared with her his plans for the future. "I'm not going to re-enlist," he added, taking a bite of the delicious cinnamon and raisin bread Rita had packed. "I've decided that New Mexico is a good place to raise horses. It's not too hot in the summer, and from what I've been told, it's not bad in the winter."

Too soon their picnic was over, but instead of heading back, Sayer picked up his cane and walked slowly toward the cabin. "I wanted to bring you here before . . . well, before now. Thankfully, the weather has held."

He smiled encouragingly, even though she caught a glimpse of dark clouds gathering to the south. "I wanted you to be the first, except for me, of course, to see it." He pointed to a tree-covered hill. "I own that for as far as you can see, and there." He pointed to a sloping meadow, where she could see a stream winding down and out of sight. "That's mine, too, clear past the creek."

When she glanced at her soldier, she saw him with a new clarity. He was no longer a man in a uniform, but a man with hopes and dreams of making this piece of land his home. She remembered how he had teased her about finding the right woman and raising a bunch of kids, and suddenly the little house didn't look so bad. She pictured herself in his arms, wearing a white gown as he carried her over the threshold.

Once on the porch, Sayer extended his hand to help her up.

She took a step back and shook her head. "It looks like it might rain," she said, turning toward the buggy. "We should pick up our things and head back before we get wet."

"I want to show you the inside."

"Another time," she said, fully aware that her rejection wounded him.

"I know it looks like hell now, but someday . . ." She felt him close the gap, then he stood next to her, yet still she couldn't bring herself to look into those fathomless blue eyes. Only when he stopped and turned her, only when he put his knuckle under her chin, did she lift her eyes to his. "Becky, what's bothering you?" he asked, searching her face. Thunder rumbled in the distance as tears pooled in her eyes, causing his brows to snap together tightly. "If it's not to your liking, I'll sell—"

"No," she cried, blinking back tears. "It's beautiful here. It's what you told me you wanted . . . to raise horses and children . . . and—"

"Yes, I do, but none of that's important unless it's shared." Lightning cracked above and the earth seemed to shake with the thunder, but he held her fast, his eyes searching hers. "Becky, I—"

She held her breath, waiting for him to say the words she longed to hear. A cold rain began to pelt them. He hesitated for a moment longer then took her hand and pulled her toward the buggy.

"You're right. We'd better go."

The rain was icy, quickly drenching them as he helped her up into the seat then came around and settled next to her. He took the reins this time while she reached back and pulled the blanket over both their shoulders. By the time the ranch came into view they were soaked. "We should have waited another week," she confessed as he pulled the horse up to her door. "Don't you dare get out of this buggy until I can help you," she scolded.

She hurried around and helped him down and into the house. "What if your fever comes back?"

"It won't. I'm fine."

"I insist that you rest by the fire." She threw some kindling on the dying coals, and in a matter of moments they burst into flames. "I'm going to take the horse to the barn. I'll be back in a few moments."

Rebeccah opened the door, drenched and shivering. The room felt warm and toasty. Sayer dozed before the fire, the pup curled in a ball by his side. Though she tried to close the door as quietly as possible, his eyes slowly opened as she placed the borrowed basket on the table.

"Has it stopped raining?" he asked, leaning his head against the back of the settee to gaze at her.

"It's sprinkling. Are you warmer?" she asked as she came over to stand by the cheerful fire.

"Yes, but you won't be if you don't get dry soon." He stood and forced her to turn around. "Here, let me help you with those buttons." His fingers were warm against her wet skin. Before she could protest, he placed a kiss on her neck, just below her ear.

"I haven't thanked you for saving my life."

"Sayer, please," she whispered, cupping his cheek, but he placed his finger on her lips to quiet her.

"I haven't thanked you, because I can't find the words to express how I feel." He bent his head and kissed her at the same time he slipped the wet gown off her shoulders. The thin, wet chemise clung to every curve.

"God, but you're beautiful," he whispered when he pulled back and let his gaze wash over her. When she started to speak, his warm finger pressed against her lips once more. "I would have us share this time without you thinking about what's right or what's proper," he said, his voice soft and reassuring. "It's not right that I see in your eyes something different than what comes out your mouth." Once more he quieted her protest with a long, intoxicating kiss. "I don't care if you belong to someone else. He's not here, and if he were, I'd challenge his right to have you."

He stroked her cheek with his fingers, drawing them down her neck, then ever so lightly between her breasts. She sucked in her breath and caught his hand.

"Please," she implored, yet the moment she spoke the word, she wondered if she'd said it to make him stop or yearned for him to continue. His breath mingled with hers as he brushed his lips over her mouth for a moment before he kissed a path to the sensitive spot below her ear.

"Tell me you want me to stop," he whispered. "Say it, Becky. Tell me you want me to stop and I will."

But she didn't. And, even though she had been taught that a lady never surrenders to a man who isn't her husband, she couldn't deny that she wanted what he was doing to her—wanted his hands on her body and his sweet words of love whispered in her ear. He took her hand in his and led her into the bedroom.

He kissed her again then began to slowly undress her. His hands were warm, his fingers nimble, and where he touched her, her skin tingled. He tenderly pushed her down on the bed and began to remove his clothes. She trembled as he slowly removed his scarf and unbuttoned his shirt. A small bandage served as a reminder of how close she had come to losing him.

When he unbuckled his belt, she looked away, feeling the heat of a blush warm her neck and cheeks. Once he lay next to her, he pulled her close to receive his kiss. His gaze caressed every inch of her body as his hands smoothed over her skin.

"What of your wounds?" she whispered. His smile was answer enough.

"Tell me, Becky," he said again, his warm breath like velvet against her skin. "Tell me you want me as badly as I want you."

She gasped when his hand closed ever so gently around her breast, kneading and caressing as her nipple hardened against his palm. "I'm here and you're here, and that's all that matters."

Thunder rumbled, and the steady pelting of the rain mingled with his harsh breathing as his hand skimmed the silky plane of her belly, slowly, seductively inching lower. He caressed her hips and thighs, banishing any thought she might have had to resist. Her whole being ached to be with him, yet he lingered, taking his time, prolonging his pleasure and her anticipation.

When all she could think about was the delicious way he made her feel, he moved over her, warming her with the weight of his hard, muscular body. When she begged him to take her, he entered her, his gaze as soft as the finest silk, his expression incredibly tender as he told her everything would be all right, that the pain would go away; and she clung to his words while her body adjusted to his welcomed invasion.

Slowly, Sayer began to move, each thrust bringing her untried senses to life, awakening in her a need that drove all rational thoughts from her mind. All she could think about was Sayer. All she wanted was him, deeply inside her, his strong arms holding her as if he'd never let her go. With each driving thrust, she spiraled upward, the tension ebbing, then intensifying, until she arched against him, clinging to him as he drew her with him to the very brink of ecstasy. Whispering her name, he gently urged her over the edge to soar as if she had suddenly sprouted wings.

Sayer groaned in pleasure as he found his own release, tightening his hold until she could feel his heartbeat—feel his harsh breath hot against her neck. When at last his breathing calmed, slowly, reluctantly, she drifted back to reality.

She was his now, completely, and the thought brought happy, satisfied tears to her eyes. It was done. Her decision finally made.

"Don't cry," he urged, his brow creasing with concern. "I didn't want to make you cry."

This time she put her fingers against his mouth to stop him. "Don't," she pleaded. "Don't talk. Just hold me."

And he did, until the sinking sun chased all the warmth from the room and it was time for him to dress and leave.

The next morning, Rebeccah awoke to the smell of fresh coffee. Shrugging on her robe, she entered the kitchen and found Sayer busy preparing their breakfast as if it was an everyday occurrence. He caught her watching and flashed a bright smile. "Good morning."

He filled two cups and carried them over to the table. His limp was pronounced, but his smile chased away her concern as he motioned for her to sit down. "I hope you don't mind, but I was hungry and you left the door unlocked."

"I don't mind at all," she replied. She added some cream and sugar to her cup.

"Even though you live close to Fernando, you should lock your door."

Before she gave it any thought she replied. "Why? Do you think the Indians who attacked you are still in the area?" The moment the words left her mouth, she wished she hadn't mentioned them. "I mean . . . I remember you told me they would leave when it got cold."

He gave her an understanding smile. "You're right. It'll be snowing soon. I expect they'd be doing as much hunting as possible to have meat for the winter."

He returned with two plates of bacon and eggs. When he sat

down, his expression grew more somber. "How long has it been," he asked, but she sensed he didn't mean for her to answer. "A month? And still I can't remember."

He took a sip of coffee, but by the tiny muscle twitching above his jaw, she knew he was far from finished with the subject. They ate in silence until finally he heaved a long sigh and pushed his plate away. "Becky, honey, I've decided that the only way I might remember is to go back up there and see where it happened."

"But . . . but you're in no condition to go back to work or to travel that far alone. It's out of the question, at least for now."

"I've already decided."

"But who will take care of you?"

"Sergeant Carmichael. I didn't tell you because I didn't want you to worry, but he and some of my men will be here in a little while." Finished eating, Sayer stood and picked up their plates, pausing a moment to place a kiss in her hair. "How come you always smell so good?"

"Don't change the subject," she admonished. He put down the plates, pulled her into his arms and gazed deeply into her eyes. Memories of their lovemaking melted the ice that had only moments ago formed around her heart. "Give me one good reason you have to leave so soon."

Sayer heaved a patient sigh. "I'll give you two. First, I'm better. Second, my orders came in. I've got thirty days to report to Fort Union."

He must have sensed her despair, because he put his arm around her and gave her a gentle squeeze. "I'd stay if I could, Becky, but it can't wait. If it snows, I may never know what happened. It's bad enough we got rain."

"Why are you so determined to remember? I should think it's best forgotten."

"Maybe, but there's something not right," he said, growing

more serious as he placed the dishes in the sink. "I've been remembering bits and pieces of things, but nothing for sure. Yet I can't shake the feeling that it wasn't Indians who attacked me. Just as you said, they'd be heading for the reservation, not wasting their time trying to kill one white soldier."

"But the arrow—"

"I don't know . . . can't explain it. That's why I have to go back."

"What makes you think returning to the place where it happened will help?"

His smile was smug. "It can't hurt."

She turned away, unwilling to let him see her disappointment. Then she voiced what she feared the most. "What if it was Indians, Sayer, and what if they're waiting for you?" She felt his presence, knew he stood behind her.

"They won't be," he whispered, placing a kiss in her hair. When he turned her around, she didn't resist.

"I don't want you to go."

"Becky, honey, don't make this any harder than it already is. Until February, I'm still the property of the United States Government."

She wanted to speak, but Kaiser waddled up and whined at her feet. Sayer picked him up, scratched the pup's ears, then placed him in her arms. "I won't be gone long—no more than a week or two. But, I'll be back this way before heading to Santa Fe, I promise you, and when I do, I'm going to ask you to marry me."

His words shook her to the very core of her being. When she couldn't find her voice, he hesitated for several moments, and then kissed her. He smiled his goodbye as he took his hat from the hook by the door then left.

She snatched up her shawl and ran outside.

"Sayer," she called, torn between doing what was right and

doing what she wanted, which was to run into his arms and beg him to stay. But Sergeant Carmichael had arrived and waited by the hitching rail with ten other men. She began to doubt the benefits of being a lady, for surely Sayer's expert touch last night had awakened something more primal, something she longed to experience again before he left. The moment he stopped and turned, flashing his usual lazy smile, she lost her nerve. "Stay safe."

Sayer entered the barn to find that Don Fernando had taken Rounder out of his stall and was helping to saddle him. "Ah, I expected you to take a little longer in saying goodbye." Fernando's expression was amused. "I hope you are recovered enough to handle your horse. Though I have had him exercised every day, he is stubborn and willful, much like his master, hey?"

Sayer took the reins from his friend. "I am in your debt."

"Do not concern yourself about it. Someday I may need a favor, *si?*" The two men shook hands.

"Yes. I won't forget." Sayer led Rounder out of the barn, glancing toward Rebeccah's house. Fernando followed his gaze.

"I will take care of her while you are away."

Sayer flashed Fernando a skeptical grin. "That's what worries me."

James Randolph opened the door. A stout elderly woman stood on the step, her black plumed hat at a haughty angle atop a pile of white hair. Something about her seemed slightly familiar, but perhaps it was only her black gown that made him uneasy. "May I help you?" he asked, frowning at the rigid way she stood, the rebellious gleam in her pale green eyes . . . eyes that reminded him of—

"James Randolph, I presume?" And the moment she spoke, he knew who she was. A painful knot formed in his chest. "I've come to collect my granddaughters."

"Papa, are you all right?" Lydia asked as she came into the parlor. The color left her father's face as he stepped back from the door. A moment later Lydia's grandmother stepped inside, followed by a younger man carrying a rather hefty satchel. "What are you doing here?" Lydia asked, stunned by her grandmother's sudden appearance.

"Lydia, where are your manners?" her grandmother scolded as she strode into the parlor. "A proper lady would invite us in before assaulting us with questions." Katherine motioned to the man behind her with a wave of her hand. "This young man is your sister's fiancé, Edward."

CHAPTER EIGHTEEN

Rebeccah hummed a little tune as she finished a long letter to Edward. Although storm clouds hovered just above the peaks, her spirits were high. She wrapped Edward's ring in a small piece of velvet and dropped it in the envelope just as a knock sounded on her door. "Come in," she called, rising from her desk.

"A message has come for you," Fernando said with a frown. "It is from your sister."

"I wonder why she didn't bring it." Rebeccah opened the envelope, unaware that her hand shook ever so slightly.

"It is bad news?" he asked, his brows drawn tightly together.

"My grandmother . . . and my fiancé are here . . . in Santa Fe," Rebeccah said calmly, although it felt as if a hand had closed around her heart. "Sh-she wants Lydia and me to return with her to England as soon as arrangements can be made."

Fernando's frown deepened. "So, she has come herself, knowing you would refuse to go if she didn't." He didn't give her time to answer. "If you decide to leave, it will be a sad day for all of us, especially for the children."

Rebeccah swallowed the lump that had formed in her throat. "Yes, thank you . . . for me also." She would have turned away, but Fernando caught her by the arm.

"What will you do?" His compassionate expression was nearly her undoing.

"Lydia will come for me in two days." Sunlight from the

open door washed over her, but it couldn't chase away the chill that suddenly encased her heart. Fernando hesitated as if he wanted to say more, but he only gave her an understanding smile then left. For a long time Rebeccah stared at the envelopes while Kaiser sat by her side and looked up at her. Stepping around the pup, she went to her desk and pulled out more paper.

Sayer knelt down on one knee to get a closer look at the nearly faded prints. Carefully, he traced a mark in the dark, grassy soil, and then noticed several others. Rounder's were there, and by the looks of the still torn-up grass, the stallion put up quite a struggle—probably the reason they left him behind.

Sayer stood at the same time Fergus came over and heaved a long, impatient sigh. "It's no use, sir. Most of the tracks are ruined." Fergus looked at the clouds gathering in the sky. "If'n we don't head down the mountain soon, sir, we're goin' tae get caught in some snow."

"No, not yet. I think I made it to those trees, and I think they followed me . . . on horseback." Vivid images flashed before his eyes, and for a moment, he relived the agony. "Maybe there's a print or two still there."

Fergus followed his commander over to a brace of thick pines, frowning at the matted grass and the dark, splotchy stain that could only be the remains of dried blood that hadn't been washed away by the rain. As before, Sayer searched the ground, this time swearing softly under his breath. "What is it, sir?" Fergus asked.

Sayer's dark frown grew even darker. "There." He pointed to a deep print as he gently pushed aside the withered grass. "Indian ponies don't wear shoes, not even broken ones." He sat back on his haunches and pushed his hat off his forehead. "Have the men mount up, Sergeant."

"Aye, sir." Sergeant Carmichael turned to leave then cast one last look over his shoulder. Sayer had picked up the broken shaft of an arrow and was looking at it, and Fergus knew by his somber expression he was remembering.

Rebeccah stood before Brandy's stall, holding an apple for the mare to munch, not caring that the juice had stained her soft, grey leather gloves. Nor did she care that bits of straw clung to the grey velvet trim of her elegant traveling suit even as Kaiser tugged playfully on the hem. Lydia and her father would arrive any moment to take her to Santa Fe, and she didn't know when she would see the little mare or ruffle the pup's soft fur again.

Even though the thought of leaving her pets was painful, it didn't draw her away from the understanding that she had left matters with Sayer unfinished simply because she had been too proud to run to him in front of his men. Lost in thought, she was only vaguely aware when Don Fernando came into the barn.

"I thought that perhaps I would find you here," he said, his voice softer than usual as he bent down and picked up the pup. By his expression, he felt he was intruding.

She pulled an envelope from her bag and held it out to Fernando. "I hope to be back before Sayer, but on the chance that I'm unable to do so, could you see that he gets this? I would greatly appreciate it. It's very important, you see, because Sayer doesn't know that I'm leaving."

Fernando tucked the letter into his pocket. "But you are only going to Santa Fe, no?"

"I hope so," she said, trying hard not to cry. "But my grandmother is a very determined woman. She's used to getting what she wants, no matter whom she hurts. In her note, she says she found out that I signed a formal betrothal. If Edward refuses to release me, I shall be forced to go back to England to nullify it, regardless of how badly I want to stay in New Mexico. But, worse yet . . ." She paused and took a silk handkerchief from her bag and dabbed at a tear. "Sayer doesn't know I've decided to break my engagement."

Fernando gave her a confused look. "Correct me if I am wrong, but this is why I am to give him a letter?"

She gave him an impatient look. "Yes. You see, Fernando, I didn't have time to send Edward his ring back, or to explain why I wanted to be released from our betrothal." She heaved an impatient sigh. "I couldn't tell Sayer. Not until Edward agrees."

Fernando's expression softened. "Did you tell the colonel that you love him in your letter?"

Fresh tears pooled in her eyes. "Surely he knows how I feel."

Fernando's understanding smile faded. "I would not be so sure, if I were you. For months you have remained distant, telling us both a thousand times that you are engaged."

If it were possible to feel worse, she did. "You don't understand. Feelings are difficult to explain in a letter."

"*Ay caramba,*" Fernando said with an agitated shrug. "The man rode away thinking you are going to be here when he returns, yet you won't. And now, if what you say is correct, he might even think that you are returning to England to marry another man?"

"No, I'm not going to do that."

Fernando shook his head. "But, Sayer does not know this . . . ah, my little *señorita.*" He gave her a sad smile. "You should have told him exactly how you feel."

"I tried, but all his men were watching," she said in a miserable voice. More tears flooded her eyes. "I knew you wouldn't understand," she repeated in a broken whisper. "Propriety deems that before I declare my love for Sayer, I must first break my engagement to Edward. I was going to send a letter, but then . . . then my grandmother's arrival changed my plans."

"*Ay caramba,*" Fernando cried again. "Once more your grandmother interferes. Perhaps I should go with you and speak with her." He raked his fingers through his hair. "Why in the name of the Holy Mother didn't you tell the colonel the truth before he left?"

"I was going to . . . when he came back. I thought I had time. How could I know my grandmother would travel all this way, and worse, I certainly didn't think she'd bring Edward." Rebeccah threw Fernando a desperate glance. "Besides. Even if I wanted to tell Sayer how I feel, ladies do not discuss such things in public, and his men were there . . . waiting . . . and watching."

The next day Sayer stopped a mile from Don Fernando's ranch, then got down from his horse, wincing as healing muscles rebelled. "Sergeant, you and the others will wait here. If I need you, I'll fire two shots. Meanwhile, have the men dismount and stay out of sight."

"You should be lettin' me and the men handle this for you," Sergeant Carmichael growled after he passed on his commander's orders, dismounted, and he and Sayer had moved out of earshot. "You've no business goin' alone."

"I have to see if Fernando's involved. If Renato's there, I'll pretend I still don't remember, turn around and come back," Sayer promised.

"If'n they don't shoot you in the back first."

"Fergus, Fernando has two little girls and an elderly grandmother. Becky's there too. What do you suppose Renato would do if he saw a detail of men riding up the road?" Sayer shook his head. "I can't risk it. They're all too important to me." He pulled up the collar on his coat. "Looks like it might snow."

Fergus heaved a loud sigh. "They won't suspect nothin' if'n I

240

were tae ride along."

"I'm going in alone."

"Then I'll follow a wee ways and hide—"

"Sergeant Carmichael."

"Aye, sir?"

"I wouldn't want to have to court-martial you for disobeying my orders, so don't do anything stupid, all right?"

Fergus gave him a black look, obviously infuriated. He stood at attention and saluted. "Aye, sir. Whatever you say, sir."

Sayer swung up and settled himself into the saddle, slightly annoyed that his old friend stayed at attention, his dark hat catching the snow.

"At ease," Sayer growled as he rode away.

"Tío," Elena and Maria cried in unison as they ran up to Sayer the moment he dismounted. He took them into his arms and held them a little longer than usual, kissing each girl's cheek before placing them on the ground. A boy came and led Rounder toward the barn. "Papa is sending us to Mexico to visit Mama."

"Colonel," Fernando said cheerfully. "I was not expecting you so soon." Both girls came over to their father and after he spoke to them, they nodded cheerfully and dashed into the house. "Come inside. It is beginning to snow. I was worried that we would never finish our game, but here you are." Fernando's gaze fell to the Colt strapped to Sayer's hip.

"What did you say to the girls?" Sayer asked.

Fernando's smile faded. "I told them that if they left us alone for a little while, I would let them watch us play chess." Fernando shrugged his shoulders. "They will not bother us. I'm sure they will fall asleep on the settee."

Sayer took off his hat and coat, nodding at Rita as she hung them up near the door. "I haven't come to play chess."

"It is a cold day, and I have a well-aged glass of brandy waiting to chase away the chill. Since *Señorita* Rebeccah is visiting her sister, we will have plenty of time for a game." Fernando led the way into the familiar room where a warm fire burned. He filled two glasses and held one out to his friend. "Dinner is almost ready and I insist you stay. Come, let us sit and visit a while."

"I think I'll stand, if you don't mind," Sayer stated, sipping from his glass. He turned to the fire, staring into the flames. Once more a familiar face passed before his eyes; only this time he knew who it belonged to and why it kept haunting his dreams. "Seen Renato lately?"

"Renato? *Si*, but why do you ask?"

Sayer turned. "I remember, Fernando. I remember what happened up on the mountain."

"That is a good thing, no?"

"No, it isn't. Let's go down to the barn." Sayer put his glass on the mantel, then turned. "There's something I need to see."

"If it will appease you, then certainly." Fernando stood, retrieved their coats and hats and motioned for Sayer to lead the way through the kitchen, pausing to put Rebeccah's envelope unnoticed inside his pocket.

Outside it had begun to snow and by the time they were in the barn, their shoulders were dusted with white. "So, here we are. Your horse is out of the storm, see? Feeling better?" Fernando's tone was edged with impatient annoyance.

"Maybe," Sayer answered, looking over the horses that stood in the stalls. "Which one is Renato's?"

"That one," Fernando stated, pointing at the bay. Once more a vivid image of a man with long wild hair, dressed in buckskin and straddling a dark horse flashed into Sayer's mind. "Well?" Fernando's voice drew Sayer away from his somber thoughts. "Now what?"

Sayer lifted a halter from a hook and stepped into the horse's stall. Once the big gelding was tied, he lifted its left forefoot then swore under his breath. "I was hoping I was wrong." Sayer said tersely, placing the animal's foot back on the ground.

"Wrong? About what?"

"Where is Renato?" Sayer asked.

Fernando shook his head in irritation. "How do I know? I assume he is with the other men, having supper. You are trying my patience, *amigo*. You act as if I am trying to hide something from you."

"Are you?" Sayer challenged. "The men who attacked the stage months ago—"

"You mean the Indians who attacked the stage, don't you?" The two men stared at each other for several tense moments.

"Their horses were shod."

Fernando shrugged his shoulders. "This should matter to me?"

"Apaches don't shoe their horses."

"Regardless of what you are thinking at this moment," Fernando said, "you are still my friend."

Sayer turned toward Brandy's stall. "Really? And when you sent them up the mount—"

Fernando grabbed Sayer's arm and spun him around. "Never. I never sent them after you. You do not know what you are talking about."

Sayer pulled his arm free, his expression hard and cold. "When Becky found me, I was dying. Afterwards, every time I closed my eyes I saw the likeness of a man. But that's not all. The so-called Indian attacks were done by a man riding a horse with a broken shoe," Sayer nodded at Renato's horse, "just like the one on that bay."

His gaze stayed on Fernando for several moments. "Don't ask me to believe you knew nothing about the raids, my friend, because I can't."

Again Fernando didn't speak, he only met Sayer's heated gaze. Finally, Sayer heaved a long sigh. "I'm only going to ask one more time. Where's Renato?"

A door opened and when Sayer turned, Renato and Jose stood behind him. Jose carried a rifle hooked over his arm. "Is everything all right, *jefe?*" Renato asked, tapping a thick leather crop against his palm. Again, Sayer relived the attack, only this time the fuzzy image of the man who laughed as he pulled the trigger had a face. Renato smirked and took a step forward, patted the sleek neck of his horse, then untied him and put him back in the stall. "A man could get killed messing with another man's horse, right, Jose?"

"Renato," Fernando warned. He spoke harshly in Spanish, then turned to Sayer and forced a smile. "Come. It is cold out here. I am sure Rita is holding our supper." There was an edge to his voice, and when Sayer flicked his gaze to his host, Fernando subtly shook his head, but it was too late. Renato pulled his revolver and held it at arm's length—aimed at Sayer.

"You're not so smart, *cabron,* to come here alone."

"He is not alone," Fernando ground out, glaring at Jose until the man took a step back.

"Keep your hand away from that pistol." With a confident smile, Renato stepped forward until the muzzle was pressed against Sayer's chest in the area of the old wound, forcing Sayer's back against a post. "Maybe Fernando lied when he said you couldn't remember. I think that maybe you remember me and the way I cut you down to size . . ." He dragged the barrel of the gun down about an inch. "Only I should have aimed a little lower."

"I remember three men, not—"

Renato hit Sayer across the face with the back of his hand.

"Renato!" Fernando shouted. "What do you think you are

doing?" Fernando took a step, freezing when Renato cocked the gun.

"Let him go," Fernando said with cool authority. "It will only be worse for us if you kill him."

"Listen to him," Sayer replied calmly, even though his heart hammered against his chest. "There's no way out of this if you kill me. I've got twenty-five men waiting for me in the trees down the road. If I don't show in a very short time, they have orders to take this place using any force necessary."

"I do not think your soldiers will harm Maria and Elena, hey?" Renato's smile was as malicious as his intent. He jammed the gun harder into Sayer's chest while he slipped his knife from its scabbard. "Is this what you used when you took a scalp? I have heard stories that white soldiers took almost as many scalps as the Indians. Is this true?" he asked then pressed the sharp blade against Sayer's throat. "I'm sure you know that there are other, quieter ways to silence a man, no?"

Sayer's gaze never wavered, not even when Renato pressed the blade a little harder against his throat until a small trickle of blood stained his scarf.

"Renato, do not do this," Fernando pleaded. "So far no one has died. Killing him will ruin our chances for escape."

"It is too late." Renato's soft laughter sent a cold chill down Sayer's back. "Until he came along, no one could identify us. Now he knows who we are, and for that he must die."

Fernando's expression was unlike any Sayer had ever seen when he walked over and stood before him. "What he says is true. I did not want it to be like this, but you have left me no choice." Fernando backed away, shaking his head. "Jose, go and pack some supplies. We must ride for Mexico tonight." When the older man hesitated, Fernando shouted, "Do as I say!"

"Go," Renato ordered, but Jose lingered by the door.

"There's still time to give yourselves up," Sayer ground out through clenched teeth.

"*Silencio*," Renato shouted.

Fernando held out his hand. "Give me the gun. I will guard him while you saddle the horses. You and Jose can take your share and leave tonight."

"What about you?" Renato snarled.

"Me? I will hold the colonel hostage. When you are gone, I will kill him. When his men come, I will tell them that I tried to stop you, but you and Jose got away. After things settle down, I will pack my things and follow with my family. We will meet in Mexico."

"I do not believe you," Renato shouted, yet still Fernando crept closer, his hand outstretched.

"We are in this together. I am no fool. We will all go to jail if the colonel is allowed to live. I will not put my family in danger. After you leave, I will kill him."

"Very well. I will do as you say." Renato pulled Sayer's pistol from the holster and slammed it against Sayer's temple before tossing it to Fernando. Dazed, Sayer sank to his knees.

Fernando caught the pistol, spun and shot at Jose, who scrambled out the door. Renato swore then turned and fired at Fernando. Sayer's vision cleared enough for him to see Fernando fall.

"You son-of-a-bitch," Sayer growled as he charged Renato. He grabbed Renato's wrist at the same time he hammered his fist into Renato's ribs, doubling the man over before he wrenched the knife free. Another powerful blow to Renato's jaw sent him sprawling on the dirt floor. Winded, Sayer turned to Fernando who slowly got to his knees. "What the—" Sayer rasped, baffled when his friend raised the pistol. He saw the gun spit fire—expected to feel the impact. Only when Renato cried out behind him did Sayer realize what had happened. Renato lay unmoving in the straw.

Sayer took a moment to check Renato then knelt by Fernando's side. Blood oozed from a hole in Fernando's shirt on the top of his shoulder.

"Is he dead?" Fernando's voice was with thick with regret, his expression pained.

"He is." Sayer pulled off his scarf and pressed it against Fernando's wound.

"He was a bad man, *amigo*. Believe me when I say I am glad he's gone."

Sayer helped Fernando to his feet. "We've got to get you inside before your men—"

"There are no others, only Jose." Fernando replied, leaning heavily on Sayer as they made their way to the hacienda. Rita and Fernando's grandmother, both with worry creasing their brows, met them at the door. Sayer helped Fernando into a chair by the table where the women cut away his shirt and bandaged the wound.

"There is blood on your throat. Are you hurt?" Rita asked.

"No," Sayer muttered. "I've had worse shaving."

"What's going to happen now? Undoubtedly your men heard the gunshots."

"I'm sure they're on their way. Can he travel?" Sayer asked of Rita.

"I-I think so."

Señora Gutierrez cupped her grandson's cheek. "The children heard the guns. They are worried."

"Then go and get them." Sayer picked up a wet cloth and wiped the blood off his neck. "You've sure made a mess of everything."

Fernando started to speak, but Maria and Elena ran into the room, tears streaming down their cheeks. They would have leapt into their father's lap, but Sayer caught them, stooping to tell them that they had to be gentle, as their papa was hurt. Sniffling and trying to be brave, they scooted closer, accepting a kiss from their father along with softly spoken words of encouragement. When at last he gave each a long hug, their tears began again, and they glanced expectantly up at Sayer and then turned to their great-grandmother for an answer.

"Is it true? Papa is not coming with us to visit mama?" Elena sniffed.

"*Si, vida mia.*"

"But what are we to do without him?" Maria asked Sayer, huge tears appearing in her eyes.

"Maria, do not bother the colonel. Come with me." The old woman exchanged a worried glance with her grandson, then spoke in Spanish with Rita for a moment before the women ushered the distraught little girls down the hall.

A heavy pounding rattled the door. Sayer pushed away from the table, frowning even more. "That will be Sergeant Carmichael. You stay here and don't make a sound." He went to the door and stepped outside. After a few minutes he came back in and filled two glasses with brandy, giving one to Fernando. "I told my men that they'd find Renato in the barn."

Several tense moments of silence passed as he walked to the fire, then pressed his thumb and forefinger against the bridge of his nose as if his head hurt. "There comes a time when a man has to face his mistakes—to atone for his sins." He turned and met Fernando's dark eyes, each man unyielding. "Tell me you've changed, that you'll never do anything like this again."

Fernando shook his head. "On my honor, I swear it." Still the two men stared at each other for several long moments.

"When I was sick, I realized that in a blink of an eye my life could have been over." Sayer slowly shook his head. "And there's so much I've done wrong and so much I want to do right." He heaved a long sigh. "Then I remembered how it happened, and even though I didn't want it to be like this, you were as wrong as the others to do what you did."

"*Si*, I was. The money we took, or at least what's left of it, is hidden in the wine cellar in some kegs marked with red paint."

Sayer tossed the last of his drink down his throat. "My men will chase down Jose. No matter what happens here tonight, you'll lose your home, your children will be taken away from you, and your family sent back to Mexico. Your ranch will be sold to replace the money you took. You'll be tried in a court of your peers and if found guilty, you'll go to prison."

"*Si*. I know." Fernando whispered, his gaze locking with Sayer's. "There is no excuse for what I have done, but you must know, if I could change it . . . if I could take it all back, I would do so."

Sayer heaved a long tired sigh. "Perhaps . . . perhaps not. One thing we do agree on is that your daughters deserve better than what you have given them. And one thing I know for sure is that I won't be able to live with myself if I let those two little girls leave for Mexico without their father."

CHAPTER NINETEEN

It was nearly dawn when Fernando lifted his daughters up into the wagon. Two other wagons were filled with furnishings and several of the other women and children waited behind. Fernando's grandmother wept softly as she hugged the children to her bosom, muttering her reassurance that once they were in Mexico they would be safe. The storm clouds hovering over the peaks looked black in the pre-dawn light, and a cold wind tugged at the men's coats and hats.

Fernando took a leather-wrapped bundle and placed it in Sayer's hand along with an envelope. "This is the deed to my land. I want you to sell my ranch and give the money to the poor. The envelope is from *Señorita* Rebeccah. She asked me to give it to you before she left." Sayer nodded, then helped Fernando into the driver's seat of the hearse, then tucked the letter inside his shirt.

"This gives me the chills," Fernando said from under his large *sombrero* and *serape*. He dragged his hand over his mouth, already missing his thick moustache. "I am naked as well," he muttered, "and, if that is not enough of an insult, I am dressed like a peasant."

"Any more complaints?" Sayer asked as he put a rifle behind the seat. "At least you're alive. My men think you're dead." He motioned to the casket inside the hearse. "You could ride in there."

"That is not amusing," Fernando countered. The rancher

heaved a long sigh, stared a few moments at the casket, then turned and looked once more at his home. "I will miss it here. But, perhaps with God's help, I can build a small home for my daughters in Mexico." He looked down at Sayer. "I will miss you, *amigo.*"

Sayer grasped Fernando's hand. "Take care, and keep to the main roads or you'll never make it. If anyone asks what you're doing, you let Rita do the talking. You don't speak English, remember?"

"*Si, no hablo Ingles.*" Fernando's expression grew more serious. "What will happen to you if they learn that you have helped me escape?"

"Don't you worry about me, just get yourself and your family as far away from here as you can."

"Some day I will repay you for your kindness." Fernando picked up the reins and pulled the heavy Mexican blanket tighter over his shoulder, hunching down so he wouldn't appear too tall. "*Vaya con Dios, mi amigo.*"

Fernando called to the other drivers in Spanish, then followed them down the long drive, turning only once to wave. Sayer waited until the small wagon train was on the main road, and then walked back into the house. Stripped of many of the furnishings, there on the table, sat a single bottle of wine. Tied around the bottle was a note. *In my lifetime I never knew what friendship was until we met. This is for you and the señorita. It is the finest French wine money can buy, and it is to be saved for your wedding day. Vaya con Dios, amigo, and someday may our paths cross once more.*

Sayer folded the note, then picked up the bottle and held it for several long moments. "*Adios, amigo.*"

He put the bottle down, went into the kitchen and opened the door to the cellar. Touching a match to the lantern hanging at the top of the steps, he held it high as he descended into the musty darkness. Just as Fernando had said, there were several small kegs on a wooden rack. As Sayer got closer, he noticed by the dust-free rings that three kegs were missing. He placed the lantern on a large barrel and checked the first keg. Nothing. Then the second keg—still nothing. Sure enough, the last keg was marked with red paint. Using his knife, he pried it open and pulled out one small sack filled with money. Slowly, very slowly, he shook his head and laughed as he remembered what Fernando had said. "A small house, my ass. The son-of-a-buck has enough money to buy half of Mexico."

Back in the house, Sayer took out Becky's letter and tore it open. "Damn it," he swore under his breath after he read it, shoving it inside his shirt. He grabbed his hat and coat and ran to the barn. A few moments later, he and the stallion bolted out of the barn and down the road, churning up the freshly fallen snow.

"Diego," Fernando called once they were miles down the road.

"*Si jefe,*" the older man answered as he rode up alongside the hearse on his mule, returning his overlord's smile.

"Diego, *mi amigo,* did you pack the kegs of whiskey I told you to pack? The ones with the red Xs on them?"

The man nodded proudly. "*Si, si,* just like you told me to, *jefe.* But there is something I do not understand."

"What is it, *mi amigo?*"

"Why did you want me to leave one behind and put the others in the coffin?"

"I left one to accommodate an old friend. By putting the others in the casket, no one will bother them."

"Oh, I see." Diego nodded, but he still looked confused. "It must be very good whiskey."

"*Si, amigo,*" Fernando laughed. "The very best."

★ ★ ★ ★ ★

Rebeccah stepped out of the carriage, offering a strained smile to Edward as he helped her down, then hurried to assist Lydia. While he was busy with their grandmother, Rebeccah pulled Lydia aside. "I've decided that I'm only going as far as Albuquerque."

Lydia frowned. "I don't understand why you're leaving at all."

"Lydia, please. Don't make this any more difficult than it is."

"Then please explain to me why you feel obliged to leave at all."

"Because," Rebeccah whispered shortly. "It will—"

"Here we are," Edward said with a bright smile, escorting the dowager up the steps to the platform. He turned and offered his hand to Lydia. Once she was standing beside Katherine, he held out his hand to Rebeccah. Her sister handed her a heavy, fur-lined cloak and Edward, ever the gentleman, helped her put it on. She glanced at him as he looked down the track for the expected train. She had forgotten that he wasn't very tall, but then, she'd gotten used to looking up at Sayer—or that Edward's dark hair, though neatly combed, wasn't very thick. And, if he didn't have on such an expensive hat and overcoat, he wouldn't stand out in the crowd at all. No, she admitted, Edward Dunlap was just as boring as his letters.

"I had no idea it was so . . . so uncivilized here," Edward said, tugging on his gloves.

"I expect that by the time we return, the railroad will be finished all the way to Santa Fe." Lydia's comforting voice drew Rebeccah away from her inspection of Edward.

"Yes, that will be nice, won't it?" she replied listlessly. She heard her sister's sigh and braced herself for what she knew would come the moment Lydia gently grasped her elbow and pulled her a few steps away.

"I'll go alone if you want," Lydia offered as the train's whistle announced its arrival. "I'll even tell them about the colonel for you."

Rebeccah shook her head, tying the cords of her cloak. "No, I shan't embarrass Grandmama, nor is it fair for me to leave Edward without at least giving him my reasons in person."

"But, Becky. The train will be here in a moment."

"I'm quite aware of that. In fact, I am hoping the journey will allow me ample time to explain to poor Edward why I can't return to England to marry him. I've already written my request to be released from our betrothal. It's in my reticule with his ring."

"Oh, for heaven's sake," Lydia muttered under her breath. "Give it to me. I'll see he gets it." She picked up their satchels and prepared to board.

"Lydia, please. I can't give the poor man a note and then trot off as if nothing was ever between us." Rebeccah motioned ever so slightly in his direction. "Look at him. He's watching me this very moment with that silly love-sick expression he used when he proposed."

"I thought you—"

"Never mind." Rebeccah forced a smile as Edward grasped Katherine's elbow and helped hoist the old lady into the car and to her seat. Before he could grab Lydia's arm, she handed him both her and Rebeccah's satchels, and while he was busy storing them, the sisters entered the car on their own, taking a seat together, forcing Edward to sit with Katherine.

The sound of a galloping horse caused several of the passengers still boarding to turn their attention toward the main street in Cerrillos. A few others left their seats and opened the large windows to look out. "What in heaven's name is all the commotion?" their grandmother asked as she and Lydia tried to see around several tall men.

"Why, looky there," a man muttered, hanging out the window. "That horse has been rode plumb near to death."

"What is it?" Rebeccah asked a little breathlessly, trying to see—but she already knew.

"Not what . . . who," Lydia said a little desperately as she and Rebeccah stared out the window at the same time, nearly bumping heads.

"Oh, dear, Lydia, it's . . . Sayer."

Both sisters swallowed hard as they watched the colonel slide his sweat-drenched horse to a stop before the depot's hitching post. A second later he was down, tying the reins and at the same time searching the crowd. His features were as dark as the gathering clouds. Then, much to Rebeccah's surprise, he boarded the train, spoke softly to the conductor for a moment, then turned and stopped. His gaze riveted to hers.

"Good heavens, he's looking at . . . at Rebeccah . . . and she's—"

Sayer cast a quick glance at the man who spoke in heavily accented English. He was dressed in rich clothing, perfectly groomed. As Rebeccah slowly stood, she looked very much the sophisticated lady she was. Sayer felt base, lower than he'd felt any other time in his life, and for a moment, he doubted he was good enough for her and wondered if that was the reason she was leaving.

"Lydia," Katherine ordered stiffly. "Fetch your sister."

"I rather doubt she'd listen to me at the moment, Grandmama."

Once she stood before him, Rebeccah raised her eyes to his. "I-I thought you were still in the mountains," she said in a suffocated whisper.

"Maybe he was, but he's back now," someone muttered, drawing a few chuckles from the throng of travelers, some seated, some standing to watch.

"Did you?" Sayer replied tightly, acutely aware that the crowd was watching them with growing interest. "I was, but I found what I was looking for."

"Excuse me, but—"

Sayer turned and looked at the Englishman, inwardly wincing that in comparison he must appear reckless and crude. So this was her dandy. This was the man she was leaving him for. Sayer caught Rebeccah's elbow and pulled her to the rear, hoping the move would give them a little more privacy from the spectators, but they, as well as her dandy, were dauntless and followed.

"Your letter didn't say you were planning to go back to England, and apparently your father doesn't know either."

"I-I—"

He didn't let her speak; he only stared at her, his gaze stabbing into her. "After . . ." His voice was a harsh whisper. "After what we shared, didn't you think I'd want to know? Had the right to know?" he demanded in a louder voice.

"Yeah, I'd want to know," an old man confirmed with a nod that nearly sent his bowler tumbling. His toothless grin faded the moment Sayer shot him a glance.

"Y-yes . . . of course," she began. Sayer's gloved fingers closed around her arms, only, unlike the soft wool of Edward's, his gloves were leather, his fingers strong yet gentle. "Sayer, please, they're watching."

"I don't give a damn that they're watching," he said gruffly.

"My good man, I demand that you unhand her this instant," Edward said, lifting his chin. "I am Edward Dunlap, the lady's fiancé. The man who will defend her honor if you persist in your advances." Edward set back and raised both fists. The moment Sayer turned, Rebeccah caught sight of that familiar tick above his jaw.

"Sayer . . . Edward, plea—"

She was too late.

"No, sir," Sayer began in a cold, calculating voice. "You *were* the lady's fiancé." He drew his fist back and punched Edward square in the nose. Edward's eyes rolled up in their sockets and he fell back into the arms of two men, who eased him down on the closest seat, then turned and applauded.

"That's telling him, Colonel," one man said with a grin.

"That's more like showing him," another added.

"Oh, dear," Rebeccah cried in dismay. She would have gone to see if Edward was all right, but Sayer caught her arm.

"I've never told anyone this before—never knew anyone worth saying it to, but, I'm telling you, Becky, whether you want to hear it or not. I love you, and I think you love me too, only you don't know what real love is about."

"You tell her, sonny," a heavyset woman encouraged.

"I don't have a fancy title or an estate or much to offer except myself and a run-down shack on a small piece of land. But, I'll promise you this. When I get out of the army, I can make a good living for us."

"All aboard," the conductor shouted.

"Y-you don't understand," Rebeccah stammered, turning away. The pain of leaving him eased a little when she didn't have to gaze into his sad blue eyes.

"A piece of paper doesn't make a man love a woman." His tone was tinged with desperation. "Where are the days spent getting to know each other? Show me where he has professed his love for you, damn it. Show me that he'd be willing to die for you. Then and only then will I believe he loves you."

"Listen to him, honey," an older woman called out, joined by several others as they voiced their agreement. "I'd take a soldier over a dandy any day."

Sayer ignored them, turning her to face him. "Look at me and tell me that you don't love me."

She swallowed hard. "I do love you," she sobbed.

The crowd cheered.

"Then stay." Sayer's plea was echoed among the other passengers.

"Yeah, stay!" one man shouted.

"Stay and we'll send someone to fetch the preacher." Laughter and words of encouragement as well as the train's whistle very nearly drowned out Rebeccah's voice.

"No," Rebeccah said, throwing the crowd a desperate glance. She stood ramrod straight, aware that Sayer also thought it was that simple. "I-I can't. My grandmother is waiting. I have to go to her . . . to explain what has happened."

That muscle above Sayer's jaw jumped again. He started to speak, but instead he looked at the crowd, then at the conductor as the man called out once more, "All aboard."

The train lurched into motion, causing Rebeccah to lose her balance. He caught her.

"Your hoss is gonna break that rail," a man shouted.

"Damn it," Sayer muttered under his breath a moment before he pulled her to him and kissed her. The kiss was painfully short but excessively thorough. The travelers applauded again, and several cheered over the train's last-call whistle. "We're not through," he ground out, backing toward the door.

He jumped down, and as she watched from the door, he tried to calm Rounder. He untied the reins, and she knew he had his hands full trying to settle the frightened horse when excess steam hissed from the engine. Then Edward was there, holding a monogrammed handkerchief to his nose, telling her it was time to sit down, muttering something about being uncivilized. She looked past him, watching as Rounder dragged Sayer several more yards away from the platform. Only when Edward grasped her elbow did she turn, but she refused to leave.

"I'm sorry, miss," the conductor began. "If you're going to

ride this train, you're going to have to take a seat."

Lydia came and took tight hold of her hand. "We'll come back, Becky, as soon as we can." Rebeccah glanced at her sister, and then turned to see Sayer struggling with his horse, but at the same time looking for her. When their eyes met, the desperation in his brought fresh tears to hers.

"Becky, don't go," Sayer shouted, his voice barely audible over the slowly turning wheels of the train. "Becky!" He shouted again, swinging up on his horse. Those who leaned out the windows to watch groaned their fear for the handsome soldier when the stallion reared and nearly toppled over. Once more the whistle sounded.

"He's gonna get kilt for sure," she heard someone mutter. "Yep, that hoss of his is a wild one."

Rebeccah closed her eyes and offered a reverent prayer.

"Goodness gracious, he sure is persistent," a woman proclaimed, and when Rebeccah opened her eyes, it was as if God had answered her prayer. Rounder settled, then lunged forward as Sayer urged him into a run. In seconds they were there—beside the moving train—her uncivilized soldier on his galloping horse. Before she had time to think about her conduct, she leaned out and fell into his waiting arms.

In the distance someone shouted her name, and when she could finally look over her shoulder, Edward stood in the door, his eyes wide and his mouth open in shock. Lydia was there too, smiling and waving a lace handkerchief, and crying with joy.

Chapter Twenty

"Why I bet that fancy English lady and that poor dandy won't get over that for quite some time," the man standing next to Lydia said of Edward and her grandmother as her view of Sayer and Rebeccah grew smaller and smaller.

"Yes, I believe you're correct," she murmured. She turned and looked at the man. "How far is it to the next stop?"

The next stop was the bustling town of Albuquerque. There Lydia wired her father with the warning that she and Katherine would be returning to Santa Fe, and would he please meet them at the train station in Cerrillos. She spent the two hours they were delayed convincing her grandmother to let Edward go east alone. Obviously the man was suffering the worse kind of embarrassment, as he had refused to speak to either of them, keeping to his assigned seat as the train continued on its way. After Lydia exchanged their tickets for two seats back to Cerrillos, she stood by their luggage while her grandmother sat on a large black trunk.

When finally they were on their way, her grandmother heaved a long, troubled sigh. "I do not believe the child is in her right mind." The dowager searched through her reticule for a lace handkerchief, and then dabbed at her nose. "Letting that . . . that hooligan carry her off. She could have been killed. What could she have been thinking to do such a thing, and to be so inconsiderate to the man she professed to love?"

260

"Grandmama," Lydia asked, drawing the old woman's attention away from the window, "why did you bring Edward with you? It was my understanding that he wasn't your choice for Rebeccah in the first place."

"He wasn't, but I had hoped he would be helpful in convincing her to come back were she belongs—where you both belong." Katherine turned back to the window. "My only hope is to return to Santa Fe in time to save the poor child from ruining what's left of her rather soiled reputation. Riding off with a-a common soldier, how dreadful."

Lydia looked at her grandmother for a very long time. "Sayer MacLaren is not just a soldier. He is a colonel in the United States Army, and a very polite and considerate man. Since I'm sure he will never let Rebeccah out of his sight again, I would suggest you get to know him—that is, if you ever want to see or hear from Rebeccah again." Lydia heaved an angry sigh. "The two of you are so much alike, I can hardly bear it."

"Alike?" Katherine cried. "How can you say that?"

"Listen to yourself." Lydia glared at her grandmother. "Look at what you're doing. You're stubborn. The both of you are as stubborn as two people can be, and I'm sick and tired of it."

Katherine squared her shoulders, raising her chin in defiance. "I should never have come."

Their train soon arrived, and a kindly man helped them to board. Lydia sat next to her grandmother, smoothing her skirt. "Since you're here, you might as well stay for a while—at least through the winter."

Refusing to let her grandmother sulk, Lydia chatted on about the weather, avoiding any more talk about Rebeccah and her hooligan. Only when the train's whistle announced their impending arrival at the Cerrillos station, did Lydia begin to worry.

"I shan't have you making any unkind remarks to father," she warned in a firm but gentle tone. "Regardless of your opinion, you don't know him, and he has been most affectionate to Rebeccah and me." She spotted him among the bystanders, his fur-collared overcoat pulled up against the bite of the chilly breeze.

"Katherine," James said politely. "I have a carriage waiting." He didn't wait for her to respond; he simply took her elbow and guided her to where a black, two-seated carriage waited. He helped her to the second seat, and then assisted Lydia to the first while he took his place beside her. It began to snow when he urged the matching grays into a lively trot. "We'll be in Santa Fe in about an hour." He cast a quick glance over his shoulder. "Are you warm enough? I've a blanket behind the seat if you should need it."

A deathly quiet fell over the threesome as they turned down the road and headed north. Only when they were well on their way did James inquire about Rebeccah's whereabouts.

Lydia told him. "And then, Papa," Lydia continued, nearly at the end of her story, "the colonel galloped up and snatched her away. It was unlike anything I have ever seen, nor do I think I shall ever see anything like it again."

James gave a soft chuckle. "Well, then, it's settled. The man's going to be my new son-in-law." James gave a satisfied nod. "I couldn't ask for a better one."

"Well," came Katherine's voice from behind. "I see you've brought the girls down to your standards."

Lydia noted the slight stiffening of her father's broad shoulders. He clicked to the horses, then turned and looked at Katherine over his shoulder. "I will tolerate your insolence because of the circumstances, but let's get something straight," he began, his gaze never wavering, "my standards were, and still are, pretty damned high, or else I would never have gotten Louise to marry me."

Lydia heard her grandmother's gasp.

"And," he continued in a very calm voice, "if you think because my daughter fell in love with a soldier that she is marrying beneath her station, you, my dear lady, are sorely mistaken. Sayer is more gentleman than most men, and thanks to him, Rebeccah has a real chance at happiness."

"The same kind of happiness you gave Louise?" Katherine countered, glaring at James. Lydia felt her father's anger, but knew he'd never be rude and vent it.

"Since you brought that up," James said, "it was my idea for her to take the girls and leave for England. And one other thing, since we're digging up the past, I'd like to know what happened to my letters."

"I don't know what you're talking about."

Lydia turned slightly to see her grandmother's face. "Papa told us he wrote to Mama, but she never answered his letters. I remember mama looking through envelopes, but . . . but it was always after you had received the post."

"I still don't know what either of you are talking about. Had you written—"

"Oh, no. I wrote. Every week."

Lydia glared accusingly at her grandmother. "You kept his letters from Mama, didn't you?"

"I saw no need to add to her unhappiness."

"Grandmama, you had no right."

"I had every right." Katherine squared her shoulders, cast a quick glance at James's back, then met Lydia's stare. "Your father was a vagabond with no roots. He was a lieutenant in the cavalry, for God's sake. He couldn't provide for her as she was provided for in my home. He would have dragged my beautiful Louise from hovel to hovel with never a care for her well-being or the fact that she was a high-born lady." Katherine retrieved her handkerchief.

"No, Grandmama, you're so very wrong. He cared for her . . . deeply. He loved her." When James tried to quiet her by taking gentle hold of her hand, Lydia clutched his tightly and returned his sad smile. "He is still in love with her memory."

"I don't believe you—either of you," Katherine cried. "She had everything money could buy. I did what was best. Had I given her your letters, they would have only complicated her life."

"No, Katherine, they would have complicated yours," James said. "Louise would've wanted to come back to me, and you were afraid of being left alone."

Lydia glanced back at her grandmother. The old woman looked wretched, with tears in her eyes. "I never wanted to hurt her . . . or you, James."

"Well, you did," Lydia replied. "And Rebeccah and me, as well."

"Yes, yes, I have, and I'm so sorry," the dowager sobbed.

James cleared his throat. "I'm going to make you an offer, Katherine, but I'm going to only make it once. Don't answer until you've given it some thought." He looked at his daughter, giving her fingers another confident squeeze. "Stay. I'll find a nice house for you in Santa Fe, and you can stay and live here with us. After all, we are your family. And I don't reckon it's going to be too long before Rebeccah and Sayer make you a great-grandmama."

Rebeccah sat next to her sister as sharply dressed young soldiers placed platters of food on the long, elegant table. Crystal wineglasses twinkled in the lamplight, as did the silver bowls and china plates. Sayer had spared no expense for their engagement party. Not only were his officers groomed to perfection, but a string quartet played softly in the corner of the elegant dining room that seemed to her to house half the population of Santa Fe.

She could barely keep her eyes off Sayer, and she was aware that each time she looked at him, residing at the head of the table, her grandmother also looked. The perfectly polished brass on his uniform, as well as the medals on his chest, looked even more impressive as, near the end of the meal, he motioned one of his men over and whispered some instructions.

The young corporal clicked his heels together and strode away in a fashion that even the Royal Army would consider genteel. When the dishes were cleared away, coffee and tea were served, as well as a rich rum-flavored cake garnished with chopped pecans. When that was finished, all the tables except the head table were put away to form a very large area for dancing.

"So tell me," Rebeccah's grandmother said, sitting to the left of the colonel, sipping a cup of tea from a china cup. "What do you propose to do now?"

Rebeccah's mouth went dry, and under the table, she grasped Lydia's hand tightly in her own.

"I'm not sure I understand your question, ma'am."

Katherine raised her chin ever so slightly, her pale eyes glinting with what Rebeccah knew was rebellious fury. "Very well, I will endeavor to make it more elementary."

Her father nearly choked on his coffee, but a quick glance at Sayer eased some of Rebeccah's fears when his gaze met hers before he gave her grandmother one of his lazy smiles.

"Did I say something amusing?" Katherine challenged.

"No, ma'am," Sayer answered as he met the old woman's dauntless stare. "It is my intention to marry your granddaughter, build her a house and sire her children." When her grandmother gasped and made a move to speak, he politely held up his hand. "If you would be so kind to allow me to finish." He paused, and Rebeccah knew he was taking great care to use just the right words. "However, I would prefer to do so with your blessing, as family . . ." He looked at Rebeccah and winked, and she knew he was remembering another conversation. ". . . family is very important to both of us."

Just then the music began to play, and Sayer put down his napkin. Rebeccah's heart picked up its pace and she felt as if she couldn't draw a proper breath, but instead of asking her to dance, Sayer held out his hand to her grandmother. "Lady Strong, would you give me the pleasure of the first dance?"

The dowager's soft gasp was barely audible. By her grandmother's expression, she had been taken completely off guard. Expecting Katherine to give her beloved a harsh refusal, Rebeccah held her breath. Slowly, her eyes never leaving her host's, Katherine put down her napkin and took Sayer's hand, then rose to her feet in a rustle of black silk. "I-I would be pleased," she replied in bewilderment.

Sayer took her hand and hooked it over his arm as he led Katherine to the middle of the dance floor. The musicians struck up a slow, elegant waltz and, in total amazement, Rebeccah watched her grandmother's usually stern features became more animated. As she and Sayer gracefully glided around the room, something happened. The domineering monarch began to smile, and when Sayer said something to her that no one else could hear, the dowager actually laughed.

"Rebeccah? Rebeccah, are you watching?" Lydia asked.

"Yes." She blinked, dragging her gaze from Sayer and her grandmother. "I don't believe what I'm seeing, though, do you?"

Two weeks later, while Katherine Strong, Duchess of Wiltshire, dabbed at the happy tears in her eyes, Sayer slipped a simple gold ring on Rebeccah's finger.

"To the bride and groom!" Fergus's voice boomed over the

cheers of those gathered to watch. Dressed in a black jacket and red-plaid kilt, he lifted his glass high. "May all their troubles be wee ones."

Sayer lifted his glass and touched it to his wife's, his eyes never leaving hers. So radiant was she in the cream-colored gown she wore, he never noticed as James introduced his mother-in-law to Mr. and Mrs. Winters from the bank. Nor did Sayer notice when Lydia danced with Lieutenant Williams, not once, but twice.

Gaily decorated pine boughs filled the air in the dining room of the fort with their fragrant scent, but Sayer didn't notice. Josh Barns played love songs on his fiddle softly in the background, and Miss Bonnie and three helpers passed around plates filled with slices of savory roasted beef, cheese and strips of hot chili peppers, rolled in freshly made tortillas, but Sayer paid them no mind. While the guests feasted and conversed, Sayer was so enthralled with his new wife, he had no idea that Fergus finally found the courage to ask Miss Bonnie if she'd like to take a carriage ride next Saturday.

No, the only thing Sayer noticed as the day wore on was his beautiful bride, and the only thing he knew for sure was that he was the happiest man alive.

EPILOGUE

"What do you mean, it's sold?" Sayer ground out, following Ben Winters into his office at the bank.

"I said, it's sold, Colonel."

"Mr. MacLaren, now. I'm not in the army anymore, Ben. I thought I was in the ranching business, but now you're telling me you've gone and sold the Gutierrez ranch." He heaved an irritated sigh and pushed his hat off his forehead. He promised Becky they'd have a home by the time the baby was born, but now it looked like he wasn't going to be able to keep his promise. "Who bought it?"

"I don't know. But before you get all worked up, I can tell you this. They paid cash, and by the looks of things, spent a whole lot on fixing it and the guest house just like they want it."

Sayer heaved another disgusted sigh. "Well, that's just fine, that's just damn fine," he said. He stormed out of the bank, nearly knocking Josh Barns off the top step. Sayer gave a hasty apology, not caring that the door to the bank slammed shut.

"Well?" Fergus asked, his grin fading when he looked at Sayer's grim expression. "Did you get it?"

"Do you see any papers in my hand?" Sayer countered sarcastically.

Fergus's brows snapped together. "What happened?"

"Someone else got it, that's what happened."

"Someone else? Who?"

"Hell if I know." Sayer untied Rounder and swung up into

the saddle. "Come on," he growled. "I've got to tell Becky that she's got to stay with her father a while longer, and then we've got to get back to the ranch. I've got a roof to mend and a fence to build. I've got cattle coming in two weeks."

Three weeks later the sun was high when Sayer spotted a rider leaving down the rutted road. "Who was that?" he asked as he came over to the water barrel. He lifted the ladle and took a long drink, pouring the rest over his head to try and cool off, then filled Kaiser's water bowl.

"Your new neighbor sent over his foreman with this," Fergus stated with a disgusted snort.

Sayer dragged his sleeve down his face then accepted the folded paper. "Damn it all," he muttered then crumpled it up and tossed in into the ashes of last night's fire.

"What did it say?" Fergus asked, following Sayer over to where their saddles hung on the fence.

"It says we have ten days to move the south fence or he'll have his men tear it down."

"But . . . but we've got fifty head on that pasture."

"I know that," Sayer spat out. He grabbed his saddle and went to where Rounder was tethered in the shade of the trees. "I've been invited to supper tonight. The son-of-a-buck wants to talk to me."

"About what?" Fergus asked, pushing his hat back to scratch his head.

"He wants to buy my land."

"You aren't goin' tae sell, are you?" exclaimed Fergus.

"Hell no."

"Then what are you going tae tell him?"

"I'm going to tell him he can take his offer and—never mind. I'm going to the river to wash up."

★ ★ ★ ★ ★

By the time the sun squatted in the crevice of the mountain, Sayer turned Rounder down the familiar drive of what was once Don Fernando's ranch. Bittersweet memories darted in and out of his thoughts as his gaze swept over the paddock where Rebeccah had learned to ride and to drive a buggy. Now a herd of well-bred horses grazed, lifting their heads to watch the intruders.

"There's no room for this kind of foolishness," he muttered to himself, yet everywhere he looked, happy recollections caused him to smile. *Could you please take care of my chicken while I'm gone?* Strange, he mused as he rode up to the hitching post and swung down from Rounder's back. Doc Randolph's buggy was there.

A breeze began, rustling the treetops. Just as Sayer was about to tie Rounder to the post, a small tumbleweed blew by. Rounder pulled back on the reins and danced around nervously for several minutes while Sayer calmed him down.

"My granddaughter told me your horse is a coward."

Katherine inwardly flinched at the look on Sayer's face when he spun around. A moment later his hat was in his hand. *Yes,* she thought to herself with a very satisfied smile, *the young man is quite a gentleman.* "Don't just stand there, let me take your arm. You can help me back to the house. It gets rather cold out here at night and, in the dark, I'm not as steady as I once was."

His silence was becoming uncomfortable, yet still she kept her secret. Only when he opened the door and helped her inside did he see that some kind of a party was taking place. Lydia and Rebeccah were there, as were Fergus and James. James came around and shook his hand, and when Fergus came up, Sayer asked him how he got there before he did.

"It wasna easy, but we Scots are a crafty breed." Everyone laughed, and Sayer was directed to take the seat closest to

Katherine's, next to his wife. A grand meal was served and afterward, coffee and tea were brought in by several Mexican maids.

"I suppose I owe you an explanation," Katherine began, drawing everyone's attention. "Rebeccah has explained to me how you intend to raise horses."

"Yes, ma'am, that is my intent."

"And do you think you can make a good living at this?" Katherine's mouth twitched as if she wanted to smile.

"In time, with the right mares."

"I see. Did you notice the mares in the paddock as you rode in?"

"Yes, ma'am. I did."

"As I knew you would. You see, I, too, have a certain fondness for horses. Many do not know it, but a very long time ago, before I was married, I dreamed of owning my own farm and raising the very best horses. Of course, this was before I was told that women do not harbor such dreams." She gave Sayer a firm look. "I've a deal to make with you, young man, but as James said to me months ago, so shall I say to you. I am only going to ask once, so I suggest you think about it very carefully before you answer."

Rebeccah stood at the window gazing out over the once-barren field, Kaiser asleep near her feet. Now, instead of scrub cedar, rocks and cactus, the frame of a small schoolhouse stood. Often she'd think about the last few months and shake her head. Never in her wildest dreams did she think she'd be living in Don Fernando's big house, her grandmother taking over the guesthouse. She splayed her fingers across her back, gently massaging the annoying ache that had arrived with her eighth month of pregnancy.

"Shall I rub your back?" Sayer's deep voice penetrated her

thoughts and brought a loving smile to her lips. She heard his footfalls on the carpeted floor, and then, when he wrapped his arms around her, she leaned back against his chest. As usual, he spread his warm fingers over her round tummy. "He's sure dancing around in there," her husband said, his breath warm against her ear a second before he kissed her cheek.

"She's practicing," Rebeccah countered, casting her husband a crafty smile.

"She?" He matched her smile. "What's she practicing?"

"Her dance steps, of course." She giggled when he nuzzled her neck. "That way, when she meets the man of her dreams, she'll be prepared when he sweeps her off her feet."

"I see," Sayer answered, turning her so they could kiss. "And is that what I did to you?"

"Yes, my love," she murmured against his lips. "Twice."

ABOUT THE AUTHOR

Donna MacQuigg is a second-generation native of New Mexico and has enjoyed many years of raising and training Arabian horses with her husband and two children. Donna has spent hours in the saddle, riding trails in the beautiful Sandia and Sangre de Cristo Mountains. She was taught at an early age the skill of hand gunning and enjoys archery and knife throwing. Having taught young students horsemanship and riding skills, her experience with horses adds to the authentic flavor of her books. Donna has previously published four historical romances. This is her second Western set in the Southwest. She enjoys receiving your comments at donnamacquigg@ yahoo.com or visit her Web site at www.donnamacquigg.com.